pretzel logic

for all of my compatriots from the STR8 spouse list

When a lady's erotic life is vexed,
God knows what God is coming next.

Ogden Nash

Prologue

The lights were flashing like an August electrical storm gone wild. The air pulsated with a basso so profundo that it felt like the floor was about to give way. I could have been having a migraine. Or an orgasm, for that matter, if it wasn't for the howls and hoots emanating from the other patrons—all gay men. Half the crowd seemed ready to pounce on any one of the eight muscular, sweaty bodies in various stages of undress up on the stage.

Why can't I get into this? I sat on the aluminum folding chair, willing myself to get caught up in the excitement. Instead I sat dumbly, feeling like a geek at a debutante's coming-out party. I tried the route of empathy: If I were a gay man right now, how would I feel and what would I be doing? All I had to do was to glance around at the other patrons of the Front Line Club, most of whom had their eyes riveted to the strip show on stage, a benefit for the New Hampshire AIDS Foundation. Including the man sitting to my right, who had finally agreed to let me accompany him after I had insisted.

"Are you sure?" he responded when I asked him to take me, his voice wary. "I don't know…"

"Of course I'm sure!" I replied.

He shook his head, then cocked it to one side; perhaps if he tilted his brains in just the right angle he might be able to figure me out.

"Are you sure you weren't a gay man in a previous life?"

Now that was one tack I hadn't considered.

"Oh, please," I groaned. "I just want to see what your life is like firsthand, even a tiny part of it."

"Well, okay. But if you don't like it, it's not my fault."

Of course, now that I was sitting beside him in the noisy crowded room scrunched in at our small round table nursing our drinks, I wasn't so sure I should have persisted. Neither was he. We were two of the calmest people in the audience. There I sat, the lone woman surrounded by several hundred gay men who were shouting some of the raunchiest phrases I had ever heard.

And beside me sat Michael, my companion, letting out an occasional whoop although sounding slightly nervous about it, and unsure about what to do with his hands. First he placed them flat on his lap, palms down. A minute later they were sliding up and down on his glass, wiping away the beads of sweat that form when Dewar's meets ice.

I looked at him out of the corner of my eye. I never tired of running my eyes over his face—his too-full-for-a-man lips, untamed eyebrows, hair the color of mahogany buzzed just a bit too short on the sides. And his eyes, my God, eyes that pierced through anything in their path. They were the color of ice on the pond in deepest January with a slight bluish tinge that magically turned a warm cobalt whenever he smiled. And when he did smile, people frequently forgot to breathe. I had been witnessing it firsthand for four years now. But tonight he was a wallflower, largely unnoticed when we entered the club, mostly due to the nearly naked bodies of the dancers onstage.

I leaned over and placed my hand on his arm. "Are you okay?" I shouted above the noise.

Startled, he released his glass and wiped his hands on his trousers. "Sure," he yelled back, pulling his mouth into a smile while the rest of his face remained immobile. "How are you doing?"

"Fine, but two drinks have done their deed." I stood up. "Be back soon," I mouthed as I headed for the ladies room.

"Whose idea was this anyway?" I thought as I meandered through a path between overturned tables and roaring, drunken men. There were hundreds of them all morphed into one giant mob, yelling and laughing. I attracted an occasional glance, but the majority of eyes were glued to the wildly gyrating hips onstage. As I dodged sweaty bodies, pumping fists, and packets of condoms flying through the air, I noticed a misty cloud hovering just beneath the ceiling, an intermingled fog of cigarette smoke and droplets of sweat and cologne.

Inside the ladies room, the noise was muffled, and I had absolutely no doubt that I was in a club filled to the rafters with gay men because there was no line for the stalls. This only enhanced the unreality of the night.

I paused in front of the mirror, not that my appearance mattered one iota on the other side of the door, and stared at my reflected face. Shoulder-length dirty blond hair parted in the middle was about as fancy as things got. Light brown eyes that looked tired, a nose of indeterminate ethnicity, and a mouth that had been pressed tightly together more often than not in recent months in a valiant effort to go with the flow.

I adjusted the angle of my head until I was satisfied that the face matched the age of the body, 32 and three-quarters. Armed and ready for anything, I pushed the door open and was immediately engulfed by the decibel level. Instead of returning to my seat, I stood at the back of the room and watched. I couldn't see Michael, but at this point in the action, there was not a single wallflower in the bunch. A couple of drinks must've worked their magic on him as well.

After a few minutes, I navigated my way back to my seat. I had seen Chippendale shows when I was living in the city, but the audiences consisted of straight women who wanted to see what it felt like to have a few drinks, let their hair down, and hoot and holler just like the guys. I usually went with a bunch of women from work, and I always looked closely for evidence of at least one hard-on among the dancers during the show. No luck.

"That means they're all gay," said one of the women after the Chippendales left the stage. "No way, the way they were gyrating up there, they'd be too exhausted to get a hard-on," countered another.

"Oh please," I said. "If they're not exerting themselves to the max and they get a hard-on, *then* you have to worry. Besides, with all the hot lights, music, and screaming women, they're all too distracted."

End of discussion. Since everyone knew my best friend was a gay man, mine was taken as the final word.

Now, as I watched the dancers who clearly wanted to leave little to the imagination of the audience, I saw how wrong I was. All but one of the dancers wore big, beautiful hard-ons that they made no attempt to conceal, and the men in the audience in the front row were sticking more than dollar bills into the dancers' sweaty g-strings. Condoms were being tossed onto the stage like roses.

I was a few yards from our table when I saw that in my absence, Michael had started to loosen up. One arm was resting on the back of the chair of the guy sitting next to him; his free hand alternated between fondling his now-empty glass and punching the air. As I sat back down, I heard him yell to the guy next to him, "Look at the ass on that one!" He then let go of both the chair and glass and cupped both hands around his mouth to make a whooping sound that in all the years I had known him I had never heard him utter.

When he saw me, he quickly returned both hands to the table. He looked flustered and reddened slightly—even I could see in the dim light—and gave me a sheepish grin before turning his attention to the stage. He put one arm back on the other guy's chair.

A fresh drink was starting to sweat in front of me. What the hell, I thought, and downed half of it with two big swallows. The Scotch flooded my chest and the top of my head with heat. I put the glass down and picked out one of the leering sweaty dancers to focus on. I leaned over to say something.

"Get a load of the package on that one," I told him while pointed out my specimen, a black-haired guy who looked to be all of nineteen. "He's huge! How long you wanna bet till he falls out of his g-string, or someone helps him out?"

Michael glanced at me with surprise, but he was smiling broadly. He studied the boy in question and narrowed his eyes. I watched him take in every inch of the guy's body and I let out an occasional whoop just to let him know he needn't be intimidated by a woman sitting next to him.

The dancer couldn't see any of the faces in the audience because of the spotlights, but of course he chose that moment to grin in our general direction, rotate his hips at double speed, and wink.

The fact that the guy probably winked to avoid the trail of dust left in the wake of a condom that went sailing past his head was totally lost on Michael, who first seemed surprised by the dancer's audacity. His astonishment didn't last long, and he let loose with a shout that sounded as if he had won the war. I shouted too, albeit not as loudly or with as much enthusiasm, but he was so caught up with the action onstage that he either didn't hear me or chose not to acknowledge me. Instead, he stood up, placed his hands on his hips, and jutted his pelvis forward. He looked directly at the boy and noisily smacked his lips.

The dancer winked again. Michael sat back down in his chair, legs splayed, grinning wildly, his face covered with sweat. He saw me looking at him and shrugged in an unapologetic way as if to say, Hey, this is what it's all about. He stood up again and this time headed for the men's room.

Now I felt uncomfortable. I didn't want to sit by myself and wonder what he was doing if he took longer than the five minutes he usually took in the men's room when we went out together to get a bite to eat or go to a movie. I decided it was time to leave. He's a big boy, he'd figure it out.

And I doubt he'll have a problem catching a ride home.

I stood up, a little wobbly and disoriented by the music, two-and-a-half Scotches, and the fact that it was my idea to come here. As I headed for the exit, past screaming, dancing men in all levels of disarray and undress, I barely missed getting smacked in the head by a slight man with a pierced lip wearing a leather thong and nothing else who was standing on a chair swiveling his hips.

I found the car, turned the key, and wondered if I should have come with him after all. When I pulled into the driveway a half-hour later, I still didn't have an answer.

I guessed I would find out the next day after Michael—my husband—came home.

Chapter One

I squinted at a stack of color snapshots taken by a woman in dire need of a new eyeglass prescription, trying to find one that wasn't too blurry or didn't cut off the top of a person's head when the phone on my desk rang. The phone was one of those big red clunky things, circa 1978, that resembled the phone Batman always used to call Commissioner Gordon on the old TV show. I hate the sterile electronic buzz of today's phones, and so I had stolen one of these dinosaurs from each of the eight jobs I'd had at small daily newspapers strung throughout northern New England. My current phone once had *PROPERTY OF THE GROVETON DAILY TRANSCRIPT* stenciled on the receiver, but after years of having my sweaty hand hold it through dull-as-dirt interviews with volunteer fire chiefs and town clerks in communities with more junk cars than people, the letters were nearly invisible. Half the time the ringer didn't work. Sometimes the volume through the receiver would suddenly become twice as loud. When this happened I would tell the person on the other end to plug their ears while I delivered a good hard whack to the cradle with the receiver before proceeding with the interview.

The phone rang again. Max, the pudgy calico office cat sleeping on top of my computer monitor, opened one sleepy eye to document the interruption. I picked it up since I was the only one in the office.

"*Coventry Courier.*"

"Oh, Emily, is that you?" asked the crackly, uncertain voice of a woman.

"Yes, Mrs. Cogswell. What can I do for you?" I asked, even though I knew the reason for her call.

"My column will be a bit late today, so can you come pick it up this afternoon?"

"Certainly," I answered. "I'll be by around three."

"Oh, thank you, dear. I'll be here."

I bet you will be, I thought as I hung up. I could picture her walking through the mahogany-paneled parlor on her way to the sideboard where a silver tray laden with crystal decanters held her afternoon sherry. I moved Max's tail to check the clock on the monitor. Not even one o'clock. I smiled. The elderly have all the fun.

I was tempted to drive over early since I knew from experience that she had in fact completed her column. But I knew she needed a pick-me-up before she felt up to meeting her public, even me, who tore her column to shreds—not that she was ever sober enough to notice. The memory of the bitter silty sherry that Mrs. Cogswell preferred would keep me at my desk squinting at grainy Instamatic photos for a few more hours. Three years of editing the *Courier* had made me intimately familiar with most of the 4,213 people who lived in Coventry. It almost didn't matter that I had grown up in the town.

Mrs. Robert Cogswell belonged to the *Courier*'s Blue Hair Brigade, the group of elderly columnists responsible for filling half the space in the paper each week with chronicles of what went on in their respective towns; in a word— nothing. If you've ever picked up a weekly newspaper published in a small rural town, there's a good chance that it contained lengthy diaries of the previous week's social calendars among the local 70-and-over set. In their columns, the writers chronicle in painstaking detail the comings and goings of the musty widowed sisters who enjoyed their drive to the farmer's market or the six-year-old girl who visited her grandmother in the state-run nursing home over in Worthington, the county seat. Thousands of column inches were filled each year with a complete accounting of the menus at the Coventry Senior Center, right down to the pickled pearl onions, along with an expression of appreciation for the tone-deaf gentleman who entertained the camphor-and-Efferdent crowd with a rousing rendition of "God Bless America" after the meal. Specifics about a patient's medical condition, including the names of everyone who sent flowers or candy to the invalid, were also diligently reported by the women. Curiously, in the 70-year history of the paper, no man had ever written a weekly town report. Topping each Blue Hair column was a photo of the correspondent, her byline always listed as Mrs. Albert Swanson—never Ernestine Swanson, God forbid—and her phone number, along with a line imploring "anyone having news" to please call.

My official title at the *Courier* was editor. But because I ran the paper with my husband Michael—whose official title was publisher and advertising director—I also had to handle whatever Carrie Godfrey, the office manager we had inherited when we bought the paper three years ago, couldn't.

Coventry, New Hampshire, was the thriving hub of the region in the central part of the state known as the Central Valley, and the *Courier* covered most of the soft news and social announcements that occurred throughout the ten-town area, about 800 square miles. Half of that area was taken up by Coventry State Park, mostly known as a teenage drinking spot and not the mecca for nature enthusiasts that the state tourist board likes to promote to tourists. Every few years, usually at prom or graduation time, a local teenager would end up at the hospital with alcohol poisoning after being dragged out of the park in the middle of the night by his or her buddies. For the following three weeks, Bill LaLumiere, Coventry's chief of police, would devote his weekly police report in the *Courier* to the evils of teenage drinking. Eventually everyone would forget about the incident and his reports would return to the usual assortment of road kill, domestic spats, and drumming up donations for the next police auction: "Clean rummage and white elephants only."

The paper covered what I described as non-news. While the *Valley Standard*, the daily paper out of Fletcher 15 miles away, covered the typical hard news articles about car crashes and house and brush fires—what passed for real excitement in these parts—the *Courier* reported the aftermath: pleas for donations of food, money, and clothing; obituaries; and the fund-raising bake sales held every Saturday morning at the Coventry Savings & Loan. I knew we were frequently referred to as the *Coventry Pointless*, but I didn't care. More people read the *Courier* than the *Standard*, and not just because it was free.

We also covered the good news about the community and its people. The scholarships, the weddings, the birth announcements—and the deaths. The letters to the editor revealed the petty little feuds, fights, and truces that are never far beneath the surface in a small town. For variety we slipped in an occasional piece by one of the assorted local heretics who thought the world would be infinitely better off if they could rant in print each week. Between the Blue Hair columns, minutes from the selectmen's meetings, and more poorly written press releases than anyone should have to stomach in one lifetime, we managed to fill a minimum of twenty-four pages each week.

It wasn't exactly what I had in mind when I went to journalism school in Boston with dreams of covering the crime beat for the *Globe*, but at least the paper gave me the chance to return to the town I grew up in and to bring my new husband with me. I'm sure that making small talk with the shoe repair shopkeeper and the bank manager in order to cajole them to advertise isn't what Michael had in mind when we decided to buy the paper, but we were running our own show and we were happy.

Michael and I met four years ago in Groveton, Massachusetts, a hardscrabble dying mill town in the central part

of the state that, at the time, was a couple of empty downtown storefronts away from taking its last breath. Word had
it that a desperate landlord had struck a deal with a cash-
strapped local thug to take a nighttime stroll downtown with
a can of gasoline and a Bic lighter and see what transpired. I
reported the rumor, which earned me a few death threats but
saved the entire block from singeing the sky.

I had been on the job at the *Groveton Daily Transcript* for
just over six months and was already on hundreds of local
shit lists. On the first warm spring day of 1992, when the
roadside salt-and-pepper snowdrifts had shrunk nearly a foot
by noon, I headed for Sutton's Town Hall to get my car
registration renewed. There was only one other person there,
sign of a town on its last gasp.

Inside, I greeted the woman standing behind the counter.
"Doris, before you type this up, maybe you should see if
Mayor Giardina has issued an executive order prohibiting me
from renewing my registration," I said with a smirk. Diplo-
macy in journalism or my personal life was not my strong
suit. My primary nemesis was Groveton's mayor of 30 years,
widely believed to be backed by the local band of Mafioso,
thugs so amateurish that instead of recruiting local restaurants for protection money they went after the flower shops
and pet stores. While I was only half joking with the town
clerk, it wouldn't be a surprise if Giardina had issued some
bogus summons to keep me from driving and, therefore,
from doing my job. Doris laughed nervously, glancing at the
man who had entered after me. "I believe I might just do
that, Emily Spencer," she said, rustling through some papers
on the counter.

I felt a tap on my shoulder. "Excuse me, but are you *the*
Emily Spencer?" I turned to see a man who, I noted, was too
handsome—in both face and dress—for scruffy Groveton.

"What if I said I was?" My standard cocky reply. I hated it
when people recognized my name in public because it
usually meant I had written something to piss them off.

The man appeared taken aback at my response, but

extended his hand anyway. "Then I'd say I was glad to meet you," he said. I reached for his hand, but just as I was about to shake it, he retracted his hand, burying it deep in the pocket of his trenchcoat.

"On second thought, since I'm not sure of your identity, I think I'll rescind the offer," he said with a slightly crooked smile. He gestured to Doris. "According to Mrs. Reilly here, you may be a convicted felon and I don't want to be considered an accomplice."

I turned back to the counter, ignoring his comment. Another nut job, I thought. A common occurrence when a reader who thought he had something to say called the news hotline only to be snubbed by an overworked editor under deadline. Doris started pawing through the drawers of endless filing cabinets. I exhaled, loudly. She'd be busy for awhile, since Giardina was too cheap to computerize the town clerk's office. I considered my options: Leave now and waste even more time here tomorrow with no guarantee that I'd get my registration renewed, or stay and listen to a crazy, albeit handsome, man spout off.

There was a third alternative. I had to struggle against my natural resistance, but I turned back around to face the man behind me. The situation was impossible to resist: I simply couldn't remember the last time I had talked to a man who didn't have grease stains on his tie. Or, for that matter, was even wearing a tie. Piercing ice-blue eyes stared back at me surrounded by bemused wrinkles, punctuated by a rugged jawline that's only seen in the photos of beefcake mountain climbers in *Outside Magazine*, the only reason I subscribe. And he was tall, at least six feet. What the hell. I rested a fist on my hip and assumed my best most cynical look.

"Yeah? Well, assuming I *was* her, why would you be glad to meet her?"

"Well—" He crossed his arms and tilted his head slightly. A few chestnut-brown strands of hair fell out of place, partially obscuring his eyes. "Aw, forget it. He suddenly pivoted on his heel. "I'll write her a letter, that is, *if* I get around to it."

Reflex took over. "Wait!" I said, grabbed his sleeve. My tug released a faint cologne smelling of cucumbers. He turned toward me with a mask of mock horror.

"Madam Whoever-You-Are, do you always walk around grabbing strangers' arms?" With a delicate motion, he plucked my hand from his sleeve. "Even if the Massachusetts Press Association did vote you most difficult reporter in the entire state..."

I looked at him hard. Had I met him before? He had to be in the newspaper business if he knew about the dubious award I won the year before when I was at the *Wolfeboro Times*. First prize was a muzzle.

In the background I heard Doris opening and closing one file cabinet drawer after another, searching for the edict handed down from on high that declared I had lost the right to register my car due to a surfeit of unpaid parking tickets. I had never actually received a parking ticket—apparently every time one was tucked onto my windshield it miraculously blew away.

The man burst out laughing and extended his hand again. When I saw he wasn't about to pull it back, I took it tentatively. "Michael Rogers, sales director at the *Groveton Ledger*," he said. "Pleased to make your acquaintance. Boy, the stories that make the rounds about *you*."

I scrunched up my face. "Yeah, what have you heard?"

He shifted his weight and scratched his head. I noticed he didn't wear a wedding ring. "Oh, we heard about the time you sent a decoy into the park to see how long it would take for the high school toughs to hit on an old man sitting by himself in the park at night."

I smiled. "Yeah, well, I wanted to prove to the people in this godforsaken town that their kids weren't the darling little angels they imagined. One safety pin would have done the trick, you know." On that assignment, I couldn't find anyone to act as stand-in. As I didn't want to do it myself, I got one of those inflatable Mister Safety Mans—the kind that single women put in the passenger seat of their cars to discourage carjacking and commuters use to speed their morning drive in the carpool lane—while I hid in the bushes with an infrared camera and waited. When the story came out the next day complete with a photo of the little darlings caught red-handed splashed above the fold on the front page, outraged parents threatened to file charges of entrapment against me. The subscription cancellations poured in. The incident was quickly forgotten, and the only fallout was that the pizzeria owner pulled his advertising contract because we spelled his daughter's name wrong: she was one of the rogues featured in the photo.

Michael was studying me. "Well, what about the time you—"

I raised my hand. "You can stop right there, mister," I said, turning back to the counter. Only Doris' rear end was visible as she rummaged through the files.

"Doris?"

"Still checking!" she chirped.

I turned back to Michael and shrugged. "My problem is that I get bored easily. The newspapers would be much better off if they assigned me to lifestyle instead of city hall, but hey, we all get bored, you know?"

"Somehow, I think you'd manage to piss people off if you wrote the bridge column."

Did word really travel that fast around here? I thought the gossip up in Coventry was bad when I was a kid.

Enough time on this subject. I gestured at the thick manila file in his hand. "So, Michael Rogers, Mister Sales Director of the Competition, are they gonna give you a hard time with whatever *you* need to do here?"

The crinkles fell out of his eyes along with his smile. "Oh, *this*." He shrugged. Just finishing up probate for my mother's estate. She died over a year ago. I never thought it would take this long to sew everything up."

"Oh, I'm sorry," I mumbled. To me, death was something that I always expected, no matter where it landed. I was never surprised when it flew in on sudden wings and claimed a pet, a grandparent, or even an oak tree like the one that supported the treehouse I built the summer I was eleven. A freak thunderstorm the November after I finished it zapped the lightning rod on the barn, which winged the bolt over to the oak, killing it instantly.

Old London Martin, the logger who lived next door, showed up the following spring brandishing his chainsaw. When it was all over and patches of ground that hadn't seen the sun in decades were abruptly exposed, I held a funeral for the tree. I wrote a brief memorial service, thanking the tree for the hours I had spent in its branches while I plowed through hundreds of musty dog-eared library books. I buried the nails I could salvage in a cigar box in my mother's garden beside the scarecrow's right foot. My mother used to worry that I looked forward to death too much. To me, death was an event and provided me with an excuse to hold a ceremony and to memorialize what was no longer. That's why I think I became a reporter, to record events and people and to preserve them for history.

Despite my comfort with death, I hated how it seemed to deflate other people and how agitated they became at the mere mention of the word. I never knew how to deal with their discomfort. As a result, I usually became uncharacteristically speechless.

My brain searched for a neutral subject. "Did you grow up in Groveton?"

"No, my mother worked in the mills, so I spent most of my childhood living with my sister and grandmother in Malden. In fact, I took the job at the *Ledger* five years ago to be close to my mom." He tapped the manila file with his index finger twice in rapid succession. "That's when she first got sick."

"I found it!" Doris yelled from behind the counter. Michael and I looked at her, grateful for the interruption. Doris emptied the contents of an oversized envelope onto the counter and started leafing through the papers. Michael stood behind me, leaning slightly to the right to peer over my shoulder.

"Boy, you sure do go through a lot of parking tickets," he said. "Funny, but I've never seen your name at the top of the list when the *Transcript* prints the list of Sutton's Top Ten Parking Scofflaws."

I whirled around to face him. I hate being teased, especially by strangers who do it to justify their criticism of my column, and I hated it even more coming from a handsome, apparently single male who was working for the competition. "So what business is this of yours?"

I was only joking, but I must have looked pretty angry because he quickly stepped back. "Whoa, I was only kidding," he said. "Truthfully, anyone who can piss off the town enough to amass a file like that in only six months and still be gainfully employed within its borders, well, I'm impressed."

I didn't say a word. I could hear Doris flipping through the papers. He stared at my still angry face, not blinking, not even when Doris cleared her throat.

"Well, Emily, I'm going to have to check with my supervisor. I'm not sure what to make of all this," she said. I turned around and felt two blue eyes boring into the back of my head.

Doris lowered her head to look at me over the top of her glasses. "I must say, though, I've never seen anything like this before, and I've been here for 28 years."

"Well, I hope this hasn't changed your opinion of me any, Doris. You know," I said, lowering my voice to a whisper, but keeping it loud enough so Michael could hear, "I'd hate to have you stop giving me all those hot tips about what's really going on in Giardina's office."

Doris's face turned crimson and she began fumbling with the file. "Oh, no, Emily," she said in a voice loud enough for anyone in the vicinity to hear. "I don't do anything like that. I never let any secrets get out."

I patted her hand. "I know, Doris, I know. I'm just teasing you."

She smiled broadly. Her teeth looked startingly white against the flush of her cheeks. "Oh, I knew that. Listen, I'll call you at the paper when I can straighten all this out," she said, tilting her head to look behind me.

"Next?" she said to Michael as I stepped away from the counter and headed for the door.

"Oh, on second thought, I think I forgot some papers," he told Doris. "I'll be back." Michael followed me out.

I continued walking, trying to appear oblivious to him as I wondered what was wrong with *this* one. Besides my need to chronicle death, I think I picked my line of work so that I could OD on people every day, leaving me too exhausted to pursue any kind of normal social life. Twenty-eight years old and my penchant for pissing people off had followed me through five jobs in four years. I wasn't interested in pursuing a relationship with a man, or so I told myself. I tended to pick the safest men I could find: they were married and I met them at the publishing conferences I attended twice a year.

But I couldn't even get *this* right. The married men I scoped out were either prime candidates for Viagra—except they didn't believe in drugs of any kind—or were born-again Christians. The glass of pineapple juice with a paper parasol in it should have been the tip-off for the latter group. Out would come the wallet and the school snapshots of eight children, all looking slightly dazed in that way you know was caused not so much by a photographer's flash but by too many Bible school classes. Just the idea of having moribund sex once or twice a year made me feel I was still part of the human race, for whatever that was worth.

Little wonder, then, that my best friend was a gay man. Through the trajectory of my multiple jobs, Eddie Trager was with me through it all. I don't mean that he moved from job to job with me or lived with me. But no matter where I lived, I was never more than a two-hour drive from his home in Concord, New Hampshire's capital. We both grew up in Coventry and both of us had moved away immediately after graduation. Eddie was one of those people I always felt comfortable with, but didn't make the time to get to know better in school.

I bumped into him one night in a bar in Woburn, Massachusetts. I had gone with a friend from work who didn't tell me until I was halfway through my second drink that we were in a gay bar.

"No shit," I said, swiveling around on my stool. At the 180-degree point, I recognized one of the men as Eddie, and from that night on, our friendship went from zero to 60 in less than a week and sustained us both through our frequent crises. We went on long, aimless drives through the countryside, ate and drank like fools, and dished and commiserated about the lack of decent men. We hung out in gay bars because Eddie didn't feel comfortable in regular bars, and I soon discovered they were the only place where I felt I could totally relax.

Sometimes, we'd camp out at one of the trashier gay bars in Manchester, New Hampshire, or Lowell, Massachusetts. By our third round, if a new specimen walked in the door, we'd start arguing over him.

"Oh, honey, he's for you. Look at the confusion on his face. I don't think he's ready for someone like me," Eddie would say, flashing me an evil grin. "But once you're done with him, *I'll* take him."

"Naw, he's yours. Look at the way he's wearing his hair," I'd point out. "Newly shorn for the occasion of his first venture into a gay bar." We would mouth the word gay in a loud whisper while looking straight at the newcomer.

I noticed that a lot of the men in the bars wore a permanent sneer, regardless of whether they were having a few drinks, out on the dance floor, or trying to pick someone up.

"They all look so, oh, I don't know, so negative," I mentioned to Eddie one night.

"Oh, that," he said. "That's the *Fuck You, I'm Gay* look. The old calling card used to be a bandanna stuck in a back pocket or a having a particular ear pierced. Today, it's the sneer."

One of the downsides of hanging out with Eddie was that I became extremely cynical about the chances of ever having a decent relationship with a man. That, combined with my utter failure to have a purely sexual relationship with a total stranger—where *were* these men with a penchant for one-night stands and how come I could never find them?—had almost cemented it for me.

This is what was running through my mind as Michael followed me out of the town hall. I decided to have some fun with him.

The hall reeked of *eau de library paste,* smothering his hint-of-cucumber aroma. "Oh, go away," I said without turning around, waving at him as I would a fly. "I'm not going to reveal any of my secrets to you so that you can go back to the *Ledger* and blab everything to Rochelle." Rochelle Lewis was my nemesis at the *Ledger.* Since I joined the *Transcript,* Rochelle, who covered the same beat I did, had repeatedly made not-so-veiled references in print to a certain person on the other side of town who "went to the Geraldo Rivera school of journalism." Though she never named me in print, with my reputation she didn't have to.

"Rochelle is a fat lazy ass and a snob," he told the back of my head. "Besides, I wouldn't give her the time of day."

I reached the exit, pushed open the door, and kept walking. Still he followed. "What do you want?" I said, without relaxing my pace. "I've already wasted too much time in there and I've got a deadline coming up."

The footsteps behind me ceased. I stopped short, but didn't turn around.

"I'm offended," he said. I turned around to see him rest the back of his hand against his forehead. "Talking with *me* was a waste of time?"

"No, that's not what I meant," I said quietly, looking everywhere but into his eyes. "It's just that—"

Michael took a few steps toward me. He crouched down in order to catch my eyes, then straightened up, bringing my gaze with him. One of his knees cracked as he stood up.

"It's just what?"

I couldn't answer. His eyes riveted me in place. He raised his eyebrows, appearing to enjoy seeing me speechless.

I looked away. "Oh, I don't know."

"Look," he said, lifting my chin up so that I had no choice but to return his gaze. His fingers touched me a second longer than they should have. "Since you've come to town, I've admired your work. But I know they edit your spitfire to ashes, and though I wouldn't just call you up out of the blue, I always thought we'd have lots to talk about. And now, I think that you work overtime to keep up your hard-ass reputation."

He glanced at his watch. "Look, I know you have a deadline—5:20, to be precise. No, no," he said as I tried to interrupt, "I just know these things. Besides, you've said I've wasted too much of your time already. But I really would like to talk with you more, not about business or to ferret out sources for our side, because God knows, they wouldn't know what to do with it at the *Ledger* anyway, but just to talk. How about it?"

Those eyes. "I'd like that," I said, whispering almost, before shaking a finger in his face. "But if you ever let it get out that I'm not the fierce tigress that everybody thinks I am, I'll, I'll—"

He smiled at me. "You'll what?"

I pulled my finger back. "I'll—oh, I don't know."

He handed me his business card. "I'll call you at 5:21, after your deadline. Very nice to meet you, Emily Spencer," he said, and walked away.

Back at the office, I buried myself in my story and promptly forgot all about Michael Rogers. But at precisely 5:21 that afternoon, three minutes after I had sent my vitriolic story for tomorrow's paper to the composing room, the phone rang. Michael asked if I had any plans for the evening. I mumbled something noncommittal and quickly hung up before he could offer any ideas. Those eyes unnerved me. The last time I'd had sex was at a conference back in January. I had imbibed one too many gin and tonics and slept with a guy with the same blue eyes that turned an iridescent green when he got a hard-on. When he turned out the light, I swear they glowed in the dark. My thoughts immediately flew to Mia Farrow and "Rosemary's Baby."

I extricated myself from his sweaty grip shortly after the guy had dropped off into Lala Land and headed for my hotel room three floors down. Though I had an IUD and he had used a condom, I didn't want to take any chances. The next day, I made an appointment with the nearest Planned Parenthood clinic to get the morning-after pill. I spent the afternoon in a darkened room, a damp washcloth on my forehead. I went back to the hotel only after I was sure the conference had ended and I wouldn't run the chance of seeing him again.

"Emily, you have an overactive imagination!" my mother used to tell me when I was growing up.

It wasn't until after she died when I was 17 and I entered J-school that I started to get an inkling of the strange ways people could act—provoked or not. Every so often, I would sass back at Mom in my mind: "Fortunately, Ma, in this business, I don't *need* an overactive imagination. Human nature provides me with more material than I could ever hope to use."

Michael's voice was still resonating in my head as I made my to-do list for the next day. I pushed some notes into my bag and headed out the door. I tried to remember whether I needed to pick up a few cans of Friskies for Chaos and Chainsaw, the two lethargic housebound felines that commandeered my apartment, and figured I'd pick up something at the 7-11 on my way home.

As I crossed the parking lot, I saw a man leaning against the car next to mine.

It was Michael. He was leaning against the hood of a VW Karmann Ghia hardtop—circa 1972, I supposed, the kind my father had craved but settled instead for a Beetle to appease my mother—and two things popped into my mind. One, with his height, how did he ever fit into that thing, and the second I quickly forgot because the man was so handsome he looked as if he belonged in a cologne ad.

I briefly smiled at him but averted my glance as I neared my car, a 1979 Mercedes 240 diesel. With 372,000 miles on the original engine, it had lost its luxury lustre about 200,000 miles ago. But with no rust to speak of due to the inch-thick tar-based undercoat that I faithfully slathered on the undercarriage every year, it got me where I wanted to go without developing the natural brand of air conditioning in the floor panels.

As I opened the door, I looked up to see him leaning on the passenger side of my car.

"Did you forget something this afternoon, Mr. Rogers? You must do well at your job since you seem to be remarkably persistent."

He nodded and leaned across the roof of my car. I noticed that a stubborn piece of rubber gasket was sticking up through the sunroof like a cowlick. "No more persistent than you in your chosen profession, Ms. Spencer. That makes at least one thing we have in common."

I threw my bag on the passenger's seat and glared at him across the roof of my car. "You haven't answered my question," I said.

"Well, you haven't answered *my* question, either. In fact, there are an awful lot of questions I'd like to ask you, but my original one was along the lines of what are your plans for dinner tonight."

I laughed out loud. "What a line!" I said. "Can't you do any better than that?" He looked confused for a second. "Then again, I'm a writer, but you're just some lowly sales hack."

"It's us lowly sales hacks who help pay your salary."

"Correction: you're a lowly sales hack who helps pay the salary of my clearly inferior competition at the *Ledger*," I explained. "But touché. You win this one."

Michael stretched himself across the roof of my car so that his face was inches from mine. "You *still* haven't answered my question."

I threw up my hands. "All right, it's a good thing for you that I just happen to be starving. But I should warn you, I do skin-blistering Szechuan or nothing."

"Good," he said. "Let's see who gives up first."

"Ah, are you tossing down the gauntlet, sir?"

"If that's what you call it."

We got into our cars and drove the two miles to the Szechuan Saloon, the best Chinese place in town, which wasn't saying much. We talked, argued, ate, and drank until we closed down the place. Once outside, he kissed me lightly on the lips before we got into our cars again and drove off.

After that night, we were inseparable, but whether it was as friends or lovers, he kept me guessing. For the first two weeks, after every dinner Michael kissed me in the same way, with the same intensity—that is to say, *none*—and lasting the same amount of time. Then, on the fifteenth night in a row that we'd gone out, I realized I had fallen in love with him. When he leaned over to kiss me in the usual way, I kissed him back harder. I half-expected him to pull back, but he didn't, though I felt the surprise in his body. For a split second, he loosened his grip on my waist, then grabbed me, harder than before.

I pulled away, a mischievous grin on my face. "Watch out, I bruise easily!"

"Oh yeah?" he asked, pulling me back so our hips touched. "*How* easily?"

It was as if I had pushed a button in Michael, giving him permission to act sexually toward me. Later on, I couldn't decide what would have happened if I hadn't taken the initiative that night. He kissed me harder than before. If I didn't sit down, my knees were going to buckle. I clung to him more tightly.

"I want you, Michael," I whispered in his ear. "I want to take you home."

For the first time, we got into one car—his—and drove to his apartment, our hands firmly on each other's thighs. We didn't talk.

Once we got inside his apartment, all hell broke loose. We barely made it to the bedroom. Each time he removed a piece of my clothing or touched a part of my body for the first time, he glanced at my face for my reaction. We slept maybe two hours that night. Four years later, I would hold that night and the sex we had for the next year against the bare light bulb of my emotions as proof of what Michael could be.

About two months after that first wild night, we went to the Szechuan Saloon as usual, and then drove back to his apartment. After we made love, we lay entwined in each other's arms. I listened as our breathing returned to normal.

Michael reached over to turn out the light. I began to stroke him, lightly at first on his stomach, then I increased the pressure and my hand moved lower. He didn't respond. In fact, he seemed to freeze up. I started rubbing him where his balls met his legs, a sensitive spot that he loved. I placed my palm around his testicles while I caressed them with my fingers.

Nothing happened. Zippo, nada. I took it personally. All the bad memories of being rejected by legions of men—that is, before I learned to reject them first—washed over me like a flood. I was helpless to staunch my anger when the question flew out of my mouth in a sneer before I could think:

"What are you, *gay* or something?"

Michael sat bolt upright and flipped the light on. He glared at me, his mouth a grim, tight line. Needless to say, the mood was pretty much dead.

"Why would you say something like that?" he almost growled.

"Oh, it's nothing, Michael. Don't go crazy. I know you're tired." While I spoke, I rubbed his shoulder, but he pulled away.

"Honey, I told you, it's nothing. No big deal." I reached across him to snap off the light. I scrunched up next to him and brought the covers up over my shoulder, but he remained sitting up. My mouth was next to his hip. I felt my hot damp breath ricochet off his hip and hit me in the face. I closed my eyes.

"Please, Michael, I'm sorry if I said something that bothers you. Please, let's go to sleep."

He said nothing. I was so exhausted—the irony is that I had no interest in going another round with him, I had just wanted to play—that I fell asleep within minutes. I'm not sure how long Michael stayed awake that night, but when I woke up the next morning, he had already left for work.

That night, when we talked on the phone, it was as if it had never happened. Had I imagined the scene from the night before? Maybe, but I knew enough not to bring it up with him again, even as a joke. In fact, I even stopped going out with Eddie for awhile because I thought that Michael didn't like him. I actually thought Michael was a bit homophobic, and because I loved him so much, I trained myself to overlook it. We're all biased toward and against at least one particular group of people, I reasoned, and this was his particular nemesis. I let it go at that.

From the first time we made love, I saw Michael as a bit of a challenge because, clearly, sex didn't drive our relationship. And because he did not regard me as a sexual being before everything else, I felt that he respected me and that he didn't want to just use me for my body and then toss me aside when he grew tired of me. The more interesting aspect of it was that I couldn't do the same thing to him. My philosophy was that it was always better to be the dumper than the dumpee. Sometimes it involved split-second timing since the trick is to beat the guy to it. That's what I liked most about the one-night stands I had—or at least, *tried* to have—at the conferences: I was usually able to get rid of the guy first.

But with Michael, the tables were turned. He didn't want

me just for sex, and vice versa, so I had no reason to want to be the dumper. In fact, it was the first time in my life I could say I was truly, rollickingly, madly in love. Needless to say, my mood around the paper improved considerably and, as such, was cause for comment from my colleagues.

Tom, my editor, was a gruff old fart, at least four times as acerbic as the Lou Grant character on "The Mary Tyler Moore Show." He even bore more than a passing resemblance to Ed Asner. Tom belonged to the old school of journalism, where the more brusque you were and the more you could smoke, drink, and curse, the better you could write. There was never any secret as to why he had hired me.

About a month after my first dinner with Michael, Tom called me to his office and closed the door. "Emily," he said, staring at his computer monitor. "What's going on?"

I decided to play dumb. "What do you mean?"

He coughed and looked around for a spittoon. "You've calmed down."

"What do you mean?" I repeated.

He looked directly at me. "You can drop the Little Miss Innocent act with me, Spencer. I hired you for your ruthlessness, to put some bite into the paper. I haven't gotten a cancellation from a subscriber for over a month. What gives? Are you getting laid regularly now, or what?"

In some offices, a more sensitive employee would have slapped a sexual harassment complaint on him or else quit. But I had developed such a thick skin from working at cheesy newspapers in third-rate cities that if I wasn't considered to be one of the boys within weeks of starting work, I would have been offended. The women reporters usually hated me since I lacked the stomach for the games they played. We basically ignored each other, and that way nobody got hurt.

"Well, no," I told him, which was true at the time, "but I do have a social life now."

"Oh?" he asked. "Anyone I know? Setting up one of your sources for a big story?"

"No." I smiled and headed for the door. "Just someone from the competition." I was reaching for the knob when Tom jumped up from his seat.

I turned around. "Relax," I told him. "Someone from the sales side."

He squinted at me. "You don't talk in your sleep, do you?"

I pasted a look of mock horror onto my face. "If you weren't so old, I'd slap you for that."

"Yeah, well, if you weren't such a hellion on wheels, I'd say something about who's on top—but I won't. Really, Emily, keep doing what you're doing. No one's said anything, I just noticed that something's different."

He sat back down. "If you ask me, I'd say it was only temporary, since something will probably come along next week to get you all riled up again and you'll be back to your old self."

I figured as much as well, but I didn't want to tell him that. But I never did regain my previous piss-and-vinegar stance at the paper. Oh, we still had readers call to cancel their subscriptions over something I had written, but they were becoming few and far between. Not like the old days when all it took was some offhand comment about one of Sutton's most upstanding citizens to send the accounts payable department into a tizzy writing refund checks.

Michael and I became regulars at the Szechuan Saloon, having dinner there at least four nights a week. Our who-can-stand-it-hotter contest turned a bit ridiculous at times, forcing us to a minimum of conversation as we spent most of the time draining our glasses and wiping our eyes.

"Hey," he said one night in between bites of a Fiery Happy Family that boasted a three hot-pepper rating on the menu. "I bet that we've built up such a tolerance we could beat all comers at a five-alarm chili contest in San Antonio."

I needed two minutes to recover from my last mouthful of Szechuan Saloon Spencer, named in my honor because I had written about the restaurant a few months earlier, but also because I was the only patron for miles around—aside from Michael—who was able to stand dishes with that heat quotient.

I was on my third Mai Tai and Michael was working on his fourth Tsing-Tao beer when I started laughing hysterically. "You flatlanders are all alike," I said.

"What flatlander?" Michael countered. "You live down here like the rest of us, so that makes you a flatlander too!"

I shook my head. "No way. You were born here. My excuse is that I'm just a temporary and reluctant boarder."

I guess I should explain. A flatlander is a derogatory term for a person who lives in the city or suburbs, typically anointed with the word by a person who lives year-round in a mountainous rural area that tends to rely on tourists for much of the region's revenue. In northern New England, locals usually reserve the term for the tourists, though I recall natives who've hurled the epithet toward another native when a fistfight was in the offing. Whenever said flatlanders visit points north in New Hampshire—like Coventry—they turn all misty-eyed upon spotting a cow or a one-room schoolhouse. They ooh and aah over every piece of weathered clapboard and hunk of genuine Vermont cheddar, which people in the Granite State usually maintain was made in *their* state, on the *good* side of the Connecticut River.

For years, my mother maintained that my first word was *flatlander.* She and my father, who died when I was seven, ran a gift shop smack in the middle of Fletcher, a few towns over from Coventry, a place described by lazy travel writers as "the quintessential New Hampshire town." When I lived in Massachusetts in my teeth-cutting reporting days, I felt like a chicken among wolves, which went a long way in explaining my combative editorial stance.

Michael, who knew he was a flatlander to the bone but denied it every chance he could, was about to throw a crispy noodle at me when he stopped suddenly and asked, "If you could do anything you wanted for work, what would it be?"

I drained my drink, removed the miniature parasol, and

began to twirl it between my fingers. Since I was introduced to my first mixed drink as a teenager, I developed the peculiar habit of molesting whatever inedible garnish the bartender stuck in my drink. When it was a tiny blue plastic mermaid, I'd drown her in duck sauce. With the parasols, I'd very neatly tear the paper from the tiny wooden slats and roll it into tiny spitballs. Then I'd arrange the naked umbrellas in whatever dish still contained some food. After a few weeks of dining out with Michael, Joanie, one of the waitresses at the Szechuan Saloon, began to studiously avoid our table. She must have found the blue mermaid that I poked through the middle of a cherry and buried in a dish of hot mustard sauce beneath a layer of cold lo mein one night.

"Oh, that's easy," I said, "I want to buy the weekly paper back in Coventry and run it myself. I worked there in high school and it's still a rag, but it's always been my fantasy. I still have a subscription to the *Coventry Courier*, and I think it would be a hoot, compared with the garbage and lies I cover down here."

Michael was halfway through peeling off the label on his bottle of beer. He hadn't shown a predilection for molesting his beer bottles the first few times we'd gone out, but it looked as if my habit had rubbed off on him.

"Like what?" he asked.

"Oh, you know, the typical small town reports from the 4-H Club, the Ladies Auxiliary, and the Blue Hair Brigade."

He stopped in mid-peel. "The what?"

"The Blue Hair Brigade." I began to work on my still-intact parasol. "Everyone always scoffs at them, but it's the first thing most people read. I keep reading in the hopes that one day a Blue Hair will slip and report who's sleeping with whom."

My parasol surgery complete, I added it to the parasol forest in my cold leftover dinner.

"Some of my old teachers are members of the Brigade. I think they consider their columns to be their way of continuing to educate the community, now that they're retired."

"Why do you call them the Blue Hair Brigade?" he asked.

"They've lived in the area all their lives, but they still dress in the style of the Forties. They never wear white before Memorial Day or after Labor Day, they always make sure their shoes match their hat, and they go to the beauty parlor once a week for a wash, set, and that bluish rinse that elderly women seem to go wild for.

"Whenever one of them dies," I continued, "the obituary and funeral makes the front page of the *Courier*, and the remaining Blue Hairs fill their columns with reminiscences and reports on the socials and visits held after the service." I tipped back my glass and crunched on an ice cube. "I'm just so sick of the bullshit that goes on down here. I'd love to go back to Coventry and run the paper."

"You're the exception, then," said Michael. "I can't stand going back to Malden. I have so many bad associations with it that I start to break out into a cold sweat as soon as I cross the town line."

"Yeah, I used to be like that too, but I've moved around so much and seen how horrible things can be in other places that now I view Coventry as a haven of sorts. Everybody from the old days still remembers me, even though there aren't many of them left. Lots of new people have moved in since the 1980s, but still the town hasn't really changed that much."

In the midst of my babbling, I noticed that Michael was staring at me.

"What?" I asked before swallowing my ice cube bits.

He grinned mischievously. "So why don't you just do it?"

"Do what?"

"Go back and run the paper."

I fished another ice cube from my glass and popped it into my mouth. "That's ridiculous," I said. "First of all, I don't have the money, and even if I did, Hal Cooper's been running the *Courier* forever. He'd *never* sell it."

"How long is forever?"

"Well, he got it from his father back in 1958, who got it

from *his* father, who started the thing back in the late teens. And Hal has kids, who are probably working there now and ready to take over the minute Hal croaks."

"Are you sure?"

I felt flustered, unable to defend myself. "Of *course* I'm sure. The only way I could run it would be if Hal went bankrupt, or had a stroke, or couldn't run it anymore and his kids didn't want it." My voice trailed off. "But that would never happen."

Michael stared at me, still smiling. "Are you sure?" he repeated.

I grinned back, but felt like slapping him. When you have a fantasy you've tucked way back in the far recesses of your mind because you know it will never materialize, yet you pull it out every so often because just the image itself is enough to lower your blood pressure…well, if you discovered it could come true you'd probably run screaming for the hills. That's how I felt about the possibility of running the *Courier*. I loved the idea but I hated the idea, well, because I *loved* the idea.

"Sometimes things can arrange themselves so that your dream can turn into reality easier than you think," Michael said. "Maybe Hal's sick of running the paper, his kids have all left town, and he fantasizes about handing it over to a hometown girl made good…except to *him* it seems too good to be true, so money is not the issue."

I waved his words away. "You're crazy. It's that extra beer talking."

He tilted his head in that way that made me breathless and mockingly shook his finger at me. "You just never know what people are really thinking. You of all people should know that."

We closed down the Szechuan Saloon and headed to his apartment. When we turned out the light, my head was buzzing. I assumed it was the fourth Mai Tai. When I woke up the next morning and the buzzing was still here, I figured it was my hangover.

A week later, the buzzing was still in my head and every single night I had dreamed of what it would be like to edit the Blue Hairs—in particular Mrs. Benton, my sadistic fifth grade teacher. I knew it was hopeless. But I had to find out.

• • •

The next afternoon, after my deadline was past and everybody was gone for the day, I called information for the *Courier*'s number. As I dialed, I envisioned Mr. Cooper angrily slamming the phone down. Like many Coventry natives, he probably thought that a decade of reporting for what he considered to be big-city dailies had permanently changed me, rendering me unsuitable for covering the banalities of small-town life in print.

"I don't know, well, Mr. Cooper, I figure you're not interested but—" I stammered after we had gotten the preliminaries out of the way.

"What is it, Em?" His voice sounded as if he had aged forty years in the last ten.

"Well—" I stammered, thinking, let's get it over with. "If you're ever interested in selling the paper or retiring, or even cutting back to part-time, well, I'd like to come back and run the paper."

No response. He didn't hang up on me, but neither could I hear any breathing.

"Mr. Cooper? Are you still there?"

He cleared his throat. "When can you come?"

I almost dropped the phone. I didn't expect this, so the first thing I did was try to talk him out of it. "But Mr. Cooper, it's your baby. You've done it for so many years. How can you give it up just like that?"

"Emily, after forty years of weekly deadlines, the paper is nothing more than a middle-aged teenager who refuses to leave the house. My kids don't want any part of it, I can't find anyone to run it for what I'm willing to pay, and I'm more tired than I hope you'll ever know. So, when can you come?"

"Wait a minute," I said, trying to stall while I considered my options. "How do you know I can do this? Besides, you haven't told me how much money you want for it."

"I don't care, pay me rent, pay me anything, we'll work something out. I know you'll be able to make a go of the editorial side, but you'll have to find someone to sell ads because you can't do it all yourself."

Up until then, I hadn't thought that Michael would come with me—after all, it was only yesterday that he asked about my dreams—but in that instant, I knew he would.

"Oh, I already know someone who could do it."

Mr. Cooper sighed. "Emily, you've dropped straight from the heavens."

At that, I panicked. My dream was about to materialize. What now?

"You can live in one of the apartments over the office," he continued. "I haven't rented them since the last tenant moved out two years ago. I just haven't had the time or the energy to fix them up. So—" He paused. "When can you come?"

I had to give notice at the paper and wrap things up in Groveton, but I figured I could be up in a month or two. I also needed some more time to think about it. Like I said, it was one thing to dream about something and something else entirely to actually get a chance to do it.

While I searched for an answer, Mr. Cooper filled me in. He had long been tired of running the paper, and none of his children had any desire to succeed him. After all, they had seen what it had done to their father.

He had frequently thought about selling the paper in the past, but the realtors in town didn't quite know how to sell a business—what they *did* know was how to sell decrepit old farmhouses to flatlanders. So he just kept at it, hobbling along. In fact, the year since his ace ad saleswoman Bea Daniels had died—my ninth-grade biology teacher—he didn't look for a replacement, figuring that a lack of sales calls would mean that advertisers wouldn't remember when their contracts expired and the number of ads in each issue would eventually dwindle down to nothing, allowing him to quietly shut the paper down.

But small towns being what they are, the advertisers reacted to Bea's death by agreeing to sign longer contracts and increasing the size of their ads. They figured that Hal was so beaten up when Bea died that he couldn't picture anyone filling her shoes. A 50 percent jump in ad sales in one month would have made any newspaper publisher ecstatic, but it had only made Hal more depressed and desperate to get out of the business. More ads meant more editorial, translating to more work for him.

But he couldn't bring himself to shut down the paper. It served as a lifeline for people in the area as well as for former residents who had moved away but kept up with the news with mail subscriptions. And of course, there were the tourists and the Coventry wannabes who, even though they lived in New York City or Boston or Washington D.C., could still get their weekly dose of vicarious rural living by paying 18 bucks a year to receive the paper.

We hung up, and I felt like screaming. With terror or joy, I wasn't sure. I thought about calling Michael, but it was such a delicious surprise that I decided to wait until I saw him that evening.

Suffice it to say that two short months later, Michael and I were partners and co-owners of the *Courier*—me as editor, Michael as publisher—and we were living together in one of the empty apartments above the newspaper offices on Main Street in Coventry. It took little coaxing on my part; as it turned out, he had always wanted to live in a small town tucked away in some bygone era. As we made our plans to leave Groveton and head north, I sometimes thought that he was more excited about the move than I was.

We were also two months away from the wedding date we had set on the last night we spent in Groveton.

Chapter Two

It really wasn't much, the proposal, I mean. We spent our last night at the Szechuan Saloon for old times' sake. After the dishes had been cleared away and Michael got down on his knees, I thought he had lost one of his contacts.

But when he grabbed my hand and looked into my eyes the way he did when we were in bed, and I noticed that the cooks had come out of the kitchen and were staring at us, well, I felt my stomach jump into my throat.

"What are you doing?" I asked, sure my voice was shuddering so much that I'd need to repeat my question.

He smiled at me briefly before glancing down at the floor. He started digging in his jacket pocket and pulled out a gumball-machine ring that he promptly displayed two inches from my nose.

"This is for you," he said. "A mere stand-in on short notice, but since we are going to be business partners we might as well make the whole thing official."

In a million years I didn't expect this. After all, we had only known each other for a few months. Up until then, the idea of marrying Michael had never entered my mind, indeed, it had never occurred to me that I would every marry *anybody*.

But as I sat there watching Michael watch me, with those blue eyes wearing the expectant look of a puppy staring at a ball in my hand, and with that ridiculous Cracker Jack ring, I started to laugh and couldn't stop.

"Yes!" I managed between cackles, fighting to catch my breath. "Yes!" The whole idea of moving to Coventry to run the *Courier* had been ludicrous from the first, but look what happened. As I continued to tell him yes, I figured our luck with each other would have no choice but to hold.

When Michael and I first landed in Coventry, we basically followed the rule of "Keep your mouth shut and your eyes and ears open." In a way, it was the equivalent of being airlifted into the middle of a life and a community that bore little resemblance to the one we had just left. When I told my colleagues at the *Transcript* about our plans, they reacted with disbelief. "You'll be bored," they said. "What are you going to write about, bake sales and craft fairs?" Michael received a similar reaction from his co-workers.

I must admit that there was a tiny part of me that bought into these accusations. After all, I had wanted to leave Coventry so much when I was a kid, I thought I must be a masochist for wanting to return. Yet, to me, even the smallest city I've lived in has always been foreign territory. A small town is familiar, manageable. It may not be as exciting as a city when it comes to the type of news that I had to write about, but it's easier to explore the fabric of a town and get to know its people when the number of square miles within its boundaries—in Coventry's case, thirty-six—is six times the number of employees who work full-time for the town.

Most importantly, I was going to realize my dream of running my own business; the icing on the cake was that I was going to do it with Michael. Our purchase of the *Courier* put us miles ahead of anyone else who wanted to do the same thing but always came up with excuses as to why it was impossible. In our business, the refrain usually leaned toward writing a book courtesy of a major New York publisher's largesse, i.e., a six-figure advance, but in ten years of newspaper work, I didn't know of one reporter who had followed through on this fantasy. Besides, I didn't want to write a book, I wanted to run a newspaper.

Hal had told us that the circulation of the *Courier* had hovered around 20,000 for the last ten years. We had no illusions about cranking up the numbers much beyond that. To accomplish this, we would have to expand the reach of the paper beyond the ten-town region that the paper always covered. We thought once we got used to running the paper, we'd decide what to do next.

I was curious to see how Michael would adjust to living in a small town with a population equal to the number of people who resided on one square block when he lived and worked in Boston. But once we became the official owners of the *Coventry Courier*, life quickly fell into a pleasant, predictable rut. Though I would have never admitted it to Tom, my editor back at the *Transcript*, I craved the white picket fence life. I was thrilled beyond words that our social life revolved around spending our evenings at home reading, going out to dinner to entertain advertisers, or attending an occasional performance at Richford College, the Ivy League college wannabe and Coventry's sole claim to fame.

During the first couple of months at the paper, we worked side by side with Hal, learning the ropes of publishing a weekly community newspaper. Even though Hal had described himself as technologically illiterate, he had fortunately converted the paper's production from the ancient method of cutting and pasting waxed strips of copy onto grid paper to a computerized desktop system two years before we arrived. We were also due to inherit Carrie Godfrey, the sole full-time employee at the paper. Carrie had been the office manager at the *Courier* when I worked there part-time after school, and neither her attitude nor her job description had changed much. She was in charge of checking up on the Blue Hair contingent, making sure that they handed their columns in on time, as well as doing the bookkeeping and wearing the umpteen hats that were part of publishing a small weekly paper. Carrie was caring without being a nudge. Hal had told me that Carrie planned to stay on when Michael and I took over, which was a great relief.

The *Courier* office was located in one of the storefronts on Coventry's Main Street, a three-block stretch of small town commerce. The building had a worn look with its dingy white clapboard exterior and scuffed pine floorboards in dire need of a coat of varnish. The front of the building had bay windows on either side of the front door with a bell that tinkled whenever it was opened and a couple of threadbare cushions on the built-in benches in the lobby. This lobby—if it could be called that—had served as a gathering place for the community in recent years, owing to the number of men in their late 50s and early 60s who tended to hang out there between jobs, warming the cushions and catching up on gossip.

I grew up in Coventry hearing that women work and men putter. Many of these able-bodied men had fathered my classmates. Apparently, they were the reason for Hal's burnout: He found it hard to resist a visit with his pals on a daily, if not hourly, basis. As a result, he'd lose track of time and then would have to work late into the night to meet his deadlines. To his credit, while Michael and I were there, Hal never once excused himself to sit among the putterers. By the end of our two-month training period, most of the men had graduated to the Coventry General Store across the street where Mary Devers, the owner, would at least make a few bucks off of them, owing to her hand-lettered sign on the door: LOITERERS MUST BUY SOMETHING OR LEAVE.

Probably the only breed of putterer allowed in the bay windows would be the two office cats we inherited from the paper along with Carrie: Lionel, a huge marmalade tom, and Max, a complacent calico, who preferred the top of my computer monitor. Chainsaw and Chaos were also world-class putterers, and aside from the first few days filled with the occasional hiss and snarl, the four cats coexisted peace-fully. At first, we lived in one of the apartments above the office, and the cats had free reign of the building. While we worked, we left the door to the apartment open so that the cats could come and go at will. But a pattern soon emerged: Max definitely was the office cat while Lionel preferred the apartment. Chainsaw and Chaos had quickly adjusted to the move north, but since they weren't used to having people around all day, kept to themselves upstairs.

Meanwhile, I kept an eye peeled for any rental houses that came through the classifieds; after all, we had first dibs. A month after we moved to Coventry, a classified ad came through for an old farmhouse on Ruggles Road three miles from the newspaper office for $750 a month, utilities not included. I called the ad the day before the paper came out and Michael and I drove out to see it. When we walked into the living room, I glanced at the wide oak floorboards and saw a dark knot in the shape of a heart near the woodstove. I reached for Michael's hand and saw that he was looking at it too. Two staircases led from the first to second floor, one in the front of the house and another in the back. Upstairs were three bedrooms, perfect for us since we both wanted to be able to work at home at least part of the time.

We signed the lease on the spot and moved in the following month. The first thing I did before unpacking the boxes was to hang my collection of 19th century photographs of Coventry village in the hallway on the first floor. The pictures had belonged to my mother, and she had given them to me when I graduated from high school. I don't know why I held onto them even when I was running like hell to escape the town, but in every apartment I had lived in I hung them up minutes after I carried the last box across the threshold.

When the house's owner, the grandmother of a classmate I vaguely remember from elementary school, died six months later, the estate offered it to us for sale and we snapped it up. We tried bringing Max back and forth with us to work a few times, but he spent most of his time at our new house brooding. Plus, it was a battle royal to lure him into the cat carrier twice a day, so Max became the office cat. Lionel stayed at home with Chaos and Chainsaw, content to spend his days sleeping in the laundry basket.

Through those first months in Coventry, Michael was unusually quiet, nodding a lot, absorbing information about his new life. Whenever a Blue Hair came hobbling into the office or an advertiser stormed in yelling and waving last week's issue in the air, irate because he had received no calls in response to his ad, Michael stood back and observed, like an anthropologist looking at a foreign culture. When I asked him about it, he'd smile and say, "I'm learning, Em, I'm learning."

For me, the most fascinating part was returning to a community where most of the people I had grown up with still lived, people I had sworn I never wanted to see again the day after graduating from Coventry High School. Girls I had infused with such power and used to steer clear of during adolescence—because of the superior attitudes they threw around so carelessly—were now slightly cowed in my presence. The tables were turned: I was now the worldly one since I had left the town while they stayed behind, hugely pregnant more often than not. The good looks they were so proud of a short decade ago were now barely recognizable under masks of poorly concealed regret and burgeoning double chins.

The biggest surprise came when Willard Blake, my best friend from high school, walked through the office door on Hal's last day. Willard had been known as a stoner in school, and we hung out together primarily because we were the two biggest outcasts around. We had lost touch after high school, and I figured he had either drifted out west or become a rehab counselor somewhere after first dealing with his own demons.

"Well, what do you know?" he said as he waltzed in the door. I noticed that Hal frowned when he saw Willard. "Emily Spencer's back in town, and running a respectable rag to boot."

We spent five minutes playing catchup with a promise to have lunch. No sooner was Willard out the door than Hal started to complain about him.

"Goddamn pothead," he grumbled. "Coventry would be better off without that good-for-nothing around. Been coming around here for years trying to sell his photos, but he's too stoned to figure out why I always say no."

It was the first time in my life that I had heard Hal Cooper curse. "He's a bad enough influence on this town to begin with, what with the poor excuses for music he plays on the radio, but no one around here has balls enough to run his sorry ass out of town," he added, sheepishly glancing at me. "Sorry 'bout my mouth, Emily, I just don't like that one."

Willard still had the Saturday morning radio show on WCOV that he had started back in high school. When I was a junior, the story was that Willard had gotten his girlfriend, Carolyn Cooper—Hal's daughter—pregnant. No wonder her father didn't like him. I wondered if Carolyn and Willard were still an item. I'd ask Willard when we got together.

Michael and I had already signed the legal papers to buy the *Courier*, which were prepared by an old classmate of mine, Ken Carville. Ken had gone away to college and law school before returning to hang his shingle on the Coventry common. Five minutes before five, we finished the layout for the next issue and Hal sent the electronic files to the printer.

"So," I said to Hal, who was perched on the edge of Michael's desk. "How does it feel to know that you'll never have to meet another newspaper deadline as long as you live?"

A broad grin covered his face. "Just wonderful, Emily," he replied. "And I feel even better after seeing that you'll be able to handle everything just fine."

He put on his coat, and headed for the door. "Can't leave it behind soon enough, can you?" Michael asked with a good-natured tease in his voice.

"I told you, but you didn't believe me, did you? I've had enough of this business. Now it's playtime. Carrie knows everything, so if you have any questions, don't call me!" The door banged behind him.

Michael and I looked at each other. Was it really ours now? I skipped toward him and he grabbed me in a big bear hug. "We did it, honey!" I said. "You were right!"

"I was right about what?"

"When you asked me about my dream and I said why I couldn't do it." I squeezed him. "You were right. I could."

"Yeah, well, just remember that the next time you think you can't have something, you're wrong," he said.

Still holding Michael in a bear hug, I could see the late-afternoon sun glinting off the engagement ring Michael had purchased a few days after surprising me with the Cracker Jack version. It was all too much too soon. Not that I was complaining, but I wondered how it could all come true within such a short period of time.

We had scheduled our wedding for the day after we took over the paper for several reasons. We were still living in the upstairs apartment and we wanted to keep the ceremony and reception simple; we knew that learning the ropes at the *Courier* would be so time-consuming that we didn't want to risk becoming attracted to the idea of a fancy wedding. As it turned out, we didn't even have the time to buy a bridal magazine, let alone read one. We wanted to keep it simple because we knew we'd have a minimum of guests. I had been out of touch with the people in Coventry for so long that I didn't know who was around anymore. And for those who did show up, I didn't want them to make a fuss.

We had a civil ceremony in the backyard behind the newspaper building with Ken Carville serving as justice of the peace. Michael's sister Stacy and her husband Patrick were there, as were Eddie and Hal Cooper. I would have invited Willard, but I wanted to leave things with Hal on a cordial note. The week before, Ken had dropped off a dog-eared paperback book of wedding vows—"Choose your own," he directed—but I was glad to not have the time to look through it, let alone write my own, which to me always crackled with fake sentimentality.

And so, with a smattering of humans and four pairs of cat eyes looking out on us from the building—Max in the office window downstairs and Lionel, Chaos, and Chainsaw pressing against the screens in the windows of our upstairs apartment—Michael and I said the *I dos* and *'til deaths* with a minimum of emotion. The whole thing was over with in less than ten minutes. We sprung for dinner at the Fletcher Country Inn where we drank too much Cabernet, ate too much duck à la orange, and talked until midnight. After everyone left, we drove home and headed up the stairs to our apartment, too exhausted to make love.

The next morning we slept until nine. After we finished our coffee, we wandered downstairs to get a headstart on the next issue. During our training period with Hal, I figured out that the quickest and easiest way to put out a paper every week was to write the whole damn thing myself, but no one would pick up a newspaper with only one writer's stories in it, and few businesses would advertise in such a publication. And so I discovered that I'd spend most of my time corralling stories and photos from contributors, laying out the paper, haranguing advertisers about getting in new copy and paying their old bills—though both Michael and Carrie also did their part in this regard—and very time little writing and editing.

We designated Saturday as our day off. Sunday was the day to get most of our work done before the phones started ringing and other interruptions began at eight o'clock sharp on Monday morning, with no respite until Friday night at eight, when the camera-ready layout was shipped to the printer. Once we moved into the house on Ruggles Road a month after the wedding, we spent Sundays working in our home offices; we rarely went into the newspaper office on Sundays.

I have interviewed enough self-employed people over the years to know that 60- and 70-hour weeks are the norm. On my side, there were town meetings and school board showdowns in the evening while Michael spent countless dinners schmoozing with advertisers. I didn't care. I was happy. I was running a business with my husband and soulmate and living once again in the town that I had loudly despised but always quietly loved. I felt as if I had no secrets. I was thrilled.

Our first three years in Coventry quickly passed in a quiet kind of delirium, a life almost monastic in its simplicity. We spent most of our waking hours either at the paper or at home—cooking, reading, or talking. We took turns making dinner every other night and switched cat box duty every other week. If I had consulted a crystal ball back in Groveton and previewed the kind of life I was living today, I would have slit my wrists to avoid the boredom. Our quiet normal lives were a novelty for both of us. In fact, we would frequently check in with each other to ask if we felt that anything was missing. For those first three years, the answer was always a blissful no.

Our sex life, while imbued with a stunned brand of passion in the early months of our relationship, had faltered off in frequency once we were married. However, since this was always considered to be par for the course, it didn't bother me. After all, our attraction was based on our minds, not our bodies.

In retrospect, I suppose I should have done a little bit of digging to see what kind of husband Michael would turn out to be. After all, he had never really told me much about his past relationships, saying, "Women don't really want to hear about these things," before changing the subject. My professional curiosity always prodded me to find out, but I was thoroughly satisfied with the WYSIWYG version—what you see is what you get—and I felt wonderfully lucky.

You know how it is when a girlfriend hooks up with the love of her life and you never see her again? I hate to admit it, but that's how I was with Michael. Why would I want to spend my precious few free moments with anyone but my husband? I began to see Eddie less and less after the wedding, even though he lived in Concord and was closer now than when I lived in Groveton. He never complained, though. The few times he and Michael met, they retreated to opposite corners of the room, so I felt less guilty about shunning him.

I learned to tune into the ever-changing rhythms of small town life again. While I was growing up in Coventry, I had always hated the way it seemed that everyone in town was watching my every move; if I wanted to cause a little trouble, my mother always heard about it before I got home. As an adult, I didn't have the same worries, though I had obviously inherited the same pair of eyes endemic to a small town where everybody knows everybody else. I called upon long-forgotten clues and instincts that I never needed in the city. For instance, if I passed by a house with a couple of out-of-state cars in the driveway and it wasn't a holiday or a weekend and the house wasn't owned by flatlanders, I knew I would receive a handwritten obituary rife with typos by the end of the day. A local death turned into a reluctant family reunion. Grown-up kids who had fled Coventry long ago would return for a few days, dragging spouses and children who had never seen their partner's or parent's childhood home. Opinions frequently changed overnight when they discovered their dad or husband grew up in a tarpaper shack.

The same truths are not as readily apparent in the city. In a small town at least an hour away from a city with more than a few options for gainful employment, desperation and changes in lifestyle reveal themselves more quickly and radically than in a populated area. When ten *For Sale* signs go up in a yard overnight, you know the names of these people, what they do and how they live, as well as the names of their kids and where they go to church. There is no such thing as quiet desperation in a rural town. People either have no qualms about letting their troubles show or else their house burns down and they hope to hell they've buried the evidence deep enough.

The only thing that worried me about owning the *Courier* was the possibility of being sued for libel or slander. The issue came up a couple of times at one of the larger papers I had worked for in Massachusetts, but the company's formidable legal team was able to buy off the slighted individual in question. One time even that wasn't necessary, since all the aggrieved reader wanted was an apology in print. Of course, the managing editor arranged for the paper's "apology" to be bumped to the middle of the Saturday night TV listings.

For me, the terror of a court battle over somebody's bruised ego was very real. Our insurance—purchased through a trade group for community newspapers—would cover costs, but I felt it would permanently drain me if we were ever sued. It just seemed like such a colossal waste of energy that I'd rather close the paper than have to fret about the legal challenges. Michael told me I had nothing to worry about, as did Hal, and though I pushed the thought away, whenever I edited a story for the next issue, I would silently ask myself, "Is somebody going to take this the wrong way?" Unless it was a blatantly nasty insult or joke, I'd leave it in, though my nervousness would remain.

Occasionally I heard curious stories through the grapevine that were no doubt true, but I couldn't print them because they were secondhand. If a family in town needed money, they'd hold on until winter when their patience and bank account would fray to the breaking point. Then, checking to see that their home insurance premiums were paid up, even if that meant eating nothing but potatoes for dinner for an entire month, they'd blame the resulting blaze on a wood-stove or chimney fire.

One tidbit that winged its way back to me was the method of smearing bacon grease on a string of Christmas tree lights sometime in December, and then arranging to visit relatives the next town over, with the dogs tied up outside in 10-below weather. Mice will smell the bacon grease and start gnawing on the wires. Within minutes there are a couple of fried mice and a house in flames. When the fire inspectors visit the next day, there are no traces, since bacon grease cannot be detected by bloodhounds.

I learned more than I ever wanted to know about human nature in running the paper. I think that's one reason why, soon after we were married, Michael and I decided not to have kids. People in general are unpredictable, messy, and overly obvious when they want something—just like children. In my reporter days, I could keep the truth about human behavior at a distance since I rarely interviewed the same person twice. But in Coventry, I got to know some people too well, and like Mary at the general store, I had to keep my mouth shut if I wanted to hold onto their business as either readers or advertisers.

So Michael and I stuck with the cats and invented amusing games to play with them, like Kitty Airport, where we'd place a piece of chicken on one end of the dining-room table and wait until one of the cats upstairs got wind of it. Usually, it took no more than a minute or two for the cats to come padding down the stairs, the click of their nails echoing off the bare walls. Then, one by one, they'd run onto the sofa cushion, using it as a trampoline to jump onto the back of the sofa and then careen down the length of the table, using their claws to stop just before reaching the end of the table. A whiff of fish took them less than 30 seconds to travel from upstairs bedroom to runway. Anything that involved a can opener, of course, didn't count since they came running even if I opened a can of beets. Curiously, only Lionel bounded down the stairs for cheese; it was his favorite.

They also invented their own games; Kitty TV was a favorite during the winter. All three would sprawl in front of the woodstove and, with heavy-lidded eyes, Chaos, Chainsaw, and Lionel would watch the fire through the glass-front door, mesmerized by the continual motion of the flames.

• • •

The first day we were on our own at the paper, a Monday, Willard showed up with three camera cases slung across his shoulders and a leather portfolio in his hand. Before I could formally introduce him to Michael, he had his portfolio unzipped and prints and contact sheets strewn across the front counter.

"I'm sorry about Hal," I told him as I began leafing through the pictures.

"Oh, that's okay. I'm used to it. Besides, I only boinked Carolyn once when we were back in high school, in the eleventh grade, though we pretty much carry on on a regular basis these days." He dug into his case and brought out a handful of photos. "And I didn't knock her up. You have no idea how difficult it is to live down your high school reputation," he said. "You were lucky. You stayed away long enough so that a lot of people forgot. Me, I came back less than a year after I left, and it was like I was right back in study hall."

I tapped the photos on the counter. "So what do you want me to do with these?"

"Publish them, of course. Old Man Cooper had no sense of humor," he said, holding up a photo of a car with its entire front end stuck in the sand so that the back was sticking up at a 45-degree angle. "This is Carhenge, some warped place in Nebraska, modeled after Stonehenge."

"Yeah? So?"

"I figured the way people are so nutso about their junk cars around here, why not have a little fun? I've seen plenty of cars in weird situations, and let me tell you, they're out there."

"Well, what, for instance?"

"This." He pointed to a shot of a 60s-vintage VW microbus stuck in the crotch of a tree.

"How'd it get there?"

"Precisely," Willard answered. "We'll print the answer in the next issue. If we put a different weird car shot in the paper every week, people will start to look forward to reading the paper again. And I wouldn't mind one bit if you decided to slap it on the front page, either. The *Courier* has gotten pretty crusty in the last few years, Emily, in one issue last year, all the Blue Hairs listed the menu at the Senior Center in their columns and not much else. Cooper didn't even catch it."

I remembered getting that issue in the mail and thought it was a joke. "Must've been a slow week," I said.

"Even slow for around here," he muttered. "Come on, you're the new owner, shake some life into this baby and get people excited about it. You still have that warped sense of humor, don't you? We'll call it Carnage, and it'll give me a reason to plug the *Courier* on the radio."

I smiled. "But I don't want to pull a Bill Clinton and alienate half the town in our first week."

"I wouldn't worry about that. Come on, Emily, at least give it a try."

"Alright," I said. "But if Moe's Used Cars pulls his ad, we'll have to forget it."

"Deal."

At first, we put the photos on page five, but as it turned out, Willard was right: Carnage was a great success. After the first couple of issues, we moved it to the front page. We had to drop off more copies at the Richford campus each week; the college students couldn't get enough of it.

Willard and I renewed our high school friendship with a vengeance. We soon confided in each other about everything, and our relationship began to have the feel of what I used to share with Eddie before I married Michael. The big difference was that Michael actually liked Willard, unlike his feelings toward Eddie.

Choosing the photos became a weekly ritual. Every Monday afternoon, Willard came into the office and spread contact sheets, slides, and prints across the conference table in the back of the office. We'd spend an hour or two pawing through them while gossiping about various people in town. It was also one of the few times that Max jumped off the monitor during the week. He was attracted to the chemicals on the prints, a fact we discovered one day when we left

Willard's photos unattended on the table and came back five minutes later to find tiny tooth marks on the corners of several of the photos.

Lionel was the same way back at the house, and I quickly learned to store all of our photos in a drawer. The two newspaper cats must have developed a taste for developer at an early age. The next week, I took out a small Baggie of catnip to distract Max.

"What a druggie," Willard muttered as Max chewed, kicked, and scratched the Baggie before passing out flat on his back under the table, paws in the air and snoring loudly enough to be heard out front in the lobby.

Though we quickly became great friends, we didn't socialize outside of those Monday afternoons. Willard was the only man I knew who was a bona fide cat nut, and he said that he didn't like to feel obligated to clean his house for visitors, but he did it anyway. In the next breath, however, he told me the real reason was Carolyn.

Carolyn Cooper had always been kind of a hippie chick in high school, and according to Willard, she had cranked up the volume about 50 decibels after leaving school. She grew organic herbs—the legal kind, he said—in a dilapidated cape on the edge of town and didn't like cats. She refused to live with Willard because he had eight. However, Carolyn liked to use the cat-fur tumbleweeds from Willard's house to weave blankets and hats to sell at the Fletcher Organic Food Coop, so she sometimes showed up to clean Willard's house when she ran out of cat fur for her projects. Plus, she was a radical vegan, a pretty unpatriotic stance in these parts.

Therefore, whenever Willard cleaned the house, it meant he had company, the female kind, and Carolyn was insanely jealous. She'd stomp around for a month if she sensed that another woman had been in Willard's house. So we kept to our Monday afternoons at the newspaper office, though I'd occasionally join him on his jaunts through town as he searched for new Carnage subjects.

I sometimes envied Willard's life. He lived in the house he

grew up in—which had long been paid off; he inherited it after his mother went into a nursing home for Alzheimers patients—and he didn't have any bills to speak of, except for film for his cameras. He worked part-time at WCOV, the local radio station that bore more than a passing resemblance to the station on the TV show Northern Exposure. The only difference is that Coventry didn't have as many moose— maybe one would amble down Main Street in broad daylight over the course of a year.

I'd occasionally catch his radio show on Saturday mornings except when he got too weird, playing music from an a capella group of men who banged the sides of their noses while humming in order to sound like a brass quintet. Most of the time, however, he stuck to a steady rotation of Phish, Tony Bennett, and Lotte Lenya, with the occasional Stravinsky thrown in for good measure.

• • •

"Why don't you do something with the letters column?" I asked, trying to keep the frustration out of my voice.

"Like what?"

"Oh, I don't know. Use your imagination."

I was talking to a fresh-faced Richford journalism major named Bethany. Michael and I had just celebrated our third anniversary at the *Courier,* and I had just about had it with the trust fund babies that the College sent us as interns on a regular basis. Girls with her age and attitude drove me nuts; they reminded me of some of the students I sat next to in J-school. These bouncy, giggly girls overdosed on journalism classes taught by paunchy, balding professors whose only claim to literary fame was a photocopied chapbook of bad poetry written in their pre-A.A. days. No matter, these idealistic female freedom fighters promptly fell in love with their cynical teachers who were so flattered by their nubile attention that they encouraged their students to use their newfound media power to free the oppressed. Jesus, give me an acne-scarred, testosterone-crazed jock who's physically incapable of looking north of my tits any day. Age and cynicism had taught me that the goal of the press on good days was to toss out a few tidbits of information before being quickly relegated to the dump or the birdcage. The problem is that no one ever told me what to do on the bad days.

The first time we had extra space to fill in the paper, Michael spent an hour writing a couple of letters to the editor expressing his views but signing them *Name Withheld*. The letters column leaned toward sparseness whenever an election wasn't pending, which was 42 weeks out of the year. The other ten weeks, I could fill the paper with nothing but bile-ridden scrawls from people who predicted an apocalypse if their candidate lost.

This week, we had only received one letter from the prolific Mr. Warren E. Byfield. This elderly gentleman prided himself on airing his beliefs on a weekly basis, which he viewed as the benchmark of a free society. He had even published and attempted to sell a bound collection of two years' of his letters to the editor—both those we published and those we ignored. That week, we still had at least two letters' worth of white space to fill.

Bethany was appalled. "You mean these aren't actually real people? Like, how can you do that?"

Michael, who was on the phone, overheard the conversation. "*Playboy* does it, why can't we?" She obviously didn't know we were kidding. He tossed a few *Couriers* from previous weeks in her direction. "Hey, the minutes from the selectmen's meeting have been pretty lame lately," he said. "They could use a little spicing up, too."

"How could you? You're a newspaper!" Her collagen-heavy top lip quivered with indignation. On top of my monitor, Max opened one sleepy eye to investigate the commotion.

"You're right, at least we were the last time I checked." Michael shrugged and resumed his typing.

Another strike in her P.C. world. I made a note to call the

journalism department for a new intern tomorrow, since Bethany obviously wouldn't stoop so low as to show her face within these heathen walls again. In fact, ten minutes later she made some excuse to leave and never came back. I began to design and write an ad highlighting next week's articles in order to fill the space. I was almost finished when I discovered I had left a few of the articles at home.

"Hey, I've got to pick up some stories back at the house," I told Michael, throwing on my coat. "I'll be back in a bit. Hold down the fort, will you?"

"No problem," Michael said. "Just as long as you're back by three. I have to go pick up the new ad from Millie." The Coventry Savings & Loan was one of our best advertisers, with one full page in every issue. Millie Connelly was the branch manager and the sister of Joel Gardner, the *Courier's* on-call computer geek. Millie had won several graphic art awards when we were in high school, but she married her childhood sweetheart and stayed in Coventry instead of attending Parsons in New York, where she had been accepted. Her creative outlet was to design all of the bank's ads for the paper. Since the bank spent so much money with us over the course of a year, Michael considered it a courtesy to pick up the new ad from her in person each week.

I passed by Michael's desk, and he craned his neck up for a kiss. When I leaned over to kiss him, my stomach jumped. Every day I marveled at how much I still loved this man, something I had thought would diminish in time.

On the way to the house, I stopped by the police station to pick up Chief Bill LaLumiere's column, if it could be called that. The cruiser was gone, and so was Bill, so I scrawled a note and tacked it on the door.

I put the 240 in reverse and swung out onto the asphalt. Sometimes I wished I could drive in reverse all the time; I only felt the power of the rear-wheel drive vehicle when I was going backwards. But I absolutely refused to break down and replace the Benz until it dropped dead. I passed the house where Eddie had grown up—his parents still lived there—and noticed several cars with out-of-state plates parked in the driveway. Bill's cruiser was also there.

Uh-oh. Last time we spoke, Eddie had told me his father wasn't doing too well since his mini-stroke last year and an advancing case of emphysema. I hated the thought, but the funeral would also give me a chance to see Eddie without having to drive south. Mid-March is that in-between time of year when I refuse to drive south for any reason. The signs of spring are more obvious south of the Mason-Dixon Line separating New Hampshire from Massachusetts, though the pollution down there probably has as much of an effect on me as the slightly warmer temperatures. I even hated to drive down to Concord this time of year. I hadn't seen Eddie since he came home for Christmas, so we had a lot of catching up to do.

I picked up the papers at the house and drove back to the paper, figuring a phone message from Eddie's mother would be waiting. I hung up my coat and nodded to Michael as I leafed through the pink message slips on my desk. On top was one from Mrs. Trager.

When I was growing up, I always wanted a mother like Mrs. Trager. I used to joke with Eddie about moving into his house. She was fun, animated, involved with her own kids in a way that, even back then, I knew was an impossible dream for my parents. She talked to her kids like people and treated their friends the same way. She never minced words when it came to the truth. "Your turtle died," she told Eddie and me one day when we were eight years old and playing in the backyard. She helped us dig a grave, locate a cigar box for the coffin, and make a grave marker that would still be legible after the first heavy rain.

I dialed the number from memory.

"Hello?" a raspy voice wheezed, catching me off guard. Eddie's father.

"Oh, Mr. Trager. It's Emily Spencer."

"Oh, Emily," was all he could manage before his voice collapsed into a violent cough, which was replaced by the dull background noise of conversation.

"Hello?" Mrs. Trager asked. "Who is this?"

"It's Emily, Mrs. Trager, what is going on?"

"Oh, Emily," she said, her voice softening to absorb her grief. "You heard, then."

"Heard about what?"

She paused. "Eddie," she whispered. "He passed away last night."

"But I thought—"

"Wait a minute," she said. The muffled conversations disappeared when I heard a door close.

"I don't want everyone to hear. I know what you're thinking, Emily, and no, it wasn't AIDS. He went into a diabetic coma, and everybody here already knows that, but you know Eddie. He wanted his buddies to think it was AIDS."

I nodded. I remembered a conversation Eddie and I had at Christmas. He didn't look well at all. His diabetes—he had carried around syringes and vials of insulin since we were in second grade—had gotten worse and was harder to control, which explained his pallor, gauntness, and lack of energy. Of course, with his flamboyance and verve, everybody thought he had AIDS; none of his friends even knew he was diabetic.

He told me that he never let on because he said that testing positive for HIV automatically bestowed a gay man with a certain honor, even awe. Eddie was lonely. As were most gay men, he told me. "But they would rather die before they'd let anyone know." His bogus illness brought him lots of love and care in what he rightfully perceived to be his last days.

Mrs. Trager filled me in about the visiting hours and the funeral, and I hung up the phone.

"What?" asked Michael.

"Eddie. He's dead."

I gave him the short version. I didn't feel like talking.

"I'm going home," I announced, putting my coat back on. It was still warm.

The funeral was held three days later at the Coventry Congregational Church. Eddie's family showed up along with faces I recognized from the days when Eddie and I were hanging out in some of New Hampshire's seedier gay bars. Michael came with me and Willard was there with his camera bag in tow. I planned to run an obituary in the next *Courier*, accompanied by the photo from his senior year. I told Willard he could take some pictures, but I couldn't imagine that we would run any from the funeral itself.

Reverend Norman Faulkner eulogized Eddie as a "unique individual, a person who wasn't afraid to be who he was." The irony was that even though Mrs. Trager had told the pastor the cause of death, Reverend Faulkner instead believed the rumors, talking of a terrible plague and playing up Eddie's individuality, a "wonderful virtue that everyone should strive for."

The service was punctuated by sniffles and a few coughs—primarily from his father—but mostly laughs when his friends and family got up to describe some of the crazier sides of Eddie's personality. His mother related how Eddie insisted he would never move out of New Hampshire because he didn't want to risk being mistaken for a flatlander. She also announced that Eddie would be cremated and his ashes scattered onto Echo Lake in the White Mountains, directly underneath the promontory of rock that was the infamous Old Man in the Mountains of license plate and postcard fame. She smiled when she described how Eddie insisted it be done on a hot, sunny Saturday in August when the place was crawling with tourists and that she should just explain to the crowd that she was scattering the ashes of an AIDS victim. That was one way to ensure that he'd have the place to himself during his favorite time of year, even though it was technically illegal to scatter ashes on water because they float and can wash up on the shore.

After the service, Michael and I drove home in silence. We ate a quick dinner of pasta and salad. At eight o'clock, I told him I was going to bed. I was exhausted and didn't set the alarm.

The next day, Carrie said she'd finish the paper that week and told me to take a long weekend. I protested, but she wouldn't hear of it. "I've been at this paper longer than you have, and it wouldn't be the first time I've done it," she said, wagging a finger in my face. I gave up and drove home.

On Saturday, I slept until nine and then spent the morning puttering around the house. I sat at the kitchen table leafing through old cookbooks. Maybe if I made something new for dinner it would cheer both of us up. Chainsaw was parked on the table, batting at each page as I turned it.

Michael came downstairs a little after eleven, which wasn't unusual for him on our days off. I thought he had slept soundly last night, but when he came downstairs he looked as if he had pulled an all-nighter.

I got up to pour him a cup of coffee. "What's the matter, honey? You look like you didn't sleep at all."

He ran a hand through his hair and yawned loudly. "Are the bags that bad?" he asked, gently pulling the skin at the corner of his eyes in the direction of his ears.

"No, but all of you looks beat."

He yawned again and reached for his cup. "Well then, I guess it's good we took a long weekend."

"Yeah, everything at the office is pretty much settled and besides, Carrie knows where I am if there's an emergency."

Michael stirred his coffee. He stared out the back window, a bit mournfully, I thought.

"The buds are still two months away, and we'll probably get socked with at least one more storm, so I wouldn't hold my breath," I told him.

"It's not that," he said. "I was just thinking about Eddie and how he felt like he needed to hide the truth from everyone, like he felt that he alone wasn't good enough. It seemed like he just had to construct these elaborate stories. Was he always like that?"

I was surprised by his comment. Although Eddie was my friend, he and Michael had seemed to barely tolerate each other. "Well, no, but he always needed an audience, and he would tell them whatever they wanted to hear, if only they would stick around. But he never said it bothered him."

Michael slumped in his seat. "Yeah, but he must have been perennially frustrated. You know, he creates this elaborate persona that has people crawling all over him but is really nothing more than an act. Then he probably had to keep creating new Eddies all the time in order to keep them all interested." He shook his head. "Not a good way to live."

Somehow, the depressing person that Michael was describing didn't mesh with the Eddie I knew. Yes, he could be bitchy and moody, but he was also one of the most genuine people I knew.

"I think that mostly he wanted to poke fun at the people who put a person with AIDS up on a pedestal and worthy of lots of attention," I explained. "Eddie told me a few years ago there were actually people who would deliberately contract AIDS because they knew they'd get a lot of attention, not only for serving as one of the foot soldiers of the gay community, but also because of the way they'd inevitably get courted by the medical establishment with all their new studies. As Eddie put it, they needed a fresh batch of guinea pigs every month."

Michael reached for his coffee. "I just think it's a shame he couldn't be who he wanted to be."

I looked at him. "Michael, you didn't even know him that well, and you barely said hello whenever he came over. I don't understand how you could say these things about someone you didn't know and never made any attempt to get to know." I got up from the table. "It shouldn't affect you so."

But it did. Though we had made plans to go out for dinner that night, Michael said he was starting to come down with a cold, so we stayed home. That weekend marked the beginning of a long stretch where Michael could barely scrape together enough energy to get out of bed in the morning. In all the time I had known him, I'd never seen him down. I was concerned, but fortunately, with all of the long-term contracts left over from Hal Cooper's reign and the new ones he had brought in since we bought the paper, we'd still make money.

A week later, Michael began to season his depression with a few pinches of anger. At first, it was the little things that set him off. He complained about finding a cat hair in his food. He used to be amused by the sight of Chaos eating off my plate on the dining room table back in Groveton. And the fact that my books were scattered around my reading chair in the living room instead of neatly stacked was enough to put him in a foul mood. Then he started slamming doors and yelling at me for not cooking dinner when it was really his turn.

I quickly learned to back off. As the weeks wore on and the days grew longer and warmer, his depression and anger deepened. At first, I asked what was bothering him. He'd shrug his shoulders and grunt. After about a week of wordless grunting, I quit asking.

He began to spend more time on the computer at home. Our computer guru Joel Gardner had set up the office system so that all the computers were networked and it was easy to access the Internet, but in truth there was always too much commotion going on at the office to take a leisurely stroll on the web. So we did the majority of our web surfing at home. Joel had hooked up our home computers a year ago and allowed us to access the network of office computers, though our two home computers were not networked to each other.

Michael was amazed at the wealth of information he could find online. In fact, when Michael first began to explore the Internet, every 10 minutes or so he'd call me over, saying, "Hey, Em, you've *got* to see this!"

But when he became depressed, his enthusiasm about sharing his online discoveries plummeted, even though he spent hours online at home. He would sit frozen in front of the computer late into the night and never once call me to see a site. If I came into his office when he was online, he'd scowl, close his browser screen, whirl around in his chair, and ask in an accusing tone, "What do *you* want?

Since he became depressed, an immutable precedent had been set for our evenings. After dinner, we'd retreat to opposite ends of the house, me in the living room reading or watching TV and Michael in his study at the computer. After an hour by myself, I'd start to get restless. I'd head upstairs and lean against the open door to his office.

"I thought you had gotten all your work done at the office today," I would say, or words to that effect, attempting but mostly failing to keep a slight whine out of my voice. "It would be nice if we could spend some time together." When I interrupted him, his lips formed a straight line, pressing tightly together. Sometimes he gave no response except for a loud wordless sigh as he clicked off his computer and dutifully padded down the hall behind me, as if the great burden of sleeping in the same room with me was too much to ask. Other times he'd say, "I'll be there soon." I'd walk over to his desk and place my hands on his shoulders. He would crane his neck up to me, and plant a perfunctory, dry kiss on my lips.

Perfunctory was the perfect word to describe it. Definition, according to Webster's: *Performed merely as an uninteresting routine; without interest or enthusiasm.* No juicy sounds here, just a dry smack, no exchange of bodily fluids possible. Even the sound of the word—perfunctory—matter-of-fact and totally without passion, suited.

On the rare nights that we went to bed at the same time, I'd use the bathroom first. Once I was in bed, it was his turn. He'd dally long enough until I warmed up the bed. He'd slide into bed besides me, rustling the sheets up like a tent before turning away from me, his back cold and hard.

Chapter Three

Despite Michael's moods, we somehow managed to put out a paper each week. I noticed that he was his old self around the office—when he managed to drag himself in—so nobody really caught on. Except for Carrie, who commented on the tension between me and Michael about a month into his depression. I noticed that she was staring at me with a funny look on her face one morning. Michael hadn't come into the office yet; when I left the house, he was still asleep.

"Emily?"

I was in the middle of deciphering Mrs. Fitzgerald's latest column, written in pencil on parchment paper, as it was every week. So far, I had managed not to smear any words, but I was pushing my luck. "Mmmm?"

"Are you two doing okay?"

I kept my head down. "Who two?"

"You and Michael."

"We're fine," I said. "Why do you ask?"

She sat across from me at Michael's desk. "You both seem a little distant lately. You don't joke around like you normally do. In fact, I don't know if I've seen you say more than five words to each other when you're both here at the same time, which is increasingly becoming a rarity."

I set my jaw and looked up at her. "Oh, Carrie, nothing's really wrong. Michael just hasn't felt well lately. You know, he's had his cold for more than a month now, and he just can't shake it."

"Do you think he wants to move back to the city?"

"Oh no," I answered. "He loves it here."

This was the only thing I was sure of. Everything else was in doubt, even his cold, though he was polishing off a family-size bottle of Nyquil every week in a vain attempt to ease his symptoms.

"Besides, I told you, he just has a cold," I said.

I knew he was sick, but I viewed it not as a cold but as more of a holding pattern, a way he could wallow in his current state of misery.

Carrie frowned, unconvinced. "I just worry about you two, you know."

"Well, don't," I told her. While I wasn't sure of the cause of Michael's malaise—and I had stopped asking—I had the feeling that if I just waited it out things would return to our previous brand of normal. After all, spring was on the horizon—in New England, it shows up in mid-May—the paper was chugging away, and no major crises loomed.

That day, I decided to keep track of Michael's moods to see if there was a pattern to them. I began to keep coded comments on my desk blotter calendar at work to chart Michael's overall disposition each day. *S* stood for a so-so day, last Thursday, for example. Michael was charming on the phone and to the Blue Hairs who came in to drop off their columns. But he'd toss a nasty glare my way if I laughed too loudly on the phone or if he didn't like where I had placed a particular ad.

He had a point: Small-town feuds can sink a business. He turned surly because the ad for the Coventry Drug Store was adjacent to a verbatim press release for an amateur theatre production of "Bye, Bye Birdie." The executive director of the county arts council who wrote the press release on the upcoming show was a lethal enemy of the woman who ran the pharmacy, and the release appeared on the same page as the ad. Sounds dumb, but Hal had drawn up a scorecard of all the long-standing feuds in town, which I came to view as one of our most valuable assets. A long-time advertiser would never tell us why he suddenly yanked his ad, he would just avoid all contact with us in the future. Small-town politics at its worst.

MB stood for Miserable Bastard, and even Max knew to stay out of Michael's way on those days. If I said even one word to him on those days, I knew he'd pick a fight. *G* was for good, which meant his mood stayed relatively calm.

After I had kept score for two months, I added up the letters on my calendar; I even kept score on the weekends. Ten *G*s, eight *S*s, and five *MB*s. I flipped back to the middle of March, when I first started to chart his moods. From April 15th until today, May 15th, I counted 18 *S*s, 11 *MB*s, and only two *G*s. Things were getting worse.

But so far, I would have graded him a rare *G* at two that afternoon. I held my breath, and by five o'clock, remarkably, the *G* had stuck. I took the bold move of asking Michael if he wanted to go out for dinner that night, just the two of us.

He didn't answer at first. Instead, he stood up and stretched. I watched his jacket part, revealing a snugly fitted dress shirt underneath. This simple motion made me catch my breath, though I had to suppress it, since he had ignored any signs of physical desire that I showed toward him lately. The last time we had sex was the beginning of March.

Michael walked over to my desk, stood behind my chair and hugged me. "Sure, Em, whatever you want," he said. "I think we both need it." Then he kissed me wetly on the cheek and sat back down at his computer. "Just give me 15 minutes, okay?"

I almost marked a great big *G* in indelible ink for the day, but not only would I be pushing my luck, it also went against my rules, since I always graded each day the following morning. After all, there were still more minutes in the day left for him to blow up at something.

"Sure, hon, you want me to call and make a reservation at Studebaker's?"

"We probably don't need one," he said, his modem rasping in the background. "Just got to check my email."

Joel had arranged our email so that we had two separate accounts—one for business, one for personal—that we could check whether we were in the office or at home. We liked to keep them separate because it made it easier to determine which messages needed our immediate attention and which didn't. If we were in the office and wanted to check personal email that was sent to us at home, we had to type in a different password. Though Michael and I shared one account for personal mail, we each had different mailboxes. Michael typed a few keystrokes before he opened his email, so I knew he was checking his personal mail. He stopped typing and began to read. I was leafing through a file cabinet, out of his range of vision, and stopped to stare at him. After spending more than three years with the man, I never got tired of looking at him.

As I watched, the bluish light from the monitor reflected back onto his face, but instead of giving him a sickly glow as it did most people, it made him look calm and serene. More than once I theorized that his recent craziness was a Jekyll and Hyde game, and in some way, out of his control. Was I really imagining it all, I thought, as I watched Michael read and then respond to each email.

His face muscles seemed to be in constant motion. Smiling, furrowing his brow, crinkling his eyes, at one point even leaning in close, his nose almost touching the monitor. He threw back his head and laughed. He glanced over at my desk and pivoted around and saw me looking at him. His face abruptly switched from relaxed to angry.

"You were watching me," he said, accusingly.

I walked over and hugged him in the same way he had embraced me not ten minutes earlier. Mr. Hyde was back. Michael angrily clicked out of his email program and stared at the screen.

"Yeah, so what?" I said, whispering in his ear.

He didn't reach up to me. Instead, my husband turned

into a lead weight, not responding to my touch, my words, my love. I didn't understand; not thirty seconds earlier, he was happy and laughing. What happened?

He abruptly stood up, breaking my embrace with a gesture that bordered on the violent. "Let's get something to eat," he said in a monotone.

"Okay," I said. Even though his mood swings caught me off guard, I kept my mouth shut because I figured that if he could snap into a bad mood in a matter of seconds, he could get out of it just as quickly. I grabbed my coat and shut off the lights. Michael stood at the open door, watching me with a dissatisfied look in his eye. Whenever he fell into these moods, I seemed to be constantly rushing to keep up with a schedule that only he knew about. Once we were outside, we began walking to the restaurant; I needed three steps to keep up with his two.

A block away from Studebaker's, I stopped. "Can you tell me what's wrong?"

He stopped and turned toward me. His face had lost its nastiness as quickly as it had appeared. "Oh, nothing, Em, I truly don't know what's gotten into me." He pulled me close and hugged me tightly.

As he held me, my mind fast-forwarded through a raft of thoughts. When Michael first became depressed, I thought it was because of me, but I couldn't come up with a single way that I had changed or started to do something different in the last few months. I assumed Michael was going through some kind of premature midlife crisis and figured he would eventually want to talk about it with me.

As I'm not the most patient person, at times Michael's antics wore extremely thin. When they hit, at the office or at home, I'd step outside and gulp air until I became dizzy. Once I calmed down, I could deal with anything Michael could hurl my way, even an entire week of *MB* days. All I needed was to regain some perspective. As Michael's wife, I needed to support him in whatever he was going through, even if he chose not to discuss it with me.

One thing, though, was really starting to bug me. Just as Tom back at the *Transcript* had told me that I had become a different person after I met Michael, I felt myself changing again, but in a disturbing way this time: I was turning into a doormat, walking on eggshells, all in an effort to keep Michael from blowing up. Years earlier, in my first reporting job at a small daily in Keene, New Hampshire, I interviewed a woman at the local battered women's clinic. When I asked her how her marriage had changed her, she took a deep breath before speaking.

"I pushed down my personality because I would do anything to keep him from hitting me, and after awhile I didn't recognize myself anymore," she told me. "Today, I'm changing again because I'm turning back into the person I was before."

Her words flashed into my mind out of nowhere that night, but I decided I was different: I was not a battered woman and I can certainly recognize myself.

Michael was still holding me. He leaned down to kiss me on the lips and took my arm, holding it the rest of the way to the restaurant. This was the Michael I fell in love with, I thought as we walked the rest of the way.

Studebaker's was a decent enough restaurant, for Coventry, at least. It's the local hangout for businessmen and Richford students with fat trust funds, and for Michael when he's trying to win over a reluctant advertiser.

"How much credit do we have left?" I asked Michael after Julie, the waitress, had taken our drink order. We usually bartered ads dollar-for-dollar with restaurants, since it allowed us to entertain clients without spending real money. However, since Michael hadn't been working much, I assumed he hadn't been to the restaurant in weeks. Michael opened up his menu with a flourish. I noticed that he sat a little straighter than usual, as if a cable were holding him in place.

He waved my question away and studied the menu. "Oh, don't worry," he said. "We have plenty. I checked last week."

"Oh?" I glanced up at him. "Have you been here recently?"

"No," he said without looking at me. "I just stopped by to check for the next time I hit them up for a new ad schedule. Their contract is up for renewal, you know."

He closed his menu and quickly looked at me before turning toward the bar at the back of the restaurant. His glance lasted a second too long before he turned back to face me.

"So," he said, a bit too eager I thought, given his moods lately. "What are you having?"

I closed my menu. "What is with you tonight?"

"*Nothing*. Why?"

Julie set the drinks on the table. She wore at least two turquoise rings on each finger of both hands—including her thumbs—and had a white feather earring stuck in her right ear. She wore a Colt revolver on her hip during her shifts, since she was a part-time deputy for the town and sometimes got a call in the middle of her shift. She also wore two pagers, one from the police station and the other from the kitchen, and I often wondered how she was able to distinguish between the two. I watched her head towards the kitchen, her walk imbued with a serious sense of purpose.

"I mean that you're more animated than I've seen you in a long time."

"I've had a good day, we're out to have a good time tonight—it's been awhile—and we're together." He covered my hand with his, letting it levitate above mine so that it was touching, but just barely. He smiled at me, tilting his head slightly. "So what's the problem?"

I settled back in my chair. I didn't have to tell him that I was so used to the unspoken tension between us I was on constant alert to defend myself.

Michael sipped his drink. I noticed Doug Prior, the owner of Studebaker's, sitting at the bar. He also owned a small store in town that specialized in fancy engraved stationery and invitations, along with novelty gifts that the typical

Richford student would drop a few hundred of Daddy's bucks on without blinking. Doug was a bit greasy for my taste, but since he had a quarter-page ad in the paper every week, I couldn't complain. In fact, he was the primary sponsor of the special Richford homecoming edition of the paper each year, taking out two full-page ads, including the back cover. I nodded to him when we first came into the restaurant.

We ate dinner in silence, except that Michael wasn't wearing his usual I'm-freezing-you-out-Emily look. After our plates were cleared, Michael excused himself to talk to Doug. I tried not to look at them at the bar, but I couldn't help myself. I hadn't seen that version of Michael in a long time. In fact, the way he was laughing and talking with Doug reminded me of the way Michael looked when we first started dating. By the time he returned, almost 20 minutes later, the coffee he told me to order for him was cold and the contemptuous curl to his lip was back.

"What was that all about?" I asked.

"Oh, nothing."

We drove home in silence. When we got home, I went to bed and Michael headed for his computer. When I woke up next morning, Michael had already left the house. He didn't come into the office all day, so I figured he was out on sales calls.

Since it was Friday, I had to stay late to close the paper. Michael knew not to bother me; I liked to be by myself when doing the finishing touches. I had lost all track of time when the phone rang. The clock on my monitor read 8:20.

"*Coventry Courier.*"

"Emily," said a voice I couldn't immediately recognize.

"Yes?"

"It's Doug. From Studebaker's. I didn't expect to find you here so late."

"Oh, hi, Doug. Listen, dinner last night was great. Michael was in a better mood than I've seen him in weeks." At least he was for part of the evening. "Hey, if you're calling to change your ad for next week, you've got about 15 minutes before I zap it to the printer."

He paused and inhaled loudly. "Well, yes and no," he replied. "I figured I was too late for next week's paper." His voice sounded strange. "But you know, I was looking for Michael. It's *not* an emergency," he added.

"Did you try him at home?"

"He wasn't there, so I left a message."

That's odd; he's usually home by now on a Friday night.

"Well, I'll tell him you called."

"Thanks, Em."

He hung up before I could say goodbye. Something wasn't right. Why was he calling the office late on a Friday night looking for Michael? I thought Doug had sounded a little nervous. I sat for a minute, staring at the phone. Michael's probably at home on the computer.

I dialed our home number, and the machine picked up after two rings, instead of four, which meant there were messages. I dialed the other number, the one we used to go online, expecting it to be busy since I was sure Michael was online. It rang and rang.

Where was he? It wasn't like him to fall asleep this early, even if he'd spent a full day on the road.

I redialed the main number and punched in the code to check messages. There were four: two hangups, and one from Doug, using a decidedly different voice from the one he used with me, more upbeat, almost sing-song.

"Hey Michael, just wanted to know if you wanted to hit the town with a bunch of us tonight. You know where we'll be."

I tried to think of a reason why Michael would want to go out with Doug, who he barely knew, when the fourth message began: It was Michael.

"Hey, Em, it's me." His voice was quiet, subdued, with none of the anger or depression that had filled it in previous months.

"I'm down in Malden with Stacy and the gang. Just felt

like coming down for a few days. I'll try you again later."

That was odd. He knew I'd be at the office; he obviously didn't want to talk to me. Something's not right. First Doug calling like an old buddy, then Michael splitting town without telling me. *It's nothing*, I thought, shaking it off, and returned to my work.

At a few minutes past nine, the paper was finished. I logged on and sent the file to the printer. After I got home, I almost called Michael at his sister's, but thought better of it. I poured milk into a saucepan and dribbled a glob of Bosco into it. The cats yelled as they polished my ankles. Two hours and 47 minutes past their dinnertime; by the sounds they made you'd think I was clipping their nails.

After spooning out their wet stink, I thanked the cat goddess that Max hated canned food so I didn't have to smell up the office by opening a can of Friskies. I took my cocoa into the living room and settled on the sofa. I reached for that morning's *Globe* and read for an hour before heading up to bed.

• • •

When I woke up, I decided that since I had the day to myself it was a good excuse to wallow in the history of Coventry. Though I rarely had time to write for the paper anymore, a story about an old building or a local person would occasionally spark my interest.

It was Michael's idea to run a series about the old cemeteries in town, running articles not only about their history but also about people who were buried there. The funny thing is that he initially meant it as a joke. "I've been trying to get Old Man Carter to advertise for years with no luck. Maybe if we run some stories about a bunch of dead people, he'll do it."

Old Man Carter—first name of Phineas—ran the local funeral home, which his grandfather had started back in the 1890s. He hadn't changed a thing about himself or his business for as long as I could remember. Phineas Carter dressed in an old black velvet suit, even on the hottest August days. One afternoon last year, I walked alongside him down Main Street, trying to get a few details out of him. I was writing an obituary about Eldred Furrow who, at 97, had been the oldest person in town and therefore in possession of the Boston Post Cane. The cane was an antiquity handed down to the next oldest person in town when the oldest dies. The tradition had started in many small New Hampshire towns about a hundred years ago, when the long-defunct *Boston Post* began a campaign in an ill-fated effort to increase its readership in the north. Many of the canes were lost, transported across state lines, or buried six feet under as a result of a long-running feud. Sometimes the current holder was damned if she would let the next oldest have the honor. If that happened, some towns had a new cane made to give to the newly knighted. In fact, *Boston Post Cane* is a standard line item in more than a few New Hampshire town budgets.

Eldred Furrow had had a long-running feud with Gladys Thibeault, the next oldest in town, who had spurned Eldred decades ago for marrying her best friend Lylah Donovan instead of herself. I wanted to ask Carter if he had spotted the cane in Eldred's house. In the middle of laying out the obituary, I noticed Old Man Carter breeze past the office. I burst through the door and caught up with him on the next block. Phineas Carter had the longest gait of anyone in town and I had to jog a little to keep up with him.

"Mr. Carter," I began. A slightly sweet smell washed off the man in waves, a combination of formaldehyde, camphor, and the old woolen suit that had surely belonged to his grandfather.

"Young lady, this won't do," he spoke in his clipped, slightly affected British accent. "I've informed your husband time and again that I see no need to advertise in your publication because I am the only mortician in town. Every-one knows where to come in their hour of need. Good day," he nodded as he doubled his pace. I stopped in my tracks and forgot all about the cane. It never surfaced and Coventry allotted $137 in the next town budget for its replacement.

Soon it became a running joke between Michael and me as to what we could put in the paper to make Carter advertise. Kate Nunley, Coventry's version of a soccer mom, was in charge of rounding up sponsors for Little League when she asked me to help her draw up a list of likely targets one day last winter. When she asked about Carter's, I shook my head. Besides, I couldn't envision a bunch of eight-year-olds running around the baseball field with *Carter's Funeral Home—We Pick Up and Deliver* emblazoned on their backs. This is how Michael came up with the idea for the cemetery series. The first few articles, about the graveyards them-selves, were well received, but I wanted something different. I was curious about one headstone in particular, which ironically didn't rest in any of the town's cemeteries.

Way back on a rutted, rarely used dirt road known as Campbell's Crossing is a headstone standing upright by the side of the road that looks as if it lost its way to the cemetery, just 100 yards further up on the right. Shaded by a tree and protected by a stone wall at its back, it's one of the few stones carved in the 1860s that is still legible. It's easy to find since the Coventry Historical Society places a fresh bouquet of plastic lilacs at the stone each year after the last snowdrifts melt away.

The stone reads:

IN MEMORY OF LAURA NEWTON
BORN NOV 23 1842
AGED 19, SHE FELL OFF THE WAGON
ON THIS SPOT ON JUNE 19 1862
AND DEPARTED THIS EARTH TWO DAYS
  LATER

Most people read the inscription and think that young Laura was a raging alcoholic who died of consumption, the usual fate of heavy drinkers in those days. Local lore has it that she never touched a drop in her brief life.

Laura Newton was one of three daughters from one of Coventry's better families. They lived in a well-kept farmhouse about a mile outside the village. One bright June morning in the year the Civil War began, Laura Newton took her horse and carriage up Campbell's Crossing to visit her fiancé, Mr. Thomas Jackson, a member of another fine Coventry family. Her visit was to be a surprise, two weeks before their wedding. She knew he would be in the barn tending to the cattle and she sneaked up on him. When she entered the barn, she saw the love of her life in a compromising position. With whom and/or what was never made public, though of course there was plenty of speculation. For more than a century, the rumors flew about what kind of compromising position Thomas was engaged in when Laura happened upon him. The neighbor girl, a runt lamb, or Mrs. Nellie Barton, a woman 15 years older than Thomas who had lost her husband when he deserted Coventry for the western gold rush, were the prime contenders. One of the wilder theories touched on a young laborer at the Jackson farm, a boy, but the Blue Hairs who belonged to the historical society vehemently denied that any homosexual had ever set foot in town, either today or a century or more ago.

Whatever Laura saw, she was clearly in shock. As the story goes, she stumbled out of the barn and climbed into her carriage. She raced down the road so fast that the carriage was weaving all over the road. One of the wheels caught on a rock and the carriage overturned, throwing Laura through the air to the other side of the road. She hit her head on the stone wall and never regained consciousness. Her heartbroken family erected a headstone at the exact point on Campbell's Crossing where Laura hit the stone wall to remind Thomas Jackson of the consequences of his actions every time he traveled down the road. It was all for naught; he left town after the following winter and was never heard from again.

Because of the strange placement of the headstone, Laura

Newton had become a minor celebrity/martyr in Coventry over the years. I knew I could never know everything there was to know about her, but I've always wanted to know more than the stories reveal. No one knows where she was buried, though it's said she was laid to rest in an unmarked grave somewhere on her family's property.

So Michael's sudden departure was well timed. I anticipated spending the weekend by myself, leafing through musty postcards and papers at Mrs. Fitzgerald's house, where she kept all the papers and books that belonged to the Historical Society in an unused bedroom. Mrs. Fitzgerald lived in an old Victorian on the road heading toward Fletcher. Her house served as a waystation for all the ephemera concerning the history of the town of Coventry, which like many small towns, couldn't afford to maintain a separate building for the historical society.

I was gathering up the notes I would bring to Mrs. Fitzgerald's when I heard footsteps on the porch. Immediately Chaos jumped up and scampered down the hallway, scattering throw rugs up against the walls while Chainsaw stayed behind in my easy chair in the living room. Lionel was probably upstairs, asleep in the laundry basket.

One knock and Willard walked in. "How goes it?" he asked, making a beeline for the coffeepot.

"Not bad," I said. "Help yourself."

"Don't mind if I do," he said as he sat down across from me. WCOV was broadcasting the high school baseball semi-finals, so Willard had the day off. I had been expecting him; he was going to take a few shots of books, letters, and photos strewn all over Mrs. Fitzgerald's floor, and then we'd head to Laura's stone to take a few more shots.

"You get any good Carnage shots on the way over?" I asked.

"Not unless Mrs. Bucheron enters the topless lawnmowing races again," he replied, sipping his coffee. Last week, the Carnage feature showed a head-on collision between an 86 Mercury Cougar and a telephone pole. Leona Bucheron was a sun goddess and liked to mow her lawn while going topless. The locals knew about it and took extreme caution if they happened to be driving by her house when she trimmed her hedges. Obviously, someone wasn't too careful and ran into the pole.

The phone rang. Willard was closer, so he leaned over and picked up the receiver. "Hello? Oh, hi," he said, and handed me the phone. "It's Michael."

"Hey, stranger," I said. "What is it like to be surrounded by Massholes once again?"

"Oh, fine, catching up with the old crowd, cleaning baby spitup off my clothes, you know, the usual." He sounded cheerful, happy. Maybe he was right; all he needed was a break. "What are you doing today?"

I filled him in. "Think Old Man Carter will bite this time?"

"Not likely," he replied. "But we'll keep trying."

"So what are you doing today?" I asked him.

"I'm building a new cupboard for Stacy's kitchen. Then I may go out and see Jack later. I think he's in town this weekend." Jack Gunther was an old friend of Michael's from high school who regularly kept in touch. He had come up to Coventry last year for a visit. Michael paused. "You know I miss you."

"I miss you too," I said, smiling. Had we finally turned the corner?

"So when are you coming home?"

"I'm not sure. It all depends on how late we stay out tonight, probably not past eleven—you know how exciting Malden is—and how much I can finish up here tomorrow."

"Well, say hello to Jack for me," I said.

"Oh, I will. You stay out of trouble, okay? I love you."

I marveled at how the phrase rolled off his tongue. When I was growing up, that particular term of endearment was always loaded with intent and conditions. One year at Christmas Eve dinner I ran from the dining room when my Uncle Charlie told his wife he loved her, right in front of everybody else. I was amazed. My parents came from sturdy Yankee stock, wearing a heavy cloak of stoicism and deprival to present to the rest of the world. I remember they pretended they didn't hear the exchange between my aunt and uncle, continuing to pass around the bowls of potatoes and stuffing.

"I love you," I told Michael, and hung up the phone. Whenever I said those words it felt as if they got stuck on the roof of my mouth. I wished it could be otherwise, and the one time I told Michael about it he said he hadn't noticed anything, but I always did. It felt like my brain seized up right before I said the words.

I turned back to Willard, smiling.

"I guess things are hunky dory again," he said. "Who's Jack?"

"Oh, Jack's an old friend of Michael's. Poor guy, he's 26, gay, and his parents are waiting for him to meet a girl and settle down. Jack thinks they don't have a clue, he's not out to them, but of course Michael assumes his parents *do* know, only that everyone's just too polite to bring it up."

"Well, that's normal. Michael doesn't have a problem with him?"

"A problem?"

"Yeah. Most straight men—even the ones who are *really* liberal—work like hell to keep their distance from gay men."

I smiled and shrugged. "Michael doesn't have many male friends, gay or straight. He's never felt comfortable hanging out with the typical straight man in this neck of the woods. I mean, he doesn't wear flannel, he doesn't spend his weekends working on cars, and he doesn't like Merle Haggard. Around here—well, except for you—what's left? He has more in common with my friends. The only one he didn't like was Eddie, but that's because they were so similar, and people who are too alike usually can't stomach each other. But I think that's why I married him: he was like Eddie, but straight." I drained my cup and stood up. "Now let's get moving."

I gathered up my stuff and we were halfway out the door

when the phone rang again.

"Grand Central," Willard announced.

"Why don't you head out to the car? I'll get this and then I'll be right out." I figured it was Michael calling back to tell me something he had forgotten.

"Hello?"

"Oh, Emily, hi, it's Jack. Listen, is Michael there?"

"No, I thought he was headed over to your place. He's down in Malden at Stacy's. Hasn't he called you yet? He told me he was going to see you tonight."

"Well, if he is, he hasn't told *me* about it. Besides, I'm already busy, so I guess I'll catch him next time."

"Oh, okay," I said, a bit distracted as I tried to puzzle out why Michael would tell me something different. "Why were you calling?"

"To find out when he was planning on being down here next. Tell him I called, okay?"

"Sure." I hung up the phone and headed out the door. I got into Willard's beatup Toyota pickup—held together with duct tape and Bondo—first clearing cameras, bags, film, and paper cups off the seat, brushing them onto the floor.

"Who was that?" he asked.

"A telemarketer," I said. I didn't want to say anything more until I had my facts straight. Michael would tell me when he got home.

We spent about an hour in Mrs. Fitzgerald's parlor, with me sneezing every five minutes from the dust motes that scattered into the air as I flipped through the old papers. Willard shot some film as I worked, and he got one of me in mid-sneeze.

"You can burn that one," I told him.

He shook his head. "I have a better idea. I'll blow it up and slap it on the back of my truck if you don't give me a raise." He wagged his finger at me but had a devilish grin on his face.

"Oh yeah? Like what?" We currently paid him $25 for each photo, significantly more than the going rate for a weekly like the *Courier*.

"How about a hundred bucks?"

"How about you go back to shooting class pictures of snot-nosed brats?" Before Willard came to work for the paper, he supplemented his income by driving to schools all over northern New Hampshire taking class pictures. He had told me he hated every minute of it.

Willard opened his mouth, then shut it. It was one of the rare times I had seen him speechless.

"We'll talk later," he said.

Next, we headed for Laura Newton's headstone on Campbell's Crossing. We got out of the truck and paused in front of the stone. I was clutching a few old photos and ledgers from her family's farm. I glanced at a photograph of Laura taken about a year before she died. A young woman with intense eyes stared back at me across a void of over 130 years. Her smile was hesitant, tinged with resignation. She wore her hair in the rolled-up style of the day, and her high-necked country dress looked as if it had been tugged at, revealing more of her neck than was acceptable back then.

Willard cleared his throat. "So what do you think it was?" he asked in an almost reverential tone.

I knew what he was talking about. Everyone in Coventry knew the story, and there were as many variations as there were warm bodies between the town lines. What did she see to make her go flying down the road at a speed that would be dangerous in a car on the same road today?

"Don't know," I said, kneeling down to scatter the photos and letters around the headstone. I was careful not to obscure the spray of plastic lilacs. "And I don't think we'll ever know." I stood up, brushing last fall's dried leaves off my jeans. Did Laura see something she knew she couldn't live with? I thought of Michael and the way he seemed to be back to his usual self. Willard snapped pictures until the stone cast a narrow shadow across the stone wall behind it.

• • •

I was upstairs in my office trying to make sense of the old news clippings and letters about Laura Newton when Michael's car pulled into the driveway a little after one in the afternoon the next day. I listened as he stopped in the bathroom, then in the kitchen, and then I heard his footsteps climb the stairs. He appeared in the doorway.

"Hi," he said, leaning against the doorjamb and swigging a Coke.

"Hi yourself," I said without looking up. "So how was last night? How is Jack?"

"Oh, he's fine." He headed toward me and leaned over for a hug. He started to rub my shoulders. "You know Jack, ultra-neurotic and pithy as usual."

Instead of hugging him back, I placed my hands in my lap. I lifted my head to focus on the bulletin board across the room.

"Michael, Jack called yesterday, right after I hung up with you. He told me he didn't know you were in Malden, that he hadn't heard from you in weeks, and that he already had plans for the night."

For a split second, Michael stopped rubbing my shoulders, but quickly resumed the same rhythm and pressure.

"That Jack," he said with a laugh. "You know, I was going to call him, but there was no answer at his house so I spent a few hours at the café anyway, hoping he would show up." He paused and took his hands from my shoulders. "Anyway, I told you I was going to *try* to see Jack, there was nothing definite."

"So who did you see?"

"Oh, you know, you've been there, the usual suspects and all. Nobody too interesting. I left the place around nine so I could get to bed and get an early start for home this morning."

Right, I thought. When I called down there at eight this morning, Stacy said you didn't get home until well after three.

I returned my hands to the desk. "Well, I'm glad you had

a good time anyway."

"Yeah," he said, kissing me on the cheek. "I'm a bit tired from the drive. I'm going to take a nap." He closed the door to my office behind him.

Chapter Four

I hoped Michael's trip would bring him back to earth. Instead, I felt as if I were riding a rollercoaster guided by a computer with random hiccups programmed into the operating system: I never knew what was coming next, and I had absolutely no control over the situation.

He seemed to have a classic case of manic depression: up, down, and side to side, in constant motion. He never hit the middle for any longer than it took him to travel from one extreme to another. But before long, he chose lethargy and stayed there. Since I could find no explanation for his behavior, I thought it was because of something I had done. Maybe if I took action I could snap him out of it.

A few days after he returned from Malden, I started doing things, anything that popped into my head. First I tried to cheer him up by making my version of the Szechuan Saloon's Fiery Happy Family. That didn't work. Then I dropped a few chocolates on his desk with a goofy card every few days, but he'd plop down in his chair with an exhausted sigh, see the candy, glance up at me with no change in the dull patina in his eyes, then push the offering aside.

I tried being gentle with him. "Honey, what's wrong?" I asked. "You know I love you and I hate to see you like this."

"Nothing's wrong," he shrugged without looking at me. "I'm just thinking a lot."

After two weeks of this pattern, I took a different tack and gave him the silent treatment. I rationed my words with him at home, at dinner, at the paper. I used the same approach with other people, but after spending a day at work first editing and then condensing my thoughts into monosyllabic one- and two-word answers, I got a raging headache and decided to limit my lack of wordiness to Michael.

Michael spent most of his time at home in bed sleeping or staring at the ceiling. When he wasn't in bed, he was in his study on the Internet. His angst generated a slightly sour smell that surrounded him, but only when he was awake. I could always tell when he was lying awake in bed because of that smell.

We might as well have slept in twin beds for all the physical contact between us—sex was out of the question. One night after we had turned the lights out, my hand grazed his hip as I was getting settled, sending an electric surge directly to my groin. I knew he wasn't asleep because the sour smell was hovering above him. I turned to face him and began to stroke the side of his face.

The instant I touched him, he stopped breathing. His body froze. I continued to stroke him, but I let my finger rest at his temple; his pulse slowed dramatically. A few seconds later, he finally inhaled. His temple throbbed double-time and I took my hand away. I rolled away from him and lay on my back with my eyes open, counting his breaths until sleep finally engulfed him and the sour aroma faded.

The next night, Michael went to bed early instead of working on his computer. I read for about a half hour more before going upstairs. Though we primarily used the front staircase, I headed up the back staircase because I wanted to drop a stack of papers on the back porch so I'd remember to bring them to the dump the next day. The back staircase doesn't creak and groan like the front staircase does, probably because we never use it. The moon was almost full, so I didn't need to turn on the hall light. Halfway up the stairs, I stopped. I thought I heard a rustling noise coming through the open door of our bedroom. Does Chainsaw have a mouse cornered in the curtains again?

I decided to sneak up on the cat. I stood in the doorway of the bedroom but didn't see a cat in the shadows quivering with excitement. Instead I saw Michael's bent legs forming a tent of the blankets and heard his rapid and heavy breathing. His face was turned away from the door, toward the window. He was masturbating. And he didn't hear me.

I smiled and tiptoed over to the bed. As soon as I sat down, he straightened out his legs and gasped. He turned to face me with a venomous look in his eyes.

"What the hell do you think you're doing, sneaking up on me like that?" he yelled.

I ignored his anger and reached under the blankets. "I thought you'd like some help," I said as my hand found his hip. He jumped as if a hot poker had touched him.

"Don't do that!" he snapped in a threatening voice, and rolled over onto his side.

"Michael," I said. I lay down on top of the covers, my back to him but without touching. My clothes were still on. The cats had been steering clear of Michael these last few weeks but that night, one by one, they crept up soundlessly and arranged themselves in a conga line that ran from just beneath my chin to my ankles, first Lionel, then Chainsaw, and finally Chaos. I fell asleep to the synchronized vibrations of their purrs.

The next morning, Michael was already awake and out of the house when I woke with one word in my head: *Eddie.*

Eddie's death was the catalyst. It had to be. Michael had come down with his cold the day after Eddie's funeral, but even after he stopped sneezing and sniffling, the inertia, despondency, and unpredictable emotions remained. *Eddie.* But why? Michael couldn't stand to be around the man. Yet, what had Michael remarked that I found extremely ironic at the time:

"He felt he had to pretend who he was…"

Once he saw me open my eyes, Chainsaw tentatively

placed a paw on my head to remind me it was time for a can of wet stink. As soon as I started to scratch him behind his ear, it sent a signal to the others to stampede down the stairs to the kitchen. I got out of bed and trudged along behind the scrabbling herd. In the kitchen I grabbed the first can of food I touched. It was catfish.

As I dished out the food, I smiled; I found the idea of feeding cats catfish endlessly amusing. But my mind tried to focus on the part of Michael that was trying to pretend he was someone else.

. . .

When I got to the office an hour later, Carrie met me at my car before I had even turned the engine off.

"What's up?" I said as I rolled down the window.

She was staring at the front door of the office. "I just thought I'd warn you."

What now? I pasted a look of nonchalance on my face. Lately, with Michael, I was getting a lot of practice.

"Warn me about what?"

"It's Mr. Sanders." Carrie jerked her head toward the office. "He's in there now."

Bob Sanders was one of our perennially frustrated writers, a semi-retired flatlander who had moved to Coventry three years ago to try his hand at country life, as had other disaffected urban cowboys of his ilk with rich pension plans. Like many newcomers to the area who fancied themselves to be so much beyond the locals, Bob Sanders' aim in writing for the *Courier* was to "educate the natives," as he told me the first time he showed up at the paper early last year. I found it amusing that Sanders didn't know how to deal with the quiet and darkness of the boonies. The first thing he did when he moved into his house was to install lights and motion detectors on every corner of his house. If a chipmunk scurried across his yard at 3 a.m., his entire property would suddenly light up like a used car lot.

The impression he gave me at that first meeting was one of pure arrogance. Sanders' entire tone told me I should be grateful to have someone with his experience willing to write a weekly column for us...for nothing, yet!

"Well, you're in the right place," I had informed him, "because that's just what we pay...*nothing*!" To flatlanders, at least; locals got $25 an article. Sanders had looked momentarily crestfallen, but promptly recovered enough to return to his diatribe. As he droned on, I started to think.

One of the Blue Hairs, Mrs. John LaBombard, had died the previous week, and so I had some space to fill. I figured that after one lousy column by Sanders, he'd decide not to write another after discovering that he had only succeeded in pissing off everyone in town. By then, I would have found a new Blue Hair correspondent for Dutton Flats, Mrs. LaBombard's beat.

"Okay," I interrupted him. "Give it a shot."

He stopped moving his mouth long enough to realize what I had just said. "Really?" he whispered. Then I saw it was all an act. Most of these guys were desperate to fit in up here, but when they saw how little they knew and how highly educated a lot of the geezers really were, they tended to revert back to habits that worked for them in the city: loud and obnoxious.

"Really. Get me your first column by Wednesday," I said. "Can you do it?"

"Sure!" He called his column "Out Of My Mind" since he viewed the column as a chance to periodically empty the contents of his brain for the benefit of us all. I don't think he ever caught on to the true meaning of the phrase.

Within two months, Sanders had received more hate mail than anyone in the paper's history. He took it as a sign that his views were badly needed, while everyone else saw him as yet another pompous out-of-state jackass who needed to shut his mouth. I said nothing and decided to let him hang himself, using the paper as his rope.

Even for a self-described ultra-libertarian, Sanders' views

on everything from democratizing the dump procedures—in one column he viewed recycling as a socialist plot—to electing only newcomers to town government positions were pretty radical. When he complained about what he perceived to be the narrow-mindedness of the readers of the *Courier*, I suggested that perhaps he should find something else to write about, maybe an interview with the president of the Coventry Garden Club. He ranted and raved for a few days, briefly threatening me with a lawsuit for infringing on his freedom of the press ("Tell him to get his own goddamn paper if he wants to be free," Michael said in response), until he agreed to tone it down and write about things that wouldn't rile folks.

Sanders had written two more columns before he hung up his pen. People in town were shunning him left and right. Even Mary at the store just grunted at him when he came to pick up his *New York Times* each morning. "I wouldn't give that man the satisfaction of sparing one iota of the energy it would take for me to open my mouth," she spat.

His swan song column appeared about a year ago. I thought we were done with him.

I rolled up the window, opened the car door, and stepped out. "What do you think he wants?" asked Carrie.

"He probably just wants his column back," I told Carrie as we headed for the door.

She threw an arm out to stop me. "Wait, it's not what you think. He's been ranting and raving in front of the building and waving this week's paper around."

"You should have told him to write an op-ed piece—"

"No," she said, and something in her tone made me stop. "It's something else. He said it's about the cemetery series."

I stared at her. "What about it?"

She sighed. "About the fact that we published directions to the Laura Newton stone, which just so happens to be located next to his property."

"So what? Everyone knows where it is. It's not as though we printed his address, a picture of his house, and said that

Leonardo DiCaprio had slept there."

"That's what I told him, but he says we infringed on his privacy and since there's no way to print a retraction and suck up the directions to the cemetery, he'd be content if we withdrew the series, so as to spare the other privacy-loving people in town from his unfortunate fate."

"He really said that?"

"Words to that effect, yes."

"Oh, Christ, this is just what I need on top of everything else, another flatlander asshole who wants to get a warrant article on the ballot at next town meeting to build a moat around the town." I walked toward the building and the open front door. "I'll take care of this," I whispered to Carrie.

"Mister Sanders, what a surprise!" I walked up to him and held out my hand. "You know, I wasn't sure if you were still in town, since I haven't heard from you lately."

He didn't accept my hand. "Oh, I'm still around, but I'm not sure how much longer you'll be here if you keep up this nonsense."

I dropped my arm to my side. "What nonsense is that?"

"This compulsion you have to print the home address of every person in Coventry who you don't particularly care for," he said.

I decided to play dumb. "I'm not sure what you mean."

"Your cemetery stories," he said, shaking a copy of last week's *Courier.* "Why you want to write about a bunch of bones is beyond me, but what really galls me is that you print detailed directions to each place you write about."

"What's so bad about that? Lots of people want to see these places for themselves after they read about it in the paper."

"You make it seem like the people who live along your published tourist route have nothing better to do than serve as tour guides! Just last night two strange cars turned around in my driveway, thanks to you. Before you started all this, I was able to live in peace. I didn't move here to welcome the world with open arms, Ms. Spencer, I moved to get the hell away from it. It would do no good to print a retraction, since you've already printed my address in the paper, but you can appease me if you discontinue the series right now. No more stories about tombstones and cemeteries. Got it?"

This guy belonged in Montana with some well-armed cult, not in New Hampshire. I knew he'd take anything I said and throw it back in my face. I'd met his kind before; the last one I dealt with was Mayor Giardina back in Groveton.

"Mister Sanders, you are obviously upset, and I don't blame you," I said. "But we're going to continue the series. We won't put your name or address or write about Laura Newton's stone in the *Courier* again. But no one else has complained. In fact, when their house has been mentioned along the cemetery tour, everyone else welcomed the chance to help people find the cemeteries and particular stones. They consider themselves to be ambassadors, caretakers of the graveyards, and—"

He threw the paper to the floor and angrily stomped toward the door.

"Do it, Ms. Spencer, or you'll be sorry."

I picked the paper off the floor and put it on the front counter. As soon as Sanders stormed out, Carrie returned to the office.

"I see it went well," she said.

I shrugged. "As good as it gets with the likes of him. I'm not worried, and neither should you," I said, sitting down at my desk. "He's all hot air, no action."

And I wasn't worried, well, not much. I didn't think there was anything to worry about.

• • •

The scene with Bob Sanders along with Michael's indifference and nastiness made me start to think that maybe we shouldn't have bought the paper after all. Maybe Carrie was right; maybe Michael is tired of living in a small town and wants to move back to the city.

I seethed my way through the rest of the day, barricading myself at my desk. Carrie knew enough to leave me alone. I left the office at three, figuring that I could get more work done at home. I pushed some papers into my bag and mumbled something to Carrie about going home. She nodded and waved.

When I got home, it took a minute longer than usual for the cats to amble down the stairs and start yowling for dinner since their internal clocks were telling them they should still be sleeping. All three sat in the kitchen watching me with bleary eyes. Then, as soon as I started to reach for the cupboard that contained the cat food, the realization hit, and as if on cue, all three made a beeline for my ankles and started their starving cat act.

As I ran the water over the fork, I knew I was still too wound up to work, so I decided to pay some of the bills. As was the case with our other household chores, Michael and I rotated paying the bills. We used a joint checking account and an accounting software program to handle the register. It was really Michael's month to pay the bills, but since I was in take-action mode I figured I might as well get it done.

Usually, we would update the new figures on the Quicken spreadsheet, throw it on a disk, and then toss it onto the other's desk a few days before the first of the month. During the early days of running the paper when we were especially tight on money, we tossed the disk back and forth through the house like a Frisbee, mostly to air our frustration.

I sat down at Michael's computer and turned it on. I had intended to copy the file to a disk and then prepare the new figures on his computer as a surprise. After the machine booted up, a full-color photograph of one man giving oral sex to another appeared on the screen. They were outside, squinting at the sun, and the one on the receiving end was leaning against a split rail fence that looked as if it was full of splinters. It didn't register. Why did Michael have that photograph on his computer?

I clicked on the image and closed the file. Right behind it was an email from the week before from BIGDIKKK to LUV69; I checked the path of the email and saw that LUV69 was really mrogers@coventry.net. It read:

"i want your big cock in my mouth at the same time my huge dick is in yours and then i want to slam it into your nice tight ass and then i want you to..."

I scrolled down to see more of the same, with every sentence containing a few more synonyms for *penis* and *big*. I started to close that file, but I hesitated for a second because I wasn't sure what I'd find behind *it*. I closed it and was relieved to see the aquamarine blue of the desktop.

I had forgotten all about paying the bills. I sat there in a daze, staring at the cool blue that radiated off the monitor. The truth began to sink in. I felt a tingly warm sensation start to float up the back of my neck and permeate my brain. Then everything felt numb, and my mind went blank.

· · ·

I had been lying awake in bed for at least a few hours when I heard Michael come home. He crawled into bed beside me, but as usual, he was careful to avoid touching me. My body was completely rigid, my back turned to his side of the bed.

The next day at the office was uneventful. No more intrusions from Bob Sanders and Michael was his usual surly self in my presence. I still felt stunned and thought my body gave it away. My eyes and my body made me feel like a deer caught in headlights. Numbness was the predominant emotion.

I honestly didn't know what to say to Michael, or if I should even bring it up at all. I had asked a lot of nosy questions in my reporting days, but this one had me stumped, although the few options that ran through my brain leaned towards the sarcastic.

"Honey, do you think you might be gay?"

"Michael, tell me, what does it feel like to have a nice hard dick rammed up your ass?"

"Dear, I've been thinking about having a sex change operation. Would you like that?"

Near the end of the workday, I asked Michael about his plans for the evening.

"At home," he answered. "Why?"

"Oh, nothing," I said and returned to my work. I knew I would confront him tonight. Maybe it was a good thing that Bob Sanders had stopped by yesterday; I may have to use some of his bulldog tactics. And so, after a wordless dinner, when we were sitting in the living room reading, but before he left to commune with BIGDIKKK, I began.

"Michael."

He grunted in reply.

"I wanted to pay the bills yesterday."

Another grunt.

"It's your month," I said.

He looked at me, not comprehending.

"So?" he snarled.

"I went on your computer to get the files."

His confusion was quickly overwhelmed by a look of surprise. His eyes widened and his mouth fell open. He stood up and the book fell from his lap, landing with a thud on the floor.

"You were spying on me!"

The words hit like a bomb, although by the time I finally saw his mouth form each word, it felt as if I was first filtering the sentence through some other brain to absorb it better.

"I wasn't spying on you, I wanted to do something nice for you since you've been feeling so bad and—"

"You were *spying* on me!" Then, as suddenly as his shock had appeared, it fell off his face. "I'm not gay, if that's what you're thinking."

"Then why do you have gay photos and email on your computer?"

He paused, pursed his lips, and took a breath.

"I think I have to explain my attraction to men."

I slumped into my chair. I watched Michael move his mouth, I caught a few words, but he might as well have been speaking Portuguese. I didn't know what to do with my hands, so I rested them on my lap and stared at the floor.

"Say something," he told me, and grabbed my hands.

I thought back to the time before we were married when we were in bed and I was joking around with him. "What are you, gay?" I had ribbed him, and was caught off guard by his angry response.

"But why?" I managed to say.

"Why *what?*"

Why what? That was a good question.

Why didn't you tell me?

Why do you feel this way?

Why did you marry me?

Why are we running a business together?

Why are we together?

I chose the most obvious: "Why didn't you tell me you were gay?"

"I'm not gay," he spat.

"Bisexual, then."

"No!"

Then what? It didn't make sense. If he was married and called himself straight, why did he have gay porn on his computer? What else is there?

"Say something," he commanded.

I couldn't think of anything. "Why didn't you tell me?" This time it came in a whisper.

He released my hands and sat back on the floor. "I knew you were going to say that," he said. "When are you going to realize that it's not all about you or what I do to you? Can't you see that this is my issue, it's an issue I've been fighting all my life, and that I'm having enough trouble dealing with it without you getting all defensive and blaming me for it?"

Of course he'd turn it around. "But just when did you know?" I listened to myself as I slowly and methodically spoke each word in a disembodied voice that trembled with calm.

"A long time ago," he said after a pause. "Before we met." Another, longer pause. "In high school."

He then explained that he'd had relationships with men all through college but even then he didn't consider himself to be gay. He said that I was the first woman he'd been involved with and he thought that by getting married and settling down, his attraction to men would disappear.

He reached for my hands again, but this time I didn't offer them, instead keeping my arms close to my side. "You're the only woman I've ever wanted, and even though I've been a shit to you lately, I'm still wildly attracted to you. In fact, I couldn't imagine having sex with any other woman." He looked up into my face while I kept my eyes on the floor.

The bolt struck. Eddie. Of course.

I looked at him. "Why were you such a shit to Eddie?"

He collapsed slightly in on himself. "Eddie. I felt terrible." He paused.

"Go on," I said.

He shrugged. "I always knew that Eddie knew about me. He could pick up the signals even though I had buried them for all these years, and I was amazed that he knew, but at the same time I hated him *because* he knew. And he hated me, probably because he felt I was misleading you, which I wasn't, of course."

So that's why Eddie and I drifted apart after Michael and I were married. I always thought I was the cause of our separation.

"Does anyone else know?" I asked.

"Stacy and Patrick," he said. "That's about it."

I did a quick rewind through the last couple of months. "What about Doug?"

He glanced at the floor. "And Doug," he said, quickly adding, "but no one else, and I don't want it to be made public."

My brain seized up again.

"I think I need to be by myself for a few days," he

announced. "And so do you."

"So you can screw as many men as you want with an open conscience now that your wife knows the truth about you?" was the first reply that popped into my head.

But no words came from my mouth.

• • •

I don't remember the next day at all. All I remember is feeling as if my body and brain had been dipped in Anbesol.

When I woke up on Sunday, I was aware of a faint glimmer of consciousness. Somehow I found the energy to get up out of bed, go downstairs, and make a pot of coffee. I sat at the kitchen table and drank most of the pot while staring out the window.

What now?

Whenever I asked this question in my work, there was always an answer: *Go find out.* I grabbed my cup and headed for my study. I switched on the computer and headed for the web. While the modem squawked, the cats assumed their positions: Chainsaw on top of the monitor and Chaos on the mousepad.

I typed *gay married* into the search engine. Chaos stared at the monitor, her whiskers occasionally twitching. It was the wrong choice of words. A list of gay porn sites with offerings along the lines of HOT N HORNY GUYS WANT TO SUCK YOUR COCK appeared. I scrolled down the list, but nothing for the non-gay spouse came up. I began to wonder if more men like Michael were coming out today—or at least exploring their options—because of the Internet. After all, they didn't have to skulk around gay bars in strange cities anymore; all they had to do was log on.

I clicked on a site that promised FREE XXX SHOTS. There I found a screen filled with an array of animated rainbow-striped condoms, dildos, and leather thongs that hopped across the screen. Chaos stared at the monitor, entranced by the cartoons. She batted at a jumping condom with a smiley face on its tip.

I returned to the search page and scrolled down to see GAY HAWAII/MAKE IT LEGAL! GIVE THE HETS THE FINGER!

Hets? Oh well, after all, I was in a world where being heterosexual was automatically considered suspect. I wondered if Eddie had ever referred to me as a *het*.

Further down SUPPORT FOR MARRIED GAYS popped up. "Have you thought of yourself as gay all your life, but got married anyway as a way to *not* be gay? Have you always felt forced into living a conventional, *straight* lifestyle? Here's help."

Looks like I was getting warm. I clicked on it and found a veritable encyclopedia of resources: support groups, books, magazines, therapists. An animated barbershop pole with the colors of the rainbow topped with a dancing pink triangle appeared in the frame. Chaos tilted her head and watched.

"You are not to blame," I read. "You can now come out and realize your true freedom in a world that is beginning to accept gay people in there own right's."

Where's my red pencil? Typos aside, the message here was that the gay person who attempted to live a straight life was a victim, forced against his will to push down his same-sex attractions in order to make it in the world. Nothing was said about the person that this liberated gay man just happened to be married to.

I returned to the search page and continued to scroll, but all I found were variations on the same theme: COME OUT & BE PROUD: GAY MARRIED FATHERS OF MAN-HATTAN UNITE! I was about to give up when I got an idea.

I clicked back to the main screen and typed in STRAIGHT SPOUSE.

"Should be an oxymoron," I muttered as the search engine did its thing.

There was exactly one entry.

THE STRAIGHT SPOUSE SUPPORT NETWORK. I

clicked on it.

Chaos watched as the site downloaded. It contained only text, no graphics, and no animated sex toys. Clearly, it was no match for the gay sites when it came to the cat entertainment quotient. Chaos jumped off the desk. Ten seconds later, I heard the crunch of dry Friskies coming from the kitchen. I leafed through the resource section, but compared with the gay sites, the selection was anemic. I found a couple of books for straight people who discovered they were married to gays, a few support groups, an Internet mailing list—that was it. I printed it out—it all fit neatly on one sheet of paper— and I suddenly felt very tired. The Anbesol had returned to my brain. I switched off the computer and padded off to bed.

When I woke an hour later, I was clear that whatever happened with Michael and me and our marriage would be separate from the paper. I didn't have a clue what his announcement meant for us or what our options were—if we indeed had any—or what I'd say to him the next time I saw him. I sensed, quite correctly, that I'd have at least a few days to puzzle things out on my own.

On Monday morning I woke up and went to the office as if the weekend hadn't happened. After all, we had a paper to put out—Michael and I were still running a business to-gether—and so I dove into work.

Chapter Five

When I sat down in front of my computer at the office, I behaved like Pavlov's dog: The association I had with facing the monitor and moving my fingers around on the keyboard was strong. I was glad I had come in today. My mind/body connection didn't react the same way when I worked on my computer at home.

The cemetery series was so well received by both readers and advertisers that we ran a new piece every week and decided to continue with it until we ran out of cemeteries, Bob Sanders notwithstanding. Even though I didn't change my strategy, I decided that no more pieces giving explicit directions would appear in the paper. Instead, I referred readers to the town map.

This week's installment was more how-to than travelogue: an interview with Mrs. Bernice Nicholas, a 72-year-old woman who had moved to Coventry five years ago when she and her husband Everett retired. Mrs. Nicholas was the polar opposite of the other Blue Hairs in town. She had been a business executive in the days when it was unusual for women to hold high positions. After moving to Coventry, Bernice and Everett happily spent the bulk of their time doing genealogical research on her huge extended family. One week they visited abandoned cemeteries in northern Scotland before flying to San Francisco, where the house her great-grandmother was born in once stood in the financial district. When they were in Coventry, Mrs. Nicholas spent hours leafing through dusty news clippings that she found in town historical societies around the state. As was the case with the Coventry Historical Society, most of the other collections were either located in someone's house or were only open to the public every other Saturday afternoon in July and August from two to four p.m.

In this week's article, Mrs. Nicholas related how genealogy was a sore spot in her family. No one on her father's side of the family—both of his parents were only children—had ever cared about mapping the family tree. Her mother's family was a different story. All five sisters—her aunts—had individually conducted thorough investigations into the family background. However, each one had come up with completely different results. Mrs. Nicholas described family gatherings where her aunts would hang five different charts on the wall and then stand back to watch the rest of the family fight bitterly over them. Although she suspected that they mangled the family records deliberately just to see a good fight, she saw it as her family duty to set the record straight and gave some advice to readers who used Coventry's cemeteries as a tool to create their own family trees.

Cemeteries were always a big issue in Coventry, with the only fistfight at last year's Town Meeting revolving around the topic. It used to be that whoever needed a summer job the most was elected Cemetery Commissioner. This person got paid to mow the seven public cemeteries—all except for one had been filled to capacity in the 1890s—which could pay as much as two thousand bucks over the course of the summer.

Last year, a flatlander named Marty Rothman—who had lived part-time in Coventry up until last year when he moved into town full time—ran on the platform that he would be strictly a volunteer and give his salary back to the town. This idea outraged the people who had been in town for generations. They viewed the position as a way to preserve their

town's history and at the same time provide an underem-
ployed resident with a job. We printed letters to the editor
that swirled around both sides of the issue, with the usual
parties taking their predictable sides. Rothman won when
another flatlander wrote in his letter that this would save
each taxpayer the equivalent of $5.29, the exact price Mary
charged for a six-pack of Bud at the store. Well, this won
over about half of the old-timers. Their vote, along with the
flatlander vote, had been enough to clinch the election in
favor of Rothman.

After working a few hours nailing down the contents in
next week's paper, I needed a break. No word from Michael,
but I wasn't surprised.

"I'm heading to the store, Carrie, you want anything?"

"Nope, I brought my lunch today."

The only thing that really did it for me when I was
stressed out were salty, greasy foods—chips, popcorn, anything with a loud crunch. The sound, the taste, and the
greasy film left behind on my fingers were better than
Valium. When I headed out for lunch, I knew precisely what
would be on the menu.

I walked across the street to the general store to get my
lunch fixings. After saying hello to Mary who was behind the
counter, the omnipresent cigarette hanging from her lips, I
grabbed a basket and got busy. A small bag of Fritos,
Doritos, Cheez Doodles, and Wise potato chips fell into the
basket, fulfilling my favorite four food groups: grease, salt,
red dye #4, and BHT. Perfect. Though I usually ordered a
sandwich and an iced tea for lunch, Mary mumbled something about last week's paper and didn't bat an eye as she
rang up the items. She'd been running the Coventry General
Store for more than three decades now, or at least as long as
I've been alive. The store's longevity is solely due to Mary's
total lack of judgment about the food and drink—of course,
mostly drink—that her customers choose. A rash of newfan-
gled stores had opened and closed in town over the years. I
had to think it was because the flatlander owners, so eager to

become an immediate and accepted part of the community, couldn't help but make a few comments about the number of lottery tickets, six-packs, or bags of junk food their customers set on the counter. Not to mention the scathing looks they gave to their clientele who used food stamps to pay for their purchases.

I walked back to the office and spread the bags on my desk. I planned to make them last all afternoon, opening them one at a time. I didn't know if I'd hear from Michael and wanted to make sure I had enough sedation to last the rest of the day. I munched as I worked, and my keyboard quickly became coated with a thin layer of salty grease. After a few lapses, I had to train myself to remember not to rub my eyes with my salty fingers.

When Carrie went around the office to empty the trash cans before she left for the day, she peered into my can filled with the crushed bags. quickly glanced at me, then shrugged and emptied the can. A few minutes later, I heard the front door open and knew it was Willard. He had called earlier to let me know he'd be by for our Carnage session a little after five.

"Hey, Em," he said as he headed for my desk. "I got a great one this week. Wait till you see." He was about to drop his bags on the floor when he stopped short.

"What's wrong, Em? You look terrible."

"Oh, I just ate too much junk food today," I said. "It's that time, you know." It wasn't, but I didn't want to get into the details with him. I mentally slapped myself into perky mode and said, "Okay, let's see what you've got." Willard gave me a funny look, but reached into his bag and pulled out several contact sheets.

"Okay, here we have a truck-bed garden. You know, like how some people use old bathtubs, this guy used a 1961 full-size Chevy truck bed because he couldn't bear to part with it—he had parted out the cab and engine long ago—and he was sick of hearing his wife yell about this old rusting hulk by the side of the barn."

I peered at the shots. Though it was early in the growing season, the loamy hummocks between the sides of the truckbed yielded several rows of healthy tomato plants and squash seedlings.

"It's a possibility, though it might work better on the 4-H page," I said. That was the problem with many of Willard's Carnage shots: they could fit into more than one section of the paper depending upon how ludicrous the subtext was. "What's next?"

He shuffled a few sheets. "Here," he said. He held out a closeup of the back end of a rusted-out Isuzu Trooper from the Joe Isuzu era of the mid-80s.

"So it's rusted carcass week?" I asked, squinting at the faded bumper sticker.

"Look," he said, pointing to the tailpipe. He would need to blow it up, but perched in the exhaust pipe was a tiny, scraggly nest of baby mice. One of the babies rested its head on the side of the nest and stared directly at the camera. I preferred the truck bed, but the mouse nest would win us brownie points for cuteness, as much as I hated to print stuff like that.

"Tell you what. We'll do the truck bed for Carnage and put the mice in the back next week, okay? So you can splurge on Carolyn and take her out to Mickey Dee's next week with all the extra money I'll be paying you, right?"

Willard cracked up. I placed his photos on the scanner.

"Are you sure you're okay, Em? You seem—"

"I'm *fine*, Willard, okay?"

"Jeez, you don't have to bite my head off."

"No, that's what you have Carolyn for," I said. "But wait. If she doesn't eat meat, does that mean she shuns yours as well?"

He stood up, grinning shyly. "I'll never tell," he said.

As Willard headed out the door, I glanced at the clock. Quarter after five and I still hadn't heard from Michael. I'd had enough of the office but didn't want to go home to an empty house. Since I had an open invitation from Mrs.

Fitzgerald to dig through the entire archives of the Coventry Historical Society stored in her parlor, I closed down the office and drove across town.

Mrs. Fitzgerald was acting nervous, repeatedly rubbing the index finger of her right hand over the back of her other hand, while I sat on her parlor floor sifting through files. On previous visits, she usually sat on her camelback sofa, idly turning the pages of a ten-year-old Judith Krantz novel while I sorted through papers, postcards, and old books. I kept a box of Kleenex at my side because the dust from the crumbling paper made me sneeze. Every so often, I asked her a question, which she answered immediately, eager for the conversation. Her husband, Harold, who taught geometry at Coventry High School, had died last year, and even though she tried to fill up her days with writing her column and presiding over the historical society, she was still lonely.

But today, she wasn't at all helpful. She sat on the sofa, fanning herself with an old copy of *Reader's Digest* and glancing at the clock every five minutes. After a half hour, I asked if anything was wrong. She reddened slightly and stopped fanning herself. "Oh no, dear, not at all. It's just that—" She stopped and looked away.

"What?"

"Oh, it's not such a big deal, and I don't know why I worry so—" She resumed fanning herself at twice the previous speed.

"What is it?"

"It's just that, well…"

"*What?*"

"I have a date!" she blurted out. "Oh my, please don't tell anyone, it'll end up in all of the Blue Hair columns and I'll never write for you again!"

Her face had turned beet red.

"Oh, Mrs. Fitzgerald, that's wonderful!" I cocked my head at her. "So it's not just another planning meeting at the church, with a bunch of built-in chaperones?"

"Oh, no, it's just me, and uh…" She looked at me

expectantly. "Don't you want to know who it is?"

I smiled. "Only if you want to tell me."

"Well, I don't think you know him, he lives over in Fletcher, but he moved back to New Hampshire after his wife died when they were living in Florida, and he just showed up one day at the library. He wanted to compare the collections at a few of the town libraries around here, but if you ask me, I think he wanted to check out who was currently in circulation," she said with a sly smile.

In addition to serving as president of the historical society and writing her Blue Hair column, Mrs. Fitzgerald was also town librarian, holding sway over a moldy out-of-date collection of about 5,000 books. One day, I randomly surveyed one hundred different books at the library and discovered that the average age of a book at the Coventry Public Library was twenty-two and a half years old. The library was open to the public for a grand total of three hours each week: on Wednesdays only from 10 to 11 a.m., 3 to 4 p.m., and again from 7 to 8 in the evening. The total annual budget for the library was $968 a year, which covered heat, electricity, and her $100 annual salary. Every year, the town budget contained a line item for a $300 increase in the library's budget, and every year it was voted down. Whatever was left over bought books, usually the latest hardcover novels by Stephen King and Danielle Steel from the Literary Guild five-books-for-a-buck introductory special.

This meant most of the newer books were donated by townspeople, but only after the used bookseller over in Fletcher refused to take them. There were also about 700 books in storage in the basement of the library; a book was banished to the musty unheated cellar if it hadn't been checked out for more than 25 years.

"So what's his name?" I asked, feeling like a 17-year-old girl for asking the question.

"Peter," she said, still flushed. "Mister Peter George. Emily, the first time he showed up at the Senior Center's Wednesday brunch last month, all the old biddy hens just clucked all afternoon. He *is* very handsome, you know."

"And how did you happen to win him over?"

"Well, you know me, I have to know everything about everyone, so I marched right over to him and asked for his name, rank, and serial number. We ended up talking the rest of the afternoon while all the old biddies threw poison darts at me with their eyes. They're still not talking to me. Mildred Harris was supposed to stop by yesterday to help me shelve books at the library, but she never showed. I wouldn't be surprised if she never volunteered again."

"Oh, I wouldn't worry about it. You know how women can get to fighting over a man." Especially in a town like Coventry, with ten Blue Hairs to every elderly gentleman.

"Oh, I know," she said, taking out a lipstick and compact. "He's going to pick me up around six, so don't mind me. You stay and finish your work if you want."

True to her word, Mr. Peter George was quite striking when he showed up ten minutes later, a seventy-something man who still had his height, a full head of silver-gray hair, and a full set of teeth; any one of these attributes still intact at his age was rare in these parts. Plus, he was well-dressed in clean clothes. No wonder the other women had scorned her.

When we were introduced, he bent slightly forward to greet me while taking my hand. A gentleman to boot. He held the door open for Mrs. Fitzgerald, who turned back to wink at me as she walked out. Hope he's not gay, I thought. But maybe, at their age, it doesn't matter. After they left, I tried to concentrate on the scattered papers in front of me, but I soon gave up and went home. I fixed a quick dinner, then propped myself up in bed to lose myself in a Russell Banks novel.

• • •

Over the next week, Michael and I did our best to avoid each other. The times we did run into each other, the awkwardness was so palpable I felt as if I couldn't breathe.

If Michael wasn't glued to his computer, he was out. Where, I didn't ask. But I assumed he was spilling his guts to his newfound buddies. He had started attending a married gay men's group on Wednesday nights, and between that and his other social outings, I had almost gotten used to being by myself at night. At quarter to eleven, I was about to turn the light out when I heard the crunch of driveway gravel followed soon after by Michael's shoes creaking up the stairs. He tapped on the door.

"Hi." He stood in the doorway, hesitant to cross the threshold.

"Hi."

"What are you doing up so late?"

I conjured up a yawn, big and loud, and closed my book. "Lots of work."

He cleared his throat. "Is something wrong, Emily?"

"Not really. Why?"

"Well, look at you," he said.

I glanced down the length of my body, anchored as usual by three sleeping cats, and looked back at him. I shrugged. "So? What *about* me?"

He slumped against the doorway. "Don't you want to hear about where I've been?"

"Not particularly," I said, picking up my book.

He crossed the room, sat on the edge of the bed, and grabbed my hands. "I went to my married gay men's group." He paused and looked at me. "I have a good time there, Em. I get to talk with men who are dealing with the same thing I'm dealing with, that *we're* dealing with." He squeezed my hands.

What I wanted to say: Yeah, and how many cocks did you suck?

What I said: Nothing.

He must have read my mind. "What you don't seem to understand is that it's not all about sex—"

I started to pull away, but he held tight.

"Wait a minute," he said. "I'm telling you, it's *not* all about sex, it's about spending time talking with other guys who feel the same things I do. Think about it: From childhood, maybe you got along with other kids okay, but no matter what you did, you were always one beat off, or maybe you had a big scar on your stomach that no other kids had, as far as you could tell. You knew you were different and you didn't want to be. So you learned to hate that scar, to hide it, to ignore it, and hoped it would disappear.

"But instead, it consumed your thoughts. And you did it for so many years that you just accepted you were different, but you never *really* accepted it, because you knew it would always be there. So what you did instead was try to act differently, to live as you would if you didn't have the scar to begin with. You try on another role, the one that's universally accepted and approved by society, and though it feels different, it's not so bad. And best of all, you start to forget about the scar, at least most of the time. And for the first time in your life, you feel happy and like you fit in.

"But real life starts to interfere, and before long, you discover that the scar and all the bad feelings you developed about it haven't gone away after all. They were lying beneath the surface all the time. You can't run away from it after all, no matter what you do."

He paused, releasing his grip on my arm.

"Yes, but—" I said, thinking he was done with his diatribe.

"I'm not finished," he snapped. "When it comes up again, you realize that all of the coping mechanisms that worked before don't anymore, which sends you into a tailspin. You're at the end of your rope, but then you find a group of people who have the same scars you do, and they've felt the exact same way about their scars. After years of feeling different, you can't believe there are other people out there like you. And when you all get together, you find you can talk honestly about it for the first time in your life. You can't imagine what that's like. As a result, you feel closer to these people than anyone else. *Almost* anyone else," he quickly amended.

"That's all that happened. We sat and talked for hours." He released my hands, which had turned clammy. "I have to figure out where my attraction to men fits into our life together."

"What I don't understand is how you can be attracted to men and still want to stay married."

He dismissed my words with a wave of his hand. "Not to worry, Em. These days, sexuality is a fluid thing. There are a lot of people who aren't trying to squeeze themselves into predefined boxes anymore. Besides, as I've told you, I'm not gay. I just have an attraction to men."

I looked at his hands for crib notes. When did Michael get to be such an expert in sex? After all, he certainly hadn't squeezed himself into my box in recent memory.

"I'm not going to have sex with anyone but you," he continued, though to me it sounded as if he was trying to talk himself into it. "I don't want to give up what you and I have together. I just need to learn how to integrate the two parts of me together. I'm studying a part of my life that I've always denied.

"I've never really been that comfortable with straight men, anyway," he continued. "All they do is drink beer, work on cars and get grease under their nails, and talk about football and women."

"But what does this all mean?" I asked. "I don't know where I fit into your life."

"That's all in the past, honey. I'm telling you, all I need to do is talk with other guys who are going through the same thing I am. That's *all*." He stood up and headed into the bathroom. When the door opened, he was in his pajamas. He turned off the light and curled up in bed beside me, his hands cupping my shoulders.

I felt his breath on my neck. "You don't have to worry about us, Emily," he whispered. "Just let me take the time to do this now. I need this, *we* need this." Less than a minute later, he was snoring softly.

I honestly didn't know what to think. Part of me believed him, that this was all Michael needed, to connect with other men who had the same feelings. The other part of me scoffed. After all, I knew that to a gay man, being gay means sex—lots of it. I had heard all the stories from Eddie, or as he put it, "Anything with a pulse and a dick will do."

What was the harm if Michael went to a few meetings now and then? Maybe he'd get it out of his system by airing his dirty laundry and we'd be able to get back to normal around here. A few minutes later, I had fallen asleep.

• • •

The next morning when I was drinking my coffee, a bolt hit. If Michael can find other people to talk with about this, so can I. So far, I hadn't told anyone about our situation. I was still confused and didn't know how other people would react. Maybe it would help to talk to people who knew what I was going through.

Even in rural northern New England, it's easy to find the local gay community. From the notices for gay support groups pinned to the bulletin boards in the Grand Union over in Fletcher to the occasional rainbow flag bumper sticker on a rust-encrusted Subaru, they're out there. Besides, most people already know who's gay in their town, and they treat them with the same typical Yankee reserve they'd treat any of their neighbors. As long as they keep their yards neat, pay their taxes, and vote at Town Meeting, all is well.

If it was easy to find a gay married men's group, it would be easy to find one for their wives. I returned to the straight spouse web page, checked the Manchester gay community's site, and came up empty-handed. It didn't make sense. If there's one for them, there's one for us, right?

So I did some digging. I sent out a few emails, made a few phone calls, and eventually found out that the closest straight spouse group meeting was in Burlington, Vermont, a good two-hour drive from Coventry.

"Oh, you'll have a good time," the woman at the Green Mountain Gay, Lesbian, Bisexual, and Transgender Center told me when I called. "Or so I hear. My girlfriend's husband went for a time after she came out, and it helped him a lot."

Odd, but up until this point, it hadn't occurred to me that men could be straight spouses too. The group met every Tuesday at seven o'clock. I thought about waiting another week, but figured I might as well get started today and left the office a little before five.

The meeting was held at the Green Mountain Women's Health Center, a nondescript brick building just off the pedestrian mall overlooking Lake Champlain. When I walked into the lobby, I saw a hand-lettered sign in the lobby that read STR8 SPICE RM 112 with an arrow pointing down the hall. When I reached Room 112, I poked my head in the open door and saw about fifteen folding chairs arranged in a circle. Several men and women stood off to the side holding Styrofoam cups of coffee. When one of them saw me by the door, the other heads turned in unison.

By reflex, I looked over my shoulder, and then turned back to the room. "Am I in the right place?" I asked.

A tall brunette woman in her mid-30s dressed in a business suit laughed. "Only if you're not gay," she said and held out her hand. "I'm Janet, and you are?"

"Emily," I said, shaking her hand. "I came all the way from Coventry, New Hampshire."

"Ted's got you beat," she said, pointing her plastic coffee stirrer at a skinny man in a flannel shirt and jeans who was standing in the corner talking with a grandmotherly type. "Ted drives all the way from Troy, New York, to get here, about three hours each way. That's Beverly with him. She's local, as are most of the people here."

I looked around the room. Everyone looked normal and respectable. I would never guess by looking at them that they were married to people who had changed their minds about their sexuality in midstream.

Even before the meeting started, I could see what Michael

was talking about. The chance to talk with people who knew exactly what I was going through was irresistible. I couldn't wait to hear what they discussed here, so I fixed myself some coffee and took a chair in the circle.

"Welcome to tonight's meeting of the Clueless Straight Spouse Support Group," Janet announced. "We have a newcomer with us this evening so, as usual, we'll go around the circle and tell a little bit about ourselves—first names only—and how we happened to arrive here. I'll go first.

"My name is Janet, and eight years ago, I woke up one morning and my husband Tom said to me, and I quote: 'Honey, today, I have to drop off the dog at the vet, pick up a few things at the market, by the way I'm gay, and can you get the dry cleaning on the way home?'"

The room rocked with laughter.

"Since then we've broken up and gotten back together again about eighty million times, and"—she glanced at her watch—"we're due to break up again in exactly eleven minutes. We've gotten so good at it that I don't even have to be there!"

More laughter, then she turned to the woman on her right. "Beverly?"

"Every time we do this, I feel like we're at A.A.," she said. "In a way, giving up booze was a breeze compared to being married to Phil. Anyway, we've been married 35 years, Phil came out three years ago, and we've been riding the roller-coaster of a mixed-orientation marriage ever since. Like Janet, we've decided to stay together, but every day our lives grow farther apart."

The man next to her, dressed in a rumpled suit and scuffed loafers, looked uncomfortable. He shifted in his chair and threw me a quick glance. "I'm Charlie, my wife Linda came out a few months ago, and it looks like we're headed for divorce." He turned to the man on his right, a tall skinny white-haired man in a flannel shirt who rose to shake my hand before sitting back down. I recognized the type: corporate executive with a rich pension plan retires early and moves to the country.

"Hi, Emily, I'm Ted. My wife Marie decided she was a lesbian about two years ago. We've been married for seven years—it was the second marriage for us both—and though we've had our moments, we get along pretty well, and she promised me that she'd pretty much stay out of trouble until she graduates from school and gets a job." He paused. "Then she'll move to Seattle to live with her Internet girl-friend." He patted the shoulder of the woman sitting next to him. She was slightly overweight and wore thick tortoiseshell glasses and tennis shoes.

"Hi, I'm Anita, and my soon-to-be-ex-husband Bill screwed around for most of the seventeen years we were married. I found out when one of his little boyfriends decided to send me a letter containing all the love notes and nude photos they had exchanged." She started to dig in her purse and popped a mint into her mouth. "Pleased to meet you, though too bad it has to be under these circumstances."

There was one more person left besides me. The woman sitting next to Anita looked like a farmer's wife: Her face and hands were chapped and she wore jeans and a blue and white checked cotton blouse. She coughed twice. "I'm Cheryl, my husband Paul is a Lutheran minister, and he came out a year ago. We've tried to make a go of it, but it just hasn't worked out. We're seeing the lawyer on Friday." She paused. "The congregation doesn't know. My latest argument is that they deserve to know everything, or else they'll think I was the cause. Paul, on the other hand, thinks it's none of their business. If it holds up the divorce, I'll give in, because I don't want to wait any longer, but in that case, I may decide to start a nasty rumor." She smiled ruefully. "Our twenty-third wedding anniversary is also on Friday. What a coinci-dence."

Janet nodded to me. "There are others who come to the meetings occasionally, depending on how their week went," she said. "It's your turn."

I decided to keep it simple. "I'm Emily, and this is my first time here, as you know. My husband Michael came out to me last week. He says it's just a phase, and that it will pass."

With that, everyone started to talk at once.

"That's what they all say," said Cheryl.

"You're new, you'll learn," offered Charlie.

"Not to scare you off, Emily, but we've all been through pretty much the same thing, only we're at different stages of the game as well as tolerance levels for what we have learned to live with," said Beverly. "Listen to the stories here. Don't let them influence you too much, but then again, don't be too surprised when you find yourself in the middle of something that someone else described the week before. Now, does anyone have anything they can't wait to vent?"

"I do," said Charlie, stirring his coffee. "Linda's been harping all week about this need to follow her destiny, which of course, is being a dyke first and foremost. We all know that marriage and most parts of your life involve some degree of self-denial and sacrifice. Well, I hate my job more each day. What I'd like most in the world is to quit my job and become a gourmet chef. But I can't do that because of my commitments. But if I was *gay*, according to our gay spouses, then I could theoretically do whatever I wanted— including quitting my job or busting up my family—because this is destiny and continuing to bury it would do irreparable harm. To that, all I can say is *Bullshit*."

"Well, Charlie, I think to some extent, your wife is right," said Beverly. "But in my opinion, she's handling it the wrong way, by acting like a spoiled teenager who doesn't want a curfew."

Cheryl nodded. "It all takes responsibility. Even though she buried it for who knows how many years, she obviously reached a point where she couldn't bury it any longer. I mean, you can't control your orientation anymore than you can stop a bird from flying over your head. But you *can* stop him from building a nest in your hair. And if Linda is just going to be a shit, you need to control yourself so you don't let her games get to you."

"But I'm not the one who started this whole thing, she did!" Charlie said. "I wasn't the one who came home one day and told her that I've decided not to have sex with her anymore because I really want to screw men. Why am *I* the one who has to make all the adjustments?"

"Because you're not the member of the maligned, misunderstood minority group. *She* is, and in her mind, you owe her big time for the centuries of abuse that the male sex has inflicted on women," said Ted. "At least, that's what Marie told me when she first came out. She felt like she needed to get even. Fortunately, she's calmed down a bit and has even apologized for her earlier behavior. Maybe Linda will do the same."

"Yeah, only when every man on the planet is castrated first," he grumbled.

"Well, I, for one, would welcome a little abuse," said Cheryl. "We haven't had sex for more than two years. Paul used to have a problem with impotence, so for the first year, I thought I knew the reason. That's why I let it go on for so long, because I understand that men feel bad enough when they can't get it up.

"And I could also understand that after a few times of trying and failing he'd be afraid to try anymore, because he knew what would happen. But you know what? I'm sick of understanding everything, of putting on a happy face in front of the congregation and acting like everything's just peachy. I'm at the point where I want a man to treat me like a sex object, because I forget what it's like. I want a man to love me for my body for once, and not my mind. Paul tells me that he loves me and doesn't want to divorce, but he's also said that he's one woman short of gay. I just want him to make up his mind because to me, this marriage is the same thing as settling for something that you don't really want because it's better than nothing."

"Yeah, well, the irony is that having sex with Bill was always pretty good for most of our marriage," said Anita. "There were never any signs that he was gay, even when he was fooling around, which only occurred on his business trips. But since he came out, we haven't had sex at all because he feels that having sex with me is not being true to his new gay identity and that if his queer friends knew, they'd be disgusted. Great, huh? I think what really bothers me most is that because he's now gay, he gets to decide everything, even something as personal as my sex life, which I think is totally unfair."

I was fascinated by the stories that were swirling around me, and I drank it all in. Even though I was still new at all this, I felt as if I fit right in, despite the fact that I had met these people only 30 minutes ago.

"Well," said Cheryl, reaching into her purse, "maybe this will help." She pulled out a copy of a book entitled *Sex Secrets for Straight Women from a Gay Man*. "I saw it in the bookstore last week, and I just couldn't resist."

Anita grabbed the book out of Cheryl's hands. "Let me see that," she said, paging through the book. "You know, part of the problem is that I sometimes think that if I do anything and everything that Bill wants sexually he'll be so fulfilled that he won't want a man. It's too late, of course, but maybe if I had this book a few months ago..."

"Oh, please," sighed Janet. "Don't we already get enough of this crap from our spouses? Just last night Tom went through a long diatribe describing in painstaking detail why making love to a man is oh-so-much better than boinking a woman. Whenever I initiate sex with Tom, I feel his critical fish-eye following my every move, like he's comparing it to being in bed with a man. He's basically sending me messages, 'I could do a better job of making love to a man than she is...'"

"But I still don't get it," said Beverly. "How would a gay man know about making love to a straight man? Besides, what does a gay man know about the...ahem...assets that are available to a straight woman that he hasn't got?"

"Beverly's right," said Ted. "I think most of us have decided that a gay spouse doesn't really have a place in our sex lives anymore."

"Despite the fact that we're all still married to them," Janet pointed out.

"Or maybe, like Anita said, it's been decided *for* us," said Charlie. "I've been coming here for two months now, and after hearing all the stories, I got to thinking that the straight men with lesbian wives have it worse than straight women with gay husbands."

Cheryl gave a snort. "Oh really, Charlie? And why is that?"

"Because once our wives decide they're lesbians, they totally tune us out. Even Marie did it to Ted before they arrived at their present truce. At least your husbands are still talking to you," said Charlie. "With Linda, as soon as she came out, she only spoke to me when it was absolutely necessary. It's like she felt she couldn't gain entry into the Exclusive Lesbian Club and receive her free-with-membership toaster if she was still associated with a man. I mean, we were still sleeping in the same bed, but it was as though an invisible barrier went straight down the middle of the bed. God forbid if I crossed that line, she would grunt and move away from me even if she was practically lying on the floor. Honestly, I don't know why she's still sleeping in the same bed. Probably to punish me."

He frowned and took a sip of his coffee. "One night last week, before I turned the lights out, I reached around her waist, out of habit, I guess. When she felt me touch her, she twisted and turned around and actually picked up my arm between her thumb and index finger and put it back on my side of the bed like she was picking up a dog turd. All of this was accompanied by the dirtiest look I've ever seen her give anyone."

"Well, you know," said Ted, "you *are* the enemy because you're male. It seems like a lot of the lesbian identity has to do with banding together with other like-minded women so that they don't feel like they're victimized by men anymore."

"Is that what Linda did when she came out, Charlie?"

asked Janet.

"Yeah, within a week she had gone from soccer mom to radical dyke. I mean, she gave all of her feminine clothes away except for her jeans and T-shirts, she bought a pair of Doc Martens, and cut her hair almost as short as I wore mine in the military. She also threw away her contacts and I swear she went out and got the heaviest, ugliest pair of glasses she could find."

He glanced around the circle. "You know, even though this seems to be the initial code of behavior when it comes to getting into the man-hating dyke clique, she and her girlfriends still go nuts when they see Pamela Anderson or some other bleached blond bimbo who's overdosed on silicone. I mean, I've heard Linda on the phone with her girlfriends and she's as bad as some of the guys I've hung at bars with."

I cleared my throat. "So what do you do to cope?" I asked.

"I try not to drink...much," he said. "Mostly, when she's out with her girlfriend and I'm stuck at home, I either watch too much TV or stomp around the house."

"You know what I do?" Anita asked. "In the last few weeks I've been making the rounds of the yard sales in late afternoon when the people are tired and just want to get rid of their junk. I zero in on the mismatched and chipped china sets and offer something like five bucks for a box of 200 pieces. They usually take it, because they don't want to have to lug it back into the house and store it for next year's sale. Then I bring it home and stash it in the barn."

"Why?" asked Beverly.

She smiled slyly. "When Bill starts to drive me crazy, or when August 1st seems too far away—" she turned to me and said, "that's the day he's moving out—I go out to the barn and hurl it against the wall, piece by piece. It's better than drugs. I just throw a plate or cup against the barn as hard as I can and scream and cry. Then, when he's around, I can be decent and civil and even have a conversation with him."

"Yeah, but you live out on a road with no neighbors,"

Cheryl pointed out.

"Well, then maybe we should have the next meeting at my place," she said. "Either that, or the next time any of you gets totally fed up, you can come out to the barn and smash a few dishes. Of course, you'd need to bring your own, 'cause I use up every one I get."

"I'd love to do something like that," said Cheryl. "I made a voodoo doll and stick pins in it whenever Paul starts harping on me or describing the last hot date he had."

"Well, *I'd* like to stick a pin in every person I meet who asks me, 'Well, didn't you know?'" said Anita. She snorted. "As if we're the only married people who don't have sex."

"And some of us do," Cheryl pointed out. "So it's not like we had a clue." She shook her head. "Now my mother just keeps asking me, 'But he had a high voice, didn't he?' As if that explained everything."

"Sorry," I said, "but I have to ask since this is all new to me. It seems like everyone here is staying with their spouses, at least temporarily," I said. "Does anyone just immediately break up when a husband or wife comes out?"

"Not really," answered Janet. "You'll discover there are many twists and turns to this road soon enough. But you could get through this a lot more quickly if you were to learn what most of us eventually discover."

"Which is?" I asked.

"It just doesn't work out," she said. "Oh, we all try it, but you can't teach a bird to like cats, and eventually we all gravitate toward our own. Even with Tom, we've been all over the map trying to incorporate his gayness into our marriage. It seems I spend my waking hours waiting for the other shoe to drop." She shrugged. "It's the nature of the beast."

We drank more coffee and I listened to the stories. The two hours flew by and I promised to return next week. On the drive home, I decided to keep the meeting a secret from Michael.

When I got home a little after eleven, he was sitting in the living room, waiting up for me.

"And where were you?" he asked before I had closed the door.

"Out," I answered. "Why?"

He didn't respond. But I could tell he was inwardly seething.

"I'm tired," I said, heading upstairs. "Good night."

Chapter Six

Michael and I spent the next month in a silent holding pattern. We kept our distance from each other. It was clear that neither of us knew what his disclosure meant to our marriage and we were determined not to bring it up. But we did talk about it with other people—a lot. Michael went to his Wednesday night gay married men's meetings and I went to my Tuesday night straight spouse meetings.

When we were together in each other's presence, however, we appeared to have been struck deaf and mute. I started to treat Michael like any other co-worker, and he did the same. One thing that helped me to wean myself from him was that he stopped looking at me in our previously intimate way, the *can-you-believe-this?* glance whenever an advertiser or one of the Blue Hairs said something exceedingly stupid. The atmosphere at the office suffered a bit because of the dearth of witty repartee between the owners, I'd be the first to admit, but it was the only way we could cope.

Michael began to spend most of the day away from the office, presumably on sales calls, but during that first month, my overactive imagination went wild. In my mind's eye, I saw him hanging out at every rest area on the Interstate, loitering at the sinks in the grimy men's room heavily perfumed with disinfectant, holding his hands under the running water until they turned to prunes in the hopes of scoring a three-minute anonymous fuck in one of the stalls. My rational side tried to convince me that he was staying away because he wanted to keep the arguments between us to an absolute minimum. I seesawed between the two sides for weeks.

Besides work, my Tuesday night meetings were the only thing that kept me sane. At the Clueless meetings, we had a forum where we could bitch, moan, and gripe about what it was like to live with a spouse who was in extreme denial—or extreme flamboyance—about his or her true orientation. In between the meetings, I began to pine for Tuesday nights, even though I still wasn't saying much at the meetings. I just sensed that sooner or later I'd somehow be able to use the information in our marriage.

Last week, Cheryl started the proceedings.

"You know," she said, "I figure that the fact that Paul is now living out some of his fantasies of what it's like to be a gay man—"

Janet cut her off. "The candy store phase, huh?"

Cheryl shrugged. "Yeah," she said. "The kid in a candy store where he can't stuff his pockets fast enough—or get stuffed enough." Everyone laughed. "I don't know, I thought that would help dissipate his anger and he would act friendlier toward me. But it's made it worse. He's even more hostile whenever we spend more than two minutes together in the same room."

"So how do you act when you're with him?" asked Anita.

"I try to be cordial. I use neutral language and stay away from the 'you saids' and the 'you shoulds.'"

"Is there any particular topic that gets him going?"

"No, and that's the strange part. Whether we're discussing the weather or the divorce, he flies off the handle. I try to stay calm, but I feel like he's baiting me."

"Well, he is," said Charlie.

"But why?"

He let out a deep sigh. "I've been up and down and all over this. I think part of it is because Linda has had to go from living a life that is accepted and condoned by society to one that is widely scorned by everyone, including herself. Even though it was entirely her choice to come out, I think part of her believes it's my fault that she's a lesbian."

"You mean she thinks *you* turned her gay?" asked Cheryl.

He coughed. "In a way, yes. Linda told me when her lesbian side first started to surface, she started going through the boyfriends she'd been with before me to see if there was anything about them that would have a) caused her to come out any sooner, b) helped her keep the lid on her gayness, or c) accepted her and lived in a celibate relationship with her while she screwed around. In the end, she couldn't think of anyone, and you know what she told me once when we were able to talk civilly?"

"What?" asked Cheryl.

"She told me it was because I was so damn honest. My honesty made her hold a mirror up to her own lies until it finally became too much for her. She said that right before she came out, it was too uncomfortable to even be in the same room with me." He smiled. "And of course, since great liars tend to be great actors, I didn't know anything was wrong until she started picking fights in the hopes I would kick her out. Of course, that's not what happened."

Anita piped up. "Well, as long as she's pissed off at you, blaming you for everything that's wrong in her life, this just means she doesn't have to deal with her own guilt about how her decision has affected you. Right?"

"Exactly," said Charlie. "But sometimes it's all in the way it's phrased; there are different degrees of honesty and lies. Linda used to make a big stink about how she needed to be honest with me about what's going on with her gay side, though for a while she wasn't able to call it that quite yet. Instead, it was 'her bisexuality.'"

Cheryl let out a little laugh. "Of course."

"A mere stepping stone," said Janet.

"Well, I think Bill knows he's being tactless on purpose," said Anita. I mean, when he comes home from a date, I'd rather hear, 'I liked the guy, we seemed to hit it off,' and not, 'God, what a cock! And his ass was really tight!'"

"Well, I've been thinking about Paul's lies all week, and I'm not sure what to do. We've talked about it before here, but honestly, I didn't think it applied to me. Now I'm not so sure."

"What is it, Cheryl?" Bob asked.

"Well, Paul has always told me that he's never done anything with another man that would ever put me at risk, and I've always believed him." She paused. "But now when I think about all the times I've caught him lying to me, it makes me obsess over the lies I *don't* know about."

"Like if he has acted in a way that would put you at risk?" Ted asked gently.

"Well, yes. The thing is that I've been thinking about getting tested for HIV, and there's part of me that wants to know. But the other part that's bought into Paul's denial, well, I'd probably be pissed off at him no matter how the results turned out. If I'm negative, I'd be angry because I'd think that he was lying about it anyway and I was just lucky. If I'm—well, if it went the other way, I'd be livid. Knowing Paul, he'd focus on my anger instead of the fact that it was his fault!"

"They always manage to turn it back onto us," said Janet, shaking her head.

"I've been thinking of nothing else all week, and I still don't know what to do."

"I say you get tested," said Anita.

"I agree," said Janet. "Cheryl, you've lived with his lies long enough, here's a chance to actually get at the truth."

"Yeah, but—"

Nobody said anything.

Finally, Ted asked the question. "You mean what if it turns out positive?"

The group was silent.

"You know we'll help you," said Janet.

Suddenly, Anita perked up.

"Hey, what if we *all* get tested next week? I mean, those of us who haven't been yet?"

Charlie shook his head. "Well, if you women want to do it, that's fine, but I don't think it's necessary for the men."

Janet swirled around in her chair. "What do you mean the men don't need to be tested, Charlie? No one is immune from AIDS, not even lesbians."

"Well, they *are* the group with the lowest rate of AIDS," Ted offered helpfully.

"It doesn't matter," said Janet. "This isn't a matter of who's most at risk. This is a matter of us sticking together, doing whatever is necessary to help each other." Her cheeks had reddened slightly and her nostrils were flaring.

"You make us sound like some kind of commune, Janet," said Charlie. "I've never thought of the group in that way."

"How have you thought of it, then?"

"I think of it as a place where I can talk to people who don't look at me like I have three heads because my wife decided she was a lesbian."

"But you've given help and advice whenever one of us has needed it," Janet countered. "You haven't been totally selfish here, Charlie, at least I don't *think* you have."

"Of course I haven't," he said. "It's just that in any group with a common interest, there's a tendency to go overboard when it comes to sticking together, and I think this is one of those occasions. This is where I draw the line."

"I think you just don't want to know the truth about your own status," said Janet.

"Yeah," said Anita. "What do you have to worry about? It's not as if Linda's slept with half the lesbians in Vermont."

Charlie recoiled, as if he had been slapped.

"Charlie, I'm sorry," said Anita, reaching over to rub his shoulder. "I know it's not easy, but this is one time when I think it's really important to support Cheryl."

Charlie didn't respond.

"Anita, why don't you just leave him alone?" Janet hissed.

Anita glared at her. "What's *your* problem?"

"Just lay off, okay? It's not important."

Janet looked down at her lap. "Okay, well, let's just say that whoever wants to get tested before the next meeting, should go ahead. But we're all behind you, Cheryl, whatever you decide."

After that, the meeting gradually ended as people stood up to leave. I walked out with Beverly.

"What did you think of all that?" I asked her.

"I was tested a few years ago when Phil first came out," she said matter-of-factly. "I hemmed and hawed for weeks, but in the end there was one big difference: I didn't tell Phil. Back then, I was telling him absolutely everything that was on my mind while he told me nothing about his own life. Why I blabbed so much, I wasn't sure, but back then I thought crass honesty would bring us closer. It just pushed him further away.

"When I first thought about getting tested, my impulse was to run and tell Phil. But I didn't, because I knew he'd launch into one of his *you-don't-trust-me* diatribes. So I kept it to myself and didn't tell anyone." She glanced at me. "It came out negative."

She paused, then said, "Of course, it was important, but it marked a turning point in our marriage. From that point on, I stopped telling Phil everything. We still discussed the major things, like the kids' college education and what to do when his mother couldn't live by herself anymore, but on the whole I stopped confiding in him. And you know what? He changed."

"How?"

"Once I stopped burdening him with my worries, he started to lighten up. I guess he felt that I was pulling away, which posed a threat to him, since for once he wasn't the one who was changing the dynamics of the marriage—it was me. And that scared him, because it made him think that perhaps I wouldn't be his doormat forever and that I had needs and desires too. And in all the time we've been married, I honestly don't think that had occurred to him before.

"So he started treating me better, the little things, like asking how my day went and holding the door for me when we went out." She smiled. "It's always the little things that reveal how someone really feels about you."

We had reached her car and she fished in her purse for her keys. "I still don't tell him everything, and he still treats me with respect."

I was fascinated by her story and the idea of turning someone around so much by doing *less,* which had never occurred to me.

"What about the sex?" I asked.

She looked at me and shrugged. "What about it? It never meant a lot to me, I could take it or leave it, but Phil was my polar opposite. Early on, I thought it was *my* lack of interest that sent him searching for the kind of person who could match his sexual appetite—another man—but after finding the secret notes and hearing the lame excuses, I knew it was much, much more complex than that."

"So," I said, leaning against her car, "why are you still married?" I thought my questions sounded pretty naïve, but Beverly didn't seem to mind. Everything was still so new to me that the idea of a woman choosing to stay married for years when she knew her husband was gay, well, I wasn't able to grasp that yet.

"Emily, if you've been together as long as Phil and I have, and you've already ironed all the wrinkles out of your marriage, when something like this happens—" Her voice trailed off and she glanced over my head. "Well, the first thing I did was shake my fist at the sky and scream, 'Why me? Why now?'"

"I never got a clear answer, so I decided to wait for one." She winked at me. "Let me tell you, I waited an awful long time for this particular kind of manna to fall from the heavens. There was one point when the pistols and daggers came out. I mean, Phil moved in and out of the house more often than I went to the dump. Every time we started to talk rationally about our situation, one of us would escalate it to the equivalent of a duel."

"How long did that last?"

She scrunched up her face and ticked off her fingers. "Oh, about eight months."

"Eight months? How could you stand it?"

"Well, he stormed out so often that I had a lot of time to spend in the house by myself. One night I made a list of the pros and cons of being married to him. Once I got it down on paper, the pros definitely outweighed the cons."

"Did you show him the list?"

"No, never. There was no reason to. And by then, I was withholding much more information than I was giving him. I learned to overlook the cons, because after all, they were *my* cons and largely had nothing to do with him. But I also decided that since I never cared that much about having a physical relationship with my husband, that if Phil wanted to go out and find sex elsewhere, that was okay with me.

"Over time, he began to cherish our marriage, or at least the parts he knew he would be unable to find with another man."

She smiled and unlocked her car. Then she leaned over to give me a quick hug. "And that, my dear, is how I've done it."

I walked over to my car. I was shivering despite the humidity.

I drove home wide-eyed.

• • •

When I arrived at the office the next morning, Joel Gardner was standing outside the office waiting for me. It was the day for all the office computers to have their annual checkups. Today Joel would upgrade several of the machines and clean out the dust and cat fur from the fans and hard drives. Though I would kill for my computer, the logistics of technology and how it worked was my black hole. But that never stopped me from asking too many questions, especially the dumb kind. I spent most of the day standing beside Joel as he fiddled with the innards of the various machines. When I called to make the appointment, I warned Joel not to expect me to keep my mouth shut while he worked.

He couldn't resist. "But how would that be different for you, Em?"

Joel and I had gone through school together, from kindergarten through high school. We weren't particularly close, but I'd gotten in touch with him after we bought the paper and I needed someone local to call with stupid computer questions.

Joel had married a girl from two towns away. They had two children—a boy and a girl—and he made a good living from being the only computer guy for miles around who didn't sound exasperated when answering stupid questions.

Due to his patience and his ability to describe technical terms in plain English, Joel's schedule was booked up solid at least three weeks in advance. We had an arrangement where I could call him at any time for help in exchange for a free business card ad in every issue of the *Courier*. Not that he needed it, since he always had twice as much work as he could handle, and he refused to have employees. Joel had an extreme distrust of government that he inherited from his Marxist father, who I recall spewing clouds of cigar smoke and unintelligible socialist rhetoric into the room when we were kids. No one wanted to go to Joel's house because his father would start his tirades the minute anyone walked in the door; it didn't matter if you were five years old or fifty. After a while, Joel gave up trying to have a social life and spent his afterschool hours taking apart and putting together the TVs and radios his father had long ago banished to the basement because of the capitalist garbage they brought into the house. Joel got so good at it that he graduated to performing the same surgery on early computers and he started his own business when he was still in high school. His sweetest revenge is that the kids who gave him one lame excuse after another why they couldn't play with him now are the ones who call him in a panic when their computers crash. Joel charges them twice his usual hourly rate.

I watched him pick out clumps of fur from around the hard drive.

Joel cleared his throat. "Hey Em."

"Hey what?"

"Is everything okay with you and Michael?" he asked without looking up.

His question caught me off guard. I strained to keep my voice neutral.

"Why do you say that, Joel?"

"Oh, it's just that something about the paper has changed. It's nothing obvious, but there seems to be a lot more discord between the ads and the stories," he said. "It wasn't there before."

"Really."

"It seems like there's a lot of tension between the stories and the ads, like they're bickering with each other. Car ads next to an article about the new recycling schedule. That kind of thing." He put down his screwdriver and turned around to look at me. "Like I said, it's nothing that another paper wouldn't do, but it seemed you were so meticulous about not doing anything like that." He paused. "Is everything okay?"

I couldn't lie to him. I took a breath and then held it for a few seconds. "Well, Joel, Michael doesn't know if he's coming or going."

"Oh." Joel turned back to the computer. I know he was waiting for me to offer up more details, but I also knew he wouldn't be offended if I didn't, and he wouldn't ask.

I watched him work in silence. After five minutes, he dug deep into his toolbox and came out with an oddly shaped bit of metal attached to a display card. He tore the metal from the plastic wrap and tossed the cardboard backing beside the computer. When I saw it, I laughed out loud, and once I started I couldn't stop.

GENDER CHANGER, it read. *Converts the Gender of a Cable or Device from DB25 Female to DB25 Male.*

Joel looked at me, a question on his face.

I pointed at the card. "*This* is the problem with my marriage right now."

He squinted at the card.

"Michael wants to be a woman?"

I started laughing all over again.

"No, Joel, he wishes I could change *my* gender!"

He looked confused. "Do you?"

"Of course not!"

The light bulb went on. "Ohhhh," he said. "Is he—"

I cut him off before he could say the word. "He's not sure."

"Oh." He paused. "When will he know?"

"That is the 64 thousand dollar question." I watched him work for a few minutes more, then decided to head home. Joel was still frowning at my computer. I started to gather up my things. "Hey, lock the door behind you."

"Sure, Emily, good luck," he said. "I'll let you know what I find."

"Good. So will I."

I was looking forward to a quiet night by myself since Michael was at his gay married whatever meeting. I fed the cats, poured milk into a bowl of cereal for dinner, and headed for bed to read. I was about to turn the light out when I heard Michael's car pull into the driveway. He came into the bedroom and patted the edge of the bed before sitting down beside me. Then he asked me about my day. As I talked, I saw his eyes glaze over. Another minute and they would have rolled back in his head, so I switched to the *Reader's Digest* version. When I was done, he cleared his throat and proceeded to fill me in on his day, particularly his meeting that evening.

I tuned out his words and just watched him talk. He was wonderfully animated, truly alive in a way that I hadn't seen in him in years. When he talked about his new life, the part of him he's denied all these years, his eyes no longer looked dull. His voice lacked that contemptuous edge he had perfected. And he was smiling.

Why, then, is he still denying that he's gay when the writing is all over the wall? He's not happy with being even a small part of the straight world, can't he see that? When he's on the phone with a guy from his married gay men's group, or reading the latest issue of *The Advocate*, he looks so peaceful that I start to feel sad. Once, years earlier, I was able to elicit the same spark from him. Now, when he's with me, when we're talking about something that has absolutely nothing to do with gay men, a dullness glazes his eyes and his voice turns into a monotone.

"You're his jailer, Emily. That's how he sees you," Janet said the other day when I complained about Michael's lack of energy and attention toward me.

"He chose you partly because he thought you would be able to rescue him from his gay side, to keep him safe and heterosexual, hidden from his true nature. Maybe he thought that if he spent enough time with you, in fact, married you, enough of you would rub off onto him."

"What part of me?"

"The heterosexual side, of course! The same thing happened with me and Tom. But when that didn't happen, he began to resent me for not being able to purge the gayness from his life.

"Before long, as he started to feel more comfortable with being gay, he began to see me as the prison warden who was keeping him from living the life he wanted to live. He resented himself more at first, because he expected me to be able to change him. When I couldn't, he got angry with himself for becoming so dependent on me. And of course, he blamed me even more."

I thought about her words as I watched Michael wave his arms around, crinkle his brow, and talk as if he was almost singing. Suddenly, I couldn't keep my eyes open and didn't try to hold back a huge yawn.

"I'm sorry, Michael," I said, leaning into the pillows. "It's been a long day. I'm going to sleep." I turned off the light and pulled the covers over my shoulders. I didn't notice whether Michael was annoyed that I interrupted his monologue. I was surprised to realize that I didn't care.

• • •

Two days later, I was alone in the office finalizing the stories for the next issue. Carrie had already gone for the day and I hadn't seen Michael since he left the house that morning. I was mulling over Beverly's relationship with her husband Phil and wondering whether I could live the same life. Could I overlook Michael's gay side? Was he really bisexual and not gay? I smiled at the thought. If I still had a chance, I'd fight for him. And this would win him over to my side, I was sure. Max was sleeping in my chair, wedged in between my butt and the chair back, snoring the contented snore of a neutered male cat.

Lucky cat, I thought. But what do you expect from a totally asexual *it*. I stood up to stretch my back since the lump that was Max was not the greatest thing for my posture, but I was not about to move him. I planned to stay and work for a few hours longer.

I was trying to place the stories and ads in more neutral positions when Michael came in the front door and sat down in the chair next to my desk. His eyes were red, as if he had been crying. I looked at him. He reached for both my hands. His were clammy.

"You don't deserve me," he mumbled, looking down at the floor, up at the ceiling, out the window, everywhere but at me.

I didn't know what to say.

"You didn't marry me knowing that I'd be attracted to men," he said in a strained voice.

I stared at the top of his head.

"You're trying to push me away," I whispered.

He jerked his head up. "No, I'm not. I'm giving you the choice to let me go now if you want, because I don't think you can live with the idea of me having an outside relationship. Which of course would only be physical," he quickly added.

Wait a minute. I thought he just wanted to talk with other men who were going through the same thing. When did anything physical enter into it?

I kept my mouth shut. If it indeed came to this, maybe he'd see that his attraction to me was more important than his attraction to men, and we could get back to normal. I squelched the next thought to float up—*But that would mean he's cheating on you!*—in favor of a solution I viewed as the equivalent of ripping off a Band-Aid.

It was still all a dream to me. It felt as if I had woken up a few months ago and someone else's husband had taken Michael's place. Things would return to normal if only I could wake up. The problem was that I didn't know how. Because I was in that dream state, I began agreeing to things that I never thought were possible, like the idea of my husband having sex with someone else, and a man to boot. A little voice was incessantly poking me on the shoulder, saying, "Hey, do you know what you're doing?"

I listened to the voice for a few seconds before flicking it off my shoulder. I refused to listen to anything or anyone suggesting that maybe what I was doing was wrong and that I should stand up for myself. This was my state of mind when I proceeded to utter a line I would soon come to regret. "Honey, if we could get through this," I said, waving my arm around the office, "we can get through anything. As long as the relationship between us doesn't change."

Oh, how naïve I was.

"We need to figure out what will be acceptable for both of us," I told Michael. I'd never seen him look at me like that before, a mix of awe and amazement on his face. "We'll deal with this together," I said.

Earlier that day, Carrie had mentioned she was writing a

novel, which was news to me. "How do you find the time?" I asked.

She described how her husband Stewart gave her one hour to spend alone each afternoon to work from 5 to 6 while he fixes dinner.

"After I get home, I fix a cup of tea, start dinner, and then go into my office and close the door. Stewart gets home after picking up the kids and he finishes making dinner. A little after six, I come downstairs and everyone's happy."

I looked at Michael and took a deep breath. "How about one hour a day?" I asked. "Or one night a week?"

"To do what?" he asked.

"To go out wherever and with whoever you want, no questions asked."

He scowled. "You're basically asking me to confine my gay side to one night out of seven," he said, frowning. "I don't know if I can do that. Besides, I get more than one day a week now."

I felt the storm rising in my stomach and clenched my teeth. Jesus, what did he want, free rein seven nights a week while I get the dregs the next morning when he's hung over and sucking down coffee in a futile attempt to be coherent with me?

I pushed the storm away. "Well," I chirped, "what would work for you?"

He thought for a minute. I tapped my foot. Maybe this was a mistake.

"How about two nights a week out—one weekend night and one weeknight—and an hour a night online?"

I thought about it. He'd still be spending most of his time with me. "Okay," I said.

Although it was twice what I had initially suggested, maybe he'd get it out of his system twice as fast.

"And if either of us is unhappy with it, we'll tell the other right away, right?" I asked.

"Of course," he said in a tone that said, *How could you doubt me?*

A week later, however, I was doubting myself. Though nothing changed at the office, our whole house turned into a shrine to the love that dared not speak its name, and Michael turned into Mister Gay. Overnight, copies of *The Advocate* littered the coffee table, dog-eared issues of *Out* covered Michael's nightstand, and the monthly calendar from SNEGMA—an acronym for the Southern New England Gay Men's Association out of Boston—was stuck to the refrigerator with a magnet in the shape of a pink triangle. Michael stopped just short of hanging a rainbow flag on the porch.

I started to hate the word gay. The term *bisexual* also appeared in the literature Michael brought home, but it seemed to be placed there as an afterthought. The word *gay* ruled and seemed so succinct, completely certain of where it was heading.

A couple of weeks after we made our deal, I headed home after closing the week's issue. When I opened the door, the house reeked of cat piss. It was Michael's week to change the litter, but it smelled as if at least a week had gone by since it had been done. Instead, Michael was parked in his chair in the living room, an Armistead Maupin novel in his lap and a can of Spaghetti-O's with a fork sticking out of it at his elbow.

"Hi," I said as I threw my papers on the kitchen table.

"Hi," he replied distractedly, unconsciously waving me away with his free hand.

"What's for dinner?" I asked.

"I dunno. What's in the fridge?"

It was also his week to make dinner, I thought as I peered into the refrigerator.

He was keeping to his end of the deal, but during his non-gay hours, he had returned to his distant, preoccupied state. He spent most of his non-gay evenings plowing through the stack of gay books he had ordered through Amazon.com. From his intensity, you would have thought he was studying for his doctorate.

I missed coming home to one of his home-cooked meals. I wanted to feel my stomach gurgle before I stepped onto the porch. Michael hadn't cooked a meal since we struck our deal. I sat by myself in the kitchen to eat yet another nuked dinner of mushy pasta and chicken something on a plastic plate. Even the cats weren't interested. After dinner, I sat down in my chair in the living room and let out a huge sigh.

Michael looked up, smiled briefly, and returned to his reading.

I couldn't hold back anymore. "Michael," I finally said.

"Yes?"

"Why are you obsessed with everything and anything gay? It's like somebody let the cork out of you and now you can't think about anything else."

He exhaled loudly, cracked the spine of his book, and placed it facedown on his lap. When he looked at me, his eyes were void of emotion.

"Emily," he said, "I am not, as you say, obsessed with everything and anything gay. Why would you think that?"

"Because," I managed to say in the sweetest voice I could summon up, "you've gone from devouring ten-year-old issues of *Editor & Publisher* every night to reading the complete works of Gore Vidal, Michelangelo what's-his-name, and John Preston in less than two weeks. Fliers for New Hampshire Pride Day are plastering the refrigerator and you've stuck a rainbow decal on your bumper."

Before he could respond, I added, "I miss the evenings we used to spend together."

"We still read together," he countered, a bit defensively.

"Yeah, but we also used to occasionally talk to each other, too. Now all you do is bury yourself in your gay books and magazines."

"But I don't spend hours on the Internet anymore," he said, "and you used to complain about that."

"Yes, but it seems that since you can now have all of your gay stuff out in the open, that's all you think about. I'm surprised you haven't stuck a rainbow decal on your computer monitor at work."

"No one at work is supposed to know," he said between clenched teeth as he stuck a bookmark from the Gay Men's Health Crisis center in the book and set it on the coffee table.

"Yeah, but they know something is going on," I said. "Not necessarily between us because we basically pass each other in the wind. But they have asked me if there's anything bothering you."

"Well, you can tell them that nothing's going on with me."

I didn't want to say what I really was thinking, that someone in town was bound to put two and two together about the sticker on his car. I'm sure Michael realized this, but I figured he liked playing with fire. Catch me if you can, almost as if he wanted to get caught.

"And I'm *not* obsessed with everything gay. It's just that I don't have to hide it from you anymore."

I glanced at my watch. "It doesn't matter anyway. I'm going to bed," I said, and headed upstairs. When I came out of the bathroom, he was sitting on the bed. I honestly didn't know why he was sitting there.

"You think of me as your best friend, right?" I asked as I got under the covers.

He pawed the edge of the quilt. "Of course. Why do you bring that up now?"

"Then why are you treating me like absolute shit?"

He stopped kneading the quilt and looked as if I had slapped him. "First of all, the two of us have worked together to come up with certain limits that are acceptable to us both. What I'm doing I'm doing with your full knowledge. I won't jeopardize your health or mine, and I will not fall in love with another man.

"And second, you said you wanted me to be totally honest with you and not hide what I'm thinking or feeling anymore. So now that I'm being honest, *that* doesn't make you happy either." His voice grew louder. "So what is it, Em? What do you want?"

Michael made me so mad whenever he got like this. I felt he was deliberately being an asshole so I would tell him to leave. Then I would be the bad guy and we would have broken up not because he was gay, but because of my temper, leaving him to go on his merry way absolved of all guilt.

So I shook my head. "I don't know."

And I didn't, because when it comes to the two organs with the worst judgment—a woman's heart and a man's dick—it's impossible to know what will happen, no matter how hard you try to prevent it. It's like swearing off chocolate: you might make it through the first day in good shape, but the minute you place restrictions on the body parts that are more responsible for influencing a person's judgment and actions than any other, well, it's like trying not to think of a polka dot elephant; within days, you'll be able to think of nothing else. And at that point, you'd do anything in order to get it.

"I can't be as enthusiastic as you are about your new lifestyle," I told him. "Even though I'm happy that you're no longer denying a very important part of yourself, which means that you can be totally honest with me for the first time in years, I can't help but see it as a threat to our marriage."

"But I keep telling you I'm not gay! Why can't you see that?"

I sighed. Because it's clear to me that what you're doing is one step in the long process of becoming comfortable with being 100 percent gay, and once you're able to admit it to me, you can admit it to the world.

Because I know that you're getting used to your new identity more quickly than you thought.

Because I now know if you weren't with me, you'd be with gay men.

Because you're a horny teenager whenever gay anything comes up, but around me you're a decrepit old man.

I wanted to shake the truth into him. Why can't you see it?

I was tired. I wanted the discussion to be over. I wanted things to be simple. If only Michael could tell me over coffee one morning one of two things: "I'm gay," or "I'm not gay," that would be the end of it and we'd know exactly how to proceed.

Suddenly, he slapped the nightstand, startling me from my fantasy.

"You just don't get it, do you? You don't understand how much I love you and that the way I want a man has nothing to do with the way I want you," he yelled. "How can I make you understand?"

He was panting. Every exhalation contained a hint of violence.

"Is there *anything* I can possibly do for you?"

The next thought I had was so ridiculous that I started to laugh.

"*What?*" he said, glaring at me.

"You can get me a penis!" Then I started to giggle, and I couldn't stop.

"You're not serious, are you?" He stared at me, stone-faced.

"Does it *look* like I'm serious?" I tried to catch my breath. "Oh, please. I'm not talking about a strap-on dildo. I mean, I really want a penis, a real one, because then you wouldn't need someone else."

His tone and glare softened. "Jesus, Em, you just don't understand, do you? It's not just a dick, it's that, well—"

"Well, what, Mister Experienced Gay, oh, sorry, Mister *Bisexual?*"

He exhaled sharply. "*Everything* is different, not just having a dick."

"Well, Mister Know-It-All, why don't you just show me?"

"I don't think you'd like it," he said quietly.

I felt my body tense up. "How do you know?"

The look in Michael's eye dulled. "Well," he said evenly, "why don't we just find out?"

I waved my hands in a who-cares way. "Well, then, why not?"

Ten minutes later, I knew the difference. Michael had left the room, leaving me face down on the bed on my knees. My ass was sticking up in the air and my panties and jeans were bunched down around my ankles while my shirt and bra had not been disturbed at all. Goosebumps had formed on my bare legs and ass while the blood flowed to my head and arms.

He was right. It *is* different. I was glad I couldn't see Michael's face while he fucked me—that was the only word that fit—because based on how it felt, I wouldn't want to know what he looked like.

After I made my comment, he got up to close the bedroom door, something he never did, came back over to the bed, and the dynamic instantly changed. The air was charged with an energy I had never felt with him.

I leaned against the headboard and reached for him, rising to a kneeling position in front of him. I stroked his face with one hand while the other sought the small of his back. He placed his hands lightly on my hips.

"You said you wanted to know the difference," he whispered. I nodded. With that, he grabbed my hips and turned me roughly around. I fell onto my elbows, still kneeling. No caress, no warning. He started to grind his pelvis against my ass. Instantly, he was hard, something that had never happened before.

After 22 seconds—I knew because I was so breathless with the shock of his urgency that I had to focus on something and the first thing my eyes found was the clock on the nightstand—he started to slide his cock up and down between the cheeks of my butt. I grabbed at the headboard to keep my balance. I stared at the luminous green numbers on the clock; I didn't want to see how white my knuckles were.

"You really want me to *fuck* you baby, don't you, you want to really *feel* me all the way up *inside* you and feel me *come* inside you, *don't* you, baby?"

It didn't sound like his voice. It sounded as if his voice had gone through a computer program that altered normal voices into horror-flick ones. With every thrust, Michael accentuated his words, timing the words to each lunge.

We both still had our clothes on. I thought of telling him to stop, that I got his point, but I couldn't find my voice. Besides, I doubt he would have.

"*What*'d you say, *baby*? My *cock* can't wait." More words from a stranger.

"Yes." I managed a rasp. "Yes."

Michael then shoved me so hard that I fell facedown onto the bed. He grabbed my legs and pulled them back up so my knees were bent. I heard his belt buckle click followed by the harsh buzz of his zipper.

"Pull your pants down, baby," he growled in that alien voice. "I want to see your ass."

I complied quickly despite the awkwardness of my position. I swallowed futilely to reduce the bile pooling in my throat. I heard him push his jeans off and I dug the bridge of my nose into the hard bone of my forearm and squeezed my eyes shut. Then I heard the click of a plastic cap followed by a wet, sticky sound, a sound I knew. Michael had slathered a palmful of K-Y Jelly on his penis and started to jerk off. Except this time it was faster and more urgent than the times he did it with me. I hadn't gotten my jeans far enough down my legs because Michael grabbed them with my panties and yanked. It felt as if he was tearing them from my body. Then he grabbed my hips and pushed his penis into me.

Michael was always considerate when we made love in the past, sometimes to a fault. I remember wishing that he would be a little more forceful. It was always up to me to show or tell him when he could enter me. Usually, it was when I got tired of foreplay. This was the polar opposite. He entered me in just one stroke and groaned deeply. The K-Y had obviously helped, because I was too shocked to know if I was responding or not. When he started thrusting, my front teeth pressed harder into my arm. He pumped faster than he ever had. I didn't bother to count the strokes.

This was *fucking*, not making love, and I had always discounted the differences whenever Michael—or anyone else—brought it up. "There's no difference," I had once told Eddie when we were dishing over previous boyfriends.

"Oh, yes there is," he replied in a sing-song tone.

Then it was all over. Michael shuddered, moved his hips back and forth a few times, then abruptly withdrew. I tasted blood from my arm. Fabric rustled as Michael pulled on his jeans.

"There," said the disjointed voice. "Now you know." He left the room.

My hand found the place where his right knee had been. It was still warm. I ran my hand over it, absorbing its warmth. I collapsed onto my side, pulled the covers over me, and drifted off to sleep with the light still on.

Chapter Seven

Over the next two months, Michael and I continued in our holding pattern. I figured if he wasn't sure, I'd take a wait and see attitude. After all, that's what everyone else at the Clueless meetings was doing, and some of them had been at it a lot longer than I had.

Speaking of which, I attended every Clueless meeting like clockwork. The strain in our relationship did not go unnoticed at the office, however, though Carrie was too polite to bring it up. Instead, I'd catch her looking at us more than usual whenever Michael and I were in the office at the same time.

If Carrie was overly polite, Willard took the opposite approach. Even though he only spent an hour or two at the *Courier* each week, he knew something was up. He had been prodding me for weeks, trying to get me to fess up. "What's wrong?" was his constant question.

"Nothing," I'd tell him, steeling myself to give the same answer until he got tired of asking.

But on a Monday afternoon in late September, I got tired of maintaining the charade. Willard and I were leafing through his shots of the back of a pickup truck that had seen better days and was now being used as a birdbath.

"Michael is trying to figure out who he likes better, women or men," I told him.

Willard opened his mouth as if to say something, obviously thought better of it, then closed it. He continued to shuffle through the pictures and said nothing more.

A week later when Willard arrived at the office, I cleared some papers from my desk so he could spread out his contact sheets, but instead he stood by my desk with his jacket still on.

"Let's go for a drive," he said. "I want to show you something."

I started to object, but I had been inside all day and figured this was the last chance I'd get to go for a leisurely drive without fighting the leaf-peeping tourists who would soon be clogging the roads.

"Sure," I said, grabbing a sweater.

He brushed film canisters and empty coffee cups from the passenger seat of his truck before I got in, and we headed north of town for the state park. In my opinion, late September was the best time for foliage; I think the state tourism department had long ago deliberately spread the myth that Columbus Day was the peak of foliage—the better to attract moneyed tourists with a three-day weekend—but in Coventry, the foliage had usually peaked by early October more often than not.

When Willard turned the truck onto a little-used logging road that went up the back side of Coventry Mountain, I knew he didn't want to show me anything but wanted to give me the third degree.

"Why are you staying with him?" he asked, downshifting into third when the road steepened.

"Because he's not sure."

"And how long are you going to wait for him to be sure?"

"I don't know."

The dirt road narrowed and turned into a washboard. Willard put the truck into four-wheel drive and downshifted again. We were travelling at a whopping five miles an hour. As we rode over the ruts, I tightened my seatbelt to keep my butt in the seat. If Willard thought physical torture could change my mind, he was wrong.

"You need new shocks," I said.

"Don't change the subject," he replied. "Look, I don't know what's going on, but whatever it is, I can see what it's doing to you. And you do a very good job of hiding it. I don't know why you're putting up with this, but you don't deserve this from Michael or from anyone."

"Yeah? Well, I could say the same thing about you and Carolyn."

"That's different. We're not married, we don't live together, and we're not running a business together."

"Then you should understand why I'm putting up with this, the ties we have together." I shrugged. "Besides, it may just pass."

"And what if it doesn't?" he countered. "What then? Emily, there are thousands of straight men out there who would cherish you because you are a woman. I don't understand what's going through your mind. When was the last time Michael made love to you?"

"That's none of your business," I snapped back. In my mind, the fucking incident didn't count.

Willard stopped the truck. It felt like the pause on a rollercoaster just before the cars reach the top and start careening down the track, gaining speed with each harrowing second.

"Okay, but look at it this way," he said. "If you're with a man who doesn't wonder if he really wants to be with someone else, someone more like himself—in other words, he just wants *you*—doesn't that kind of relationship make more sense than trying to convince a man that because you love him and are willing to wait for him for as long as it takes to make up his mind that he should *try* to desire you?"

He stared at me.

"Well?"

"I just want to see if it's something that Michael needs to get out of his system," I replied. "You know, like a midlife crisis, except that his is a little earlier and a little different."

"Okay, so what if he comes to you in a few months and says, 'Honey, I was wrong, I'm not gay, I'm straight, so let's pick up where we left off.'"

"I'd take him back, of course. And our marriage would be stronger because of what we went through."

"Are you sure?" he asked. "What if he just managed to push it down again, and a year or two down the road the same thing happened again?"

"He wouldn't do that," I said, "because I'm giving him enough time and space to make up his mind now so he won't have to go through this again."

"Yeah, but what about you?"

"What *about* me?"

"Don't you deserve better?" I looked out across the mountain range. This was my favorite place to hike with my father when I was a kid. I rarely came here anymore because the view made me think of him. If he were alive, I knew that he'd tell me what to do and I'd do it, no questions asked.

"Let's go back," I whispered.

Willard started backing down the road. "I just don't like what this is doing to you."

We drove to the office in silence. Willard threw a few sheets of slides onto my desk and turned towards the door.

"I ever tell you that old joke about the cow and bull having sex?" he asked.

I shook my head.

"Well, a bull is mounting a cow, while a farm boy and girl are watching. The boy says, 'I sure would like some of what that bull's getting.'

"The farm girl says, 'Go ahead, it's your cow.'"

I looked at him, uncomprehending.

"It's your cow," he shrugged, and walked out the door.

He was right. Another woman would have kicked Michael's ass out on the street by now. Why didn't I?

I still believed he would get it out of his system, though all I had to do was look around the circle at the Clueless meetings to see how wrong I was.

But all of us went through this phase. I think it was because after all these years, we *thought* we knew our spouses; it seemed like an alien had swooped down out of the sky one day to turn our spouses gay overnight. If they could change that suddenly, they could change back to straight just as quickly. *That's* why we held on, why *I* held on.

I picked up a slide at random and without looking at it, scanned it into the computer. I picked up another one and held it up to Max, in his usual spot sprawled on top of my monitor. "What do you think?" I asked him.

The cat raised his head, sniffed at one corner of the slide before tentatively batting at it and lowering his head to his paws.

"That's what I thought," I told him.

• • •

When I arrived at the Clueless meeting the next night, the air was charged with tension. Janet took control.

"Okay, kids, looks like a few of you need to vent," she said. "So let's have it. We'll go around the circle and spit out whatever has been bugging you this week. Everybody else, no questions, no judgments, no nothing. Just listen. I'll go first."

She took a deep breath. "The minute I think we've settled into our lives, Tom does something to muck it up. I wish I had never agreed to this arrangement—lately, I've been thinking about what I've given up."

She looked over at Charlie sitting to her left.

"Linda is still on the fence," he said. "This week, a woman she was dating broke it off specifically because Linda is still unsure. Part of me felt, here we go again, but another part immediately became hopeful for our marriage. I almost sent the other woman flowers with a card saying, 'Dear Dyke Homewrecker, These are to thank you for not stealing my wife.' But I wonder why I'm taking her back because she's just going to fall for another woman and we'll go through the same tired stuff all over again. This was the third one in two months. Honestly, sometimes I can't believe the levels I've stooped to." He looked at the floor and kicked the chair leg a couple of times. "Once, I even let her put makeup on me so she could fantasize that I was a woman. I just wish she would make up her mind already and pick *something*: one week she's straight, the next she's lesbian, and the third she's bisexual."

He turned to Anita.

"Okay," she said. "I was never homophobic before Bill came out to me, but now it's all I can do to keep from screaming when I see a rainbow bumper sticker on somebody's car. It feels like the world is full of shallow gay men intent on winning my husband over to their side."

Cheryl was next. "Well, this week I read somewhere that if a man ever had sex with another man that meant he was unequivocally gay," she said. "According to this line of thinking, if a man had sex with a woman, that should make him straight, right?" She looked around the circle.

"Of course not," she replied. "But I'm starting to think about what to tell our kids, two boys, eight and eleven, because they've started to ask questions. What do I tell them? I mean, there's no need to say that Daddy likes to go into public toilets and suck strange men's cocks, but if their sexuality is as central to a gay man's identity as they all say it is, then maybe the kids have a right to a straightforward explanation, even though it hurts."

"I forgot something," said Janet. "When it comes to ear piercing, which ear means the gay ear?" Her question was initially met with silence. After all, the rules were to just listen, but Beverly couldn't help herself.

"The right," she answered. "Why?"

"Well, that's a bit confusing. Tom had his left ear pierced last week, but I see that most gay men have their left pierced."

"Maybe the left ear means they were late coming out, formerly straight," offered Charlie.

"Either that, or they're still unsure," said Cheryl. "Speaking of which, Paul did something last week that made me gag. He and his cyber lover bought the same kind of boxer shorts from that gay sex toy company, Adam & Adam. You know, I should have realized years ago that he was gay since he always preferred me in flannel pajamas."

"Well, my husband used to wear boxers until he came out and now he even wears bikini briefs, Calvin Kleins, no less," said Anita. "I could never get him to wear those but now that he's gay, it's another story. Actually, I think he buys them for the pictures on the box. In many misguided attempts to turn him on over the years, I have amassed quite a closetful of lingerie. Not that he noticed, of course. I once put on a very sexy black lace nightie, and he asked, 'Is that a new dress?' before he rolled over to go to sleep."

She looked at Ted. "Sorry, Ted, we got off track. It's your turn."

"This week I've been thinking about the same thing as you, Charlie. I mean, how gay is she, anyway? Marie goes back and forth on the gay-straight continuum so many times that she's worn a rut in the front yard.

"Lately, she's been using me as her scapegoat," he continued. "Sometimes she says she's not sure about the gay thing and talks about quitting truck-driving school. I hear her tell her girlfriends, 'He gets scared when I go out,' or 'He has something he needs me to do at home.'" He shook his head. "I can't win. She says she prefers men—in other words, me—for a long-term relationship, but women for sex. Then in the next breath she sounds like a fifteen-year-old when she says if I loved her, I'd be okay about letting her have sex with a woman."

It was Janet's turn.

"Well, Tom has been coming out to some of our oldest friends lately, and the next day they call me up with the dumbest questions."

"Like what?" I asked.

"Like, 'But he doesn't *look* gay! But you have children!'"

Everyone cracked up.

"Or, 'Didn't you know when you married him?'"

"You know," said Cheryl, "after Paul came out to me, I used to beat myself up because I didn't have a clue. But it wasn't until recently, when my aunt told me that I must have been one helluva woman to keep a gay man interested for so long that my perspective changed."

No one said anything. It was certainly a different way of looking at things.

"Well, I had a friend who worked as a corporate relocation counselor for an international bank," said Beverly. "He told me he knew when a male employee was gay if he listed 57 sweaters in his inventory list. Phil has always been an absolute slob; even though I had my suspicions years ago, I believed he couldn't possibly be gay because he was such an Oscar Madison type. In all the years we've been together, he hasn't owned more than three sweaters and he's never turned on the iron by himself."

"Well, at least you know where you stand," said Charlie. "I wish Linda would make up her mind," "I just think she's afraid that when we go to court, I'm going to play the *L* card so that I'll get custody of the kids."

"The *L* card?" asked Ted.

"The *Lesbian* card," he said. "Linda says that since men have been in power for so many centuries, it would be unfair for me to jeopardize her parental rights by telling the judge that she's gay. But when I assure her that I only want her to be happy and find her way so that the kids will spend time with two calm, loving parents, then she accuses me of denying myself of my own masculine power." He sadly shook his head. "I don't know if I'm coming or going anymore."

"The Lesbian card, huh," said Janet. "What about the Celibate Martyr's Hat?"

"The *what?*" asked Charlie.

"The Celibate Martyr's Hat. Whenever I'm feeling lousy or depressed about something at work, I milk it for all it's worth, believing that it's okay to feel this way because after all I've been celibate for seven years, three months, and eighteen days. Sometimes, I take it off and throw it at Tom. Figuratively, of course. He's so into his new life that he never even bothers to ask how I feel, or to ask me what's wrong when it's clear I'm stewing."

"Well, Bill has always been such a control freak that I was kind of relieved when he came out to me, because at least now I knew why," said Anita. "But over the years, it's gotten worse. After all, if he couldn't control his own feelings and bury his gayness, he was going to do his damnedest to control someone or something else. At least, that's how it seemed."

"Marie has turned into a control freak, too," said Ted. "It seems like she's out to the world, but she doesn't want me to say anything about it. She loves her gay life, but she also wants the world—that is, the *straight* world—to think the best of her. But the opinions of her dyke friends are more important to her than anything else. She sold her Taurus last week because her girlfriend said that Henry Ford was a misogynist. There's no proof, except that it's pretty well known that he didn't like Jews. So her girlfriend said if he didn't like Jews, he also didn't like women, blacks, or cats for that matter. After that, Marie couldn't get rid of the car fast enough.

"But the thing I hate most of all is that her mother thinks we're splitting up because *I'm* having an affair, and Marie hasn't done a thing to deny it. If only I had the guts to do what I heard a guy down in Maryland did when his wife came out to him."

"What?" Anita asked.

A sly smile formed on Ted's lips. "The day after she dropped the bomb, he sent a handwritten note to his wife's boss, congratulating him on being so open-minded to work side-by-side with a lesbian. Then he took out a display ad in the local paper, congratulating his wife on her decision to come out of the closet. I also heard he held a conciliatory dinner for his wife and her new lover the night before she moved out: he used a pair of his dirty underwear to strain the pasta which, of course, he refrained from eating that night."

Everyone laughed. Though we rarely talked about it, thoughts of vengeance were always high in our consciousness.

"I'm curious about one thing," said Charlie.

"What is it?"

"When she came out to you, did she say how long she knew she was gay?"

"Only since childhood," Ted answered.

"But don't you get angry when you think of the fact that she was lying to you all those years?"

"I used to, but I couldn't dwell on it or I'd kill someone. Now I'm careful not to go there at all. I used to think of buying her an Oscar since she certainly deserves one for best supporting actress for her role as sex partner for all these years." His voice trailed off.

"Emily, you've been quiet tonight," said Beverly, trying to defuse the thick cloud of pity that was threatening to break over our heads. "Do you need to vent?"

"No thanks," I replied. I was afraid if I thought any more about my talk with Willard, the dam would burst, and I wasn't sure I could handle it.

"Okay, then," she said. "I want to tell you all a little story." Good ol' Beverly, out to save the day in all her grace and humor. "Back when Phil first came out to me, doormat that I was, he passed along all of the gay books he read after he was finished with them," she said. "And I read all of them because I thought I would find the answer to our problems in them." She smiled. "Of course you know how that turned out, but one of the books was *The Best Little Boy in the World* by Andrew Tobias, the financial writer, though back then he used a pseudonym.

"Anyway, he had a yardstick to use to measure the continuum of sexual orientation. You know, on a scale of one to ten where one is totally gay and ten is totally straight, where would you fall on the scale? Tobias wrote that he was a one, adding that the best way for him to rid himself of an embarrassing erection in public was to imagine having sex with a woman."

Everyone laughed, and after a few more of Beverly's stories and jokes, the meeting broke up.

On the two-hour drive home, my uncertainty about my marriage returned. When I got home, I fell into bed alone and exhausted.

• • •

The next morning, I opened my eyes to see Michael bound into the bedroom with a big smile. He carried a tray that held a pot of coffee, a glass of orange juice, and the *Globe*. I blinked at him. What's wrong with this picture?

"Good morning!" he said as he laid the tray across my lap and leaned over and kissed me on the mouth, lingering for a couple of seconds. What's going on? Michael couldn't stand morning breath—his own or anyone else's. I wiggled my way up to a sitting position, and he sat down on the bed by my side, placing his hand on my thigh.

"What gives?" I asked, my first thought being that maybe he had crashed his computer by downloading too many photos of naked men from gay porn sites and he wanted to buy another. I couldn't remember the last time I saw him looking so happy.

"Nothing," he replied, squeezing my thigh. "It's just that I love you so much."

I stared at him, my head slightly cocked, eyes narrowed, mouth shut. Michael had always hated this look, he called it my *where-have-you-been-and-what-were-you-doing?* look. He never failed to call me on it, always accusing me of not trusting him. Not this time; his smile stayed in place. And the skin around his eyes was crinkled up, something he could never fake.

I placed my hand on the coffeepot. I didn't know what to

say.

"Here, let me do that," he said, taking the coffeepot and pouring a cup for me. He mixed in the exact amount of milk I liked along with one-and-a-half teaspoons of sugar. Oh, he always knew how I liked it, but he rarely got it right. The few times I corrected him in the first year of our marriage, he sighed heavily as he poured the milk, as if it was too much to ask, before giving up completely.

He clinked the spoon against the cup three times, as was my habit, and then handed the cup to me. I sipped it, and it tasted as if my own hand had done the job.

"So you *have* been paying attention all these years."

He was still beaming at me as he handed me the juice, poured into a crystal goblet that I had seen last coated with a thick fur of dust and pushed to the back corner of the china cabinet. The glass had been his mother's. I drank the juice, not my usual Tropicana, but fresh-squeezed. Later, I would see the pulpy Pyrex hand juicer resting in the sink.

"What *gives?*" I repeated.

He reached over for the tray and put it on the floor. Then he kneeled next to me and embraced me with the longest, warmest, most sensual hug I could remember. He kissed me gently on my neck before pulling back slightly.

"It finally dawned on me how much I do love you," he said, looking in my eyes. "And how much you love me if you were able to tell me to go out to do what I had to do and still stay with me."

He burrowed his face in my hair. I felt his dry lips in the crook of my neck. Goosebumps began to form on my upper arms.

"You accept me the way I am," he whispered into my neck. More goosebumps, plus a faraway tingling sensation of arousal deep in my hips that, by force of habit, I immediately squelched. My body stiffened and I pulled away.

He straightened up and put both hands on my shoulders. Concern shadowed his face. "What's wrong?" he asked, a slight catch in his throat.

I yanked at a stray thread on the comforter, not looking at him. "Nothing," I mumbled, searching for another thread.

Michael grabbed my chin in his hand and pulled my head up.

"*Bullshit*," he said, his hand still on my chin. "I know what's going on. Do you think I haven't noticed? I wasn't *that* mired in my own swamp that I didn't notice what was going on with you. I just didn't care. But I do now." He leaned over to kiss me on the mouth, harder this time, and his lips parted. Then he kissed me on the forehead, my eyes, my cheeks, my neck, and down to my shoulders. My body remained stiff.

"Come on, Emily," he whispered between kisses. "I've been a fool. I've treated you badly. I almost threw away a wonderful life with you." He sucked gently at my collarbone as his hands found my breasts.

"I love you," he said. "We have a second chance. How many people can say that?"

My body and brain were still engaged in the tug of war they knew by heart: my body still knew how to react sexually, but my brain always overruled, lest it be disappointed once more. This time, I wanted to believe Michael, but the old patterns were just too entrenched. I craned my neck back and stared at the Rorschach crack in the ceiling that looked like a spider web viewed through a fun-house mirror.

"I know," I whispered. "I know, Michael. But it's been such a long time. I need to know things will be different this time and that they'll last."

His hands froze. "You don't trust me?"

"Oh, it's not that I don't trust you, but I've been used to the way things have been between us lately. I can't just snap back to how I was before."

The *Fuck You I'm Gay* look briefly flashed across his face—I don't think he knew I saw it—but he immediately replaced it with a look of concern.

"I know, Emily. I know it will take some time." He reached under the covers and began to trace a circle on my left hipbone. Instinctively I pressed my thighs together.

"But maybe I can help hasten it along," he whispered as the circle grew, and his fingers brushed against my clitoris.

My head felt as if it would burst. I didn't want to totally unleash my pent-up sexuality because, once it was out, I didn't know how I would ever get it back in. More tellingly, I'm sure I wouldn't want to. But the truth was that I had actually forgotten what being fully sexual was like, as I had censored my actions and responses since Michael had first come down with his cold, almost six months ago.

As his fingers caressed my clitoris, my body won out. Slowly, I began to relax, one part of my body at a time, my face, my neck, then my shoulders. Once the last of the tension left my shoulders—I was still sitting up in bed—I came almost immediately. I grabbed onto Michael's hair and squeezed my eyes shut just in time to see a crescent of tiny white stars. Somewhere in my hazy consciousness I heard cat nails scrabbling down the hall in between moans from a loud wordless voice I did not recognize as my own. A few seconds later, I heard the furnace kick on. I couldn't—*wouldn't*—open my eyes. Then I'd know it wasn't real.

Michael scooted down to lay his head on my lap, and I leaned back on the pillow. I must have slept for an hour because when I finally opened my eyes, my coffee was cold and the juice was warm. And Michael was gone.

I got out of bed and stood on legs made of rubber. I somehow navigated my way to the bathroom. When I was settled on the toilet, I saw a note stuck to the mirror.

"I love you," it said, written in gray eyeliner encircled by a heart of lipstick.

I showered, dressed, and sat on the edge of the bed drinking coffee, wrapping myself in the memory, committing it to the memory in my bones.

Chapter Eight

One week later, we left the office an hour early and headed down the interstate for Manchester. I wasn't overly fond of the town but people from away usually thought it was a quaint and manageable city. Compared to Coventry, however, it was one big noisy metropolis.

"You know," I told Michael as the world hurled by at seventy miles an hour, "I'm not sure if I really want to do this."

Michael reached over and squeezed my hand. "Oh, come on, it will be fun."

"I don't know," I said. "All I can picture is a bunch of men with mustaches sitting in a circle practicing putting condoms on bananas."

Michael snatched his hand away. "Oh, come on, Em, you don't really believe all the stereotypes now, do you?"

"No, it's just that when I'm going to a safe sex seminar for gay men, well, I'm just not sure that my presence will be entirely welcome."

"But it's not just for gay men, but bisexuals *and* their partners," he corrected me as he returned his hand to mine. "And since they're inviting bisexuals too, then their heterosexual partners will obviously be involved."

Bisexual. Gay. Heterosexual. There were those words again. But for once, I didn't mind. The last week had been deliriously happy, a throwback to the days when Michael and I started dating. In fact, it felt a bit *too* good, and I thought of people in similar situations who reported pinching themselves until they were black and blue to see if their happiness was for real. I wasn't pinching myself, but every night when Michael and I went upstairs together, as I reached for the light, he'd say, "Don't," and then we'd spend the next hour making love. It felt as if we were living a dream. I didn't think about waking up, however, because if accepting Michael meant a life like this, who wouldn't want him to be happy?

So when he asked me to accompany him to some of his gay events, I initially balked, but within seconds I had agreed. "Sure," I told him, which is how we ended up heading to Manchester.

He slowed at the approach to the Hooksett toll booths, within a stone's throw of a sprawling state liquor store. New Hampshire seemed to expect that every Massachusetts resident heading home after a weekend in the White Mountains would want to stop to load up on cheap booze and Powerball tickets. As Michael dug for a few coins, I saw a pink triangle sticker affixed to the coin basket.

He glanced over at me. "But that's not what you're really worried about, is it?"

I had to give him two points for perception. "Well, Michael, turn the tables. If our situation was reversed and you were going to a lesbian safe sex seminar with me, what would be the first thing on your mind?"

"Well, for one, they would never allow a man, gay or straight, in there."

"Good try, but not what I was thinking. Is there anything else that might bother you?"

He thought for a moment. "Well, I would hope that I wouldn't see you making eyes at a woman or giving out your number."

"Bingo!" With our vast improvement in communicating, I felt comfortable airing all of the questions I would have previously squashed. "You know, with all the literature you bring home and everything I hear, it's still hard for me not to believe that being a gay or bisexual man is about anything else besides sex."

Michael looked slightly disgusted. "You know, Em, I'm not even going to go there. We've been through all of this before, so I'm not going to waste the time now." He squeezed my hand again.

When we got to the meeting, it turned out I wasn't too far off the mark. Bananas, condoms, and men with exquisitely groomed mustaches. All we needed was a large wardrobe of leather accoutrements and we'd be able to stage a Village People look-alike concert. Although I questioned why we needed to attend a safe sex seminar if Michael had promised to be monogamous, after we got there I had the feeling he wanted to show me off, to make the guys jealous of me. Why, I didn't have a clue—they were all gay, or perhaps latent bisexuals—but maybe he wanted to prove a point to himself: that it was possible for him to be attracted to men and to me too.

I was the only woman in the room, but this did nothing to encourage self-consciousness among my compatriots. On the contrary, I felt like the proverbial fly on the wall. The other men did stare openly at my husband. However, as far as I could tell, Michael didn't stare back. In one of the group exercises, we passed around a piece of paper where we wrote down answers to questions about our fantasies. The fun part was listening to the fantasies, which were read aloud later.

"Name a fantasy that is the most likely scenario to come true given your current situation," read one question.

Just having Michael want to make love with me every day was better than any fantasy I could have thought of, so I dug out an old one involving sunbathing naked on the porch when the UPS man drives up. Apparently it's a popular fantasy, since half the fantasies of the men in the circle involved a delivery man in one form or another.

The drive home later that evening was exquisite: windows

down, music blasting, Michael's hand lightly rubbing my leg. Could it possibly get any better? Part of me felt as if I had my husband back, but it actually seemed more as if I had never known this man in the first place. It felt like I was having an affair. I began to think of this time as the honeymoon we never had.

The following week, we even went to a gay male strip show together, and even though it made me uncomfortable and I left early without him, he made it up to me the next morning. I had been up for an hour and a half, and my two requisite oversized mugs of coffee and a bagel were history. After I brushed my teeth, I climbed into bed beside Michael, who was still asleep. I wrapped my hand around his body to his chest, resting it on his right pectoral muscle. His skin was slightly damp. My fingers pressed on his nipple gently at first, so he probably thought I was just arranging myself in bed. But then I steadily increased the pressure in my fingers and pressed my hips against his ass, then moved my hand lower on his body.

He shifted slightly. I started to lightly trace a circle on his hipbone.

When he twisted his body around, I saw he was hard. I kissed him, my lips lingering. He didn't respond immediately, and he pressed his lips together, almost as if he was embarrassed, to say, *Stop*, I haven't brushed my teeth yet. But I didn't care, and started to probe deeper with my tongue. He opened his mouth and gave in. This was heady stuff, the way I could make him respond, something that I had always felt was missing before. Later, we showered together and left for the office.

That night, there was a Clueless meeting, but I didn't go. I almost felt that if I went, it might poison what Michael and I had rediscovered. "My husband made the decision to stay with me, and besides, we're having sex at least once a day," I thought of the others in the group, a bit smugly. "Why can't yours?"

The next few weeks passed in much the same way. We

made love every night, occasionally in the morning. Michael had his two gay nights out every week, and I stayed home or went to the office. Speaking of which, work was a blur. After three years, I could crank out the paper in my sleep. Carrie noticed the improvement in my mood.

"You okay?" she asked one morning three weeks after Michael first surprised me with breakfast in bed.

"Yes, of course," I answered. "Why?"

She smiled. "Well, it seems that things are a bit different around here."

I pushed Max's tail away from the monitor. "In what way?"

"Oh, you just seem happier, there's not as much tension around here as before. Keep it up, whatever you're doing."

I suppressed a laugh. "I will," I told her. "I will."

But I couldn't. Because I didn't want to admit to myself that tiny cracks in the foundation were starting to appear. Why would I want to dwell on the bad when there was so much good?

But the resistance, surprisingly, was coming from me. I loved the Michael I had, but I wanted to have Michael without all The Gay Shit—as Janet had eloquently described it at Clueless one evening—in my face all the time. It almost seemed as if Michael needed it in order to maintain his equilibrium. But I wanted it to be something that was private to him, tucked away and out of sight. However, given the way we were living, The Gay Shit was the polka dot elephant in the living room, and we were unable to do or say anything without first acknowledging its presence in our lives.

And so the next week I quietly started going to Clueless meetings again. At five o'clock sharp on Tuesday, I got in my car and headed for Burlington. Two hours later, I walked by the STR8 SPICE sign and into the meeting room. Everybody welcomed me back and left it at that. No raised eyebrows. All in all, my return was uneventful. Most of the people there had been through this stage, or else had witnessed it in the others. As I sat down in the circle and looked around the room, this time I didn't see people who couldn't hold onto their spouses; instead, I saw people who had gotten trampled on, some harder than others. But we were all dealing with the same thing.

Tonight there was tension in the air. No one was joking or laughing, and Charlie and Ted were both frowning. This was also the first time I had seen them sitting on opposite sides of the circle. Most of the time, they sat next to each other and were laughing and joking around until the meeting started.

I glanced at Janet, who just shrugged. Cheryl arrived a couple of minutes past seven, closed the door, and sat down. Nobody spoke, but we were all looking at Charlie and Ted, who sat with their arms across their chests, stony-faced, lips pressed so tightly together they were turning white.

Ted gestured with his head. "It was all *his* fault," he said, nodding at Charlie.

Charlie uncrossed his arms and turned toward his accuser. "Like hell it was," he shouted. "*You* were the one who suggested they meet in the first place!"

Uh-oh.

"I was just trying to help," said Ted. "Since Linda has been such a shit to you for so long, and Marie has been pretty good through this entire thing, I only thought she would be able to help your wife put everything in perspective."

"Yeah, but that was before I knew she would end up seducing her!" Charlie yelled.

A few people shifted in their chairs. I idly wondered why this hadn't happened before.

"Charlie, why are you so upset?" asked Cheryl. "I would think you'd be happy that she's got something going now so she won't be in your hair as much."

"Yeah, but now she's worse when she is around. And it's all because now she has another dyke girlfriend to commiserate with, *his* wife!" he said, pointing at Ted.

"Actually, Linda and I have been getting along pretty well

lately until all this happened!" Back went the arms across his chest and he looked around at everyone in the group except Ted.

"But Charlie, you know how fragile our marriages are," said Cheryl. "Anything can make them go *poof* with absolutely no warning. There are no guarantees in any marriage, and even fewer in marriages like ours."

Charlie shook his head sadly. "I know, I know, but I thought we were different," he said. "The last month has been pretty good for us. Counseling was going well and she was even letting me kiss her again." His face grew stormy. "Then Ted gets the bright idea to help me and look what happened! I didn't think we were here to run a dating service for our gay spouses!"

Cheryl stepped in as referee "Guys, guys, cool it, okay? Ted, it wasn't your fault, you were just trying to help, and Charlie, if it wasn't Ted's wife it would be someone else's, no matter how well the two of you were doing. I know it's hard to say you should never be caught off guard by anything your gay spouse does, but guess what? We still are. We can't help it. It's that goddamn rollercoaster again. When it's up, we delude ourselves into thinking it will stay there permanently. The next month—or next day or hour, even—we're down in the pits again, hysterical.

"So let's just deal and get on with it. Charlie, instead of feeling like we're running a dating service for our spouses, how about running one for *us*?"

He looked perplexed. "What do you mean?"

"I mean, we can't date each other here, that would be too incestuous for words. We know too much about each other. I mean, can you imagine Emily and Ted together, or you and me?" Everyone laughed, but I didn't think it was *that* funny. I was starting to feel like jumping on the first man who could provide me with a written guarantee that he was 100 percent straight.

"A dating service for straight spouses?" Anita laughed. "I know just what to call it."

"Straight from the Heart."

Everyone cracked up. Even Charlie and Ted smiled.

"How about Straight Expectations?"

Janet turned to Charlie. "I wouldn't worry about it, Charlie. You'll get your revenge when lesbian bed death sets in with Linda."

"*What?*"

"Lesbian bed death, or LBD," Janet repeated. "I've heard that after the first year or two of post-nuptial bliss in a lesbian relationship, many women don't have sex anymore. Sounds like a lot of lesbians just don't like sex, period. They also tend to move in with each other in pretty short order."

"And just how would you know so much about lesbian bed death?" asked Charlie. All eyes turned to Janet, who squirmed slightly.

"Well," she said, "my sister-in-law came out about ten years ago, and she began living with a woman almost immediately. They're still together, but she told me a few months ago that they haven't had sex for more than eight years."

"Sounds like my life," said Beverly. "What happened?"

"Don't know. It doesn't seem to bother either of them that much, though," she said. "I think they do actually have sex once a year during their annual September pilgrimage to Provincetown for old times' sake, but it sounds like maintenance, to make sure they still remember how." She smiled. "Hey, what does a lesbian bring on a second date?"

Everyone responded. "What?"

"A U-Haul." The room cracked up. "What does a gay man bring on a second date?"

Again, a resounding, "*What?*"

She paused. "What second date?" Much laughter.

I was glad to be back. These people had become close friends in a very short time. I was grateful for their companionship and advice. And though I hadn't told Michael, he knew where I was on Tuesday nights when I wasn't home.

At the office the next day, Michael let his displeasure show. "What do you mean you don't want to go to the gay/straight spouse dinner next week?" he asked, an indignant whine creeping around the edges of his voice. I was writing captions for next week's paper. Willard's Carnage photograph that week showed half a modular home that had slipped off the flatbed truck that had been towing it along the Interstate. A ratty Ford 1982 pickup with a WIDE LOAD AHEAD sign on top that had served as the rear escort couldn't stop in time and had crashed into the back of the house.

Max started to chew on a corner of the photo. I brushed him aside.

"You're just not working at our marriage as hard as I am," Michael said, continuing his tirade. "While I've been going to my meetings and talking out things and trying to learn about myself, all you've done is complain about the fact that you don't have as many places to go for support as I do, which I've never bought. I get the feeling that at these heterosexual meetings you go to, all you do is sit around and complain about your husbands and wives who are finally learning to be free. But no, you don't want to support your spouses at the picnic and spend time with other families. You'd rather sit around and bitch and moan instead of trying to change the system." He threw up his hands. "Honestly, Emily, I do all I can to help you, and you just come up with ways to fight me."

I sighed. I was resigned to the fact that Michael would never catch on.

"Walter's wife Valerie marched with the PFLAG group at the Pride Parade in Concord last June." Walter was the founder of the gay married men's meetings that Michael went to. "What's the big deal about a dinner, Emily? I don't get it. I feel like you're pulling away from me at the worst possible time."

"The worst possible time?" I asked. "For who? You? Or me? Michael, I know you didn't ask to be born gay, bisexual, or whatever you happen to be this week, but it sometimes seems that you feel you deserve all the sympathy here and that I should just continue to bow down in my role of poor-Michael-let's-give-him-everything-he-wants-because-after-all-he's-a-member-of-a-downtrodden-minority-group."

"You know," he said, "the thing that pisses me off the most about your attitude is that out of all the people in my life, I would think that you would be the most supportive. I'd think that you'd want to help the world see that the reason people like me end up married is because of the way our culture treats anyone who is attracted to his own sex."

I started to interrupt, but he was just taking a breath. "Don't you see that if you encourage everyone to be open and accept themselves, regardless of who they are or what their sexuality is, they won't end up in marriages that may eventually break up when heterosexual convention becomes too much to bear?"

"But I already get together with other people who are dealing with the same issues that I am. I don't want to get together with people I don't know to show our public support for our poor beleaguered spouses. Michael, I am not about to participate in the pity party that some of these straight doormat spouses do, like Walter's wonderful wife Valerie, who knew her husband was gay when she married him but still stands in front of the State House to shake her fist at society because homosexuality has never totally been accepted. I'm sorry, but right now it's more important for me to deal with my own experience, and not stand up and blame the world for the misfortune of it all."

I felt like slapping him, but left the room instead. I was disappointed by the change in our dynamic, but figured it was just another trip on the rollercoaster. What goes down comes up, and vice versa. I would just have to wait for the good Michael to return. We went through the next month in a precarious truce. We made love only twice, each time wordlessly and tinged with bittersweet.

Then Michael suggested we see a couples therapist.

"Look, we both know things haven't been the greatest for either of us lately," he said.

My hopes soared with his words because that meant he had cherished our brief magical month.

"If we're going to learn to deal with this, we have to learn how to communicate better," he told me after returning from his married gay men's meeting while we sat in the kitchen drinking tea. I quickly grew to despise these weekly meetings because throughout that entire tense post-honeymoon month, the only time he said anything to me was to tell me yet another idea he thought *I* could use to better deal with the fact that I was married to a gay man. Now that I had started to attend my Clueless meetings again, I didn't say a word. He never liked the idea that I was talking about our problems with total strangers, but the one time I pointed out that he was doing the same thing, he said, "But that's different," and quickly changed the subject. The therapist idea, though, was a twist because it implied that we were *both* going to do something to cope, or at least that's how I perceived it.

Chaos jumped up on the table and started rubbing against my teacup. Michael threw the cat a dirty look as he took a crumpled piece of paper from his pocket. He ironed out the wrinkles with the heel of his hand and stole a furtive glance at me as he handed me the paper, which held a faint shadow from a sweating glass.

Ronald Thierren, M.S.W., was handwritten in a clumsy scrawl along with a phone number with a Bloomfield exchange, about twenty miles away. I turned it over. For all I know, it could have been a number Michael collected from a guy who tried to pick him up at the bar his group frequented after their meeting. Someone who had immediately revealed his profession once he learned that Michael was married. I could only imagine the exchange; spending too much time with Eddie in the past had permanently poisoned my mind about the true motivations of a gay man. Curiously, I had a blind spot regarding this when it came to Michael. I saw the conversation unfold before my eyes:

"I can help, you know," Ronald the M.S.W. told Michael

as he threw back the remains of his Dewar's and water. "I'm a therapist."

This, I knew, would get Michael's interest. "Yeah? How?"

"I was married once, too, you know," said Ron. "I specialize in couples. I can help you learn how to deal with your wife if you want to stay—or leave," he hastily tacked on.

With this, I saw Michael almost but not quite slam his glass down on the bar. "Well, I love my wife, and she knows I'm here tonight, not like the rest of these chicken hawks who are sneaking around."

Ronald the M.S.W. had heard it all before, I would have to believe, but in the interest of getting into Michael's pants, he didn't dismiss Michael's protests. Instead he rested his chin in his cupped hand and appeared to hang on Michael's every word. I had witnessed enough quickie seductions with Eddie I could almost write the screenplay.

"Well, then, you are to be commended," Ronald said with the proper amount of respect in his voice, "and so is your wife." At that point, the two of them drank silently for a minute. Michael cleared his throat.

"Do you ever work with couples…like *us*?" Michael always had trouble with anything that described him with the word *sex* in it. He still maintained that he was bisexual, saying the word with great difficulty. I think he was physically incapable of uttering the words *mixed-orientation marriage*, though he was probably capable of pointing to these words in a magazine or book. More than once I thought of pretending I was Mister Rogers and asking him, "Can you say *mixed-orientation marriage?*"

Ronald signaled for another round and placed his cupped hand over Michael's when he offered a weak protest. If this was a one-panel cartoon in one of Michael's gay magazines, the thought balloon over the therapist's head would read, "Okay, I understand the poor guy has to go through it on his own to come out on the other side…*as 100 percent homosexual.*"

I fumbled with the paper while Michael looked at me, waiting for me to say something.

I won't, I won't, I won't ask. *"So Michael, is Ron gay, or what?"* If I did, it would only give Michael an excuse to launch into yet another diatribe on how I equate everything gay as bad. The question turned into the polka dot elephant in the living room, only now it started to stampede through my brain. I gulped my tea to keep the words from flying out of my mouth; tonight I was in no mood for Michael to have the satisfaction of accusing me of starting another fight.

"Sooooo, is he, er, do you want some more tea?" I asked as sweetly as I could without gagging.

"No," he said, looking slightly deflated.

Now the elephant had developed zebra stripes and was trumpeting loudly. I tried again. "Soooo, is he, uh, what is this guy like?" I poured myself more tea and bit down hard on my lip.

"Well, he works mostly with couples—"

"Like us?" I blurted out.

"Some. Matt says he's pretty good, that he and Rhonda saw him for awhile." Michael's group considered Matt and Rhonda to be one of the success stories, though I thought the woman should be listed under *D* in the dictionary for doormat. No wonder they were a success story: she agreed to anything Matt wanted and had suffered through a severe outbreak of crabs that required three cycles of A-200 before it disappeared completely.

Michael cleared his throat. "I made the first appointment for next Thursday after work, if you don't mind."

I did mind, but at that point, I didn't care. I forgot all about it until Thursday afternoon at 5:15, when I looked up to see Michael hovering by my desk.

"So, are you ready?" he asked

I looked up from Mrs. Swanson's column. She had written about having lunch with the two surviving members of the Coventry Women's Club, as far as I could make out. It looked like her arthritis was acting up pretty bad this week;

I'd have to get one of the other Blue Hairs to translate.

I glanced up at the clock. "Ready for what?"

He looked hurt. "Our appointment," he said. "With Ron. *Remember?* I'll drive."

I didn't, not immediately. Then it kicked in. I stood up and followed Michael to his car by the ring in my nose, like a cow headed for her last milking before her big date at the slaughterhouse.

I cleared a copy of *Out,* several crushed paper cups festooned with rainbow flags, and a tape cassette case for the audiobook version of *Easy As Cake: Coming Out Clean* from the passenger seat. As soon as Michael turned the ignition, the tape started blaring. I caught a few words in a voice that had taken the strains of the *Fuck You, I'm Gay* intonation to a new level before Michael stabbed the stop button. I stared straight ahead, and we drove in silence.

Once we reached Bloomfield, Michael weaved through the side streets. I coughed once before assuming my best nonchalant voice. "Spending a lot of time in Bloomfield lately?" I asked.

It was his turn to stare straight ahead. "No, but I know where his office is."

He stopped in front of a Victorian house that had seen better days. We walked up a creaky set of porch stairs with peeling paint. This guy can't be gay, I thought. Then Michael opened the door and we entered the reception area. The coffee table was littered with copies of *Bay Windows, New England Homo,* and *Queer Power!* while a bookshelf literally groaned under the weight of *Loving Someone Gay, Radically Queer,* and *The Bisexual Option.* A quick glance showed that the books were for gay men, none for straights, women, or even lesbians, for that matter. One lonely copy of *The Other Side of the Closet: The Coming-Out Crisis for Straight Spouses and Families,* still in its shrinkwrap, was shelved upside-down on the far end of the bottom shelf, next to *Final Exit.*

Before we had a chance to sit down, a door opened and Ron Thierren, M.S.W., appeared.

"Thanks for coming, Emily, Michael," he said, shaking my hand first. He didn't *sound* gay. I began to relax. "Could you fill out these forms and then bring them with you when you come inside? If you have any questions, let me know. I'll be back in five minutes." He was gone as quickly as he had appeared, abruptly shutting the door behind him.

We sat down and I looked at my sheet of blue paper. Not much more than name, rank, and serial number, and I was done. I glanced over at Michael and noticed that he was filling out at least five different sheets of paper, all pink. I started to tell Michael we should switch papers—blue is for boys, pink is for girls—but I squelched the impulse. Think of where you are, Emily: pink is for the gay people, blue is for everyone else.

I pretended to continue to write while Michael finished. When the door opened again and Ron poked his head out, Michael stopped writing and stood up. He took my hand and we walked through the door.

Ron sat down in a director's chair that was placed between two easy chairs directly facing each other. Michael and I stood, uncertain of where to sit.

Ron waved at the chairs. "So you can talk to each other, remember?" he said. "And I'm in the middle to show you how to communicate better. So Michael, you sit there, and Emily, this one's yours.

"Now," he said once we got settled, "why don't you tell me why you're here. Emily, why don't you go first?"

He's going to earn his one-hundred-and-twenty-five pennies a minute, isn't he, I thought, and dove right in.

"Well," I said, talking with Ron as if Michael wasn't there, "it was Michael's idea that we see a therapist. He told me he wanted to explore his attraction to men back in May. We had a few real good fights, then we settled down for awhile, and then we had one wonderful month together." I smiled at Michael before turning back to Ron. "And now, we're having problems again." I paused.

"Go on, Emily, but as you talk, I want you to look at

Michael and tell him, not me," he said. "Acknowledge that you're giving your opinion by starting each sentence off with the statement, 'I feel,' or 'I believe.' That way, when you start to venture into tinderbox areas, you'll be less likely to blame Michael by accusing him with sentences that begin 'You always,' or 'You never.' And Michael, the same goes for you. Got it?"

I looked at Michael and we both nodded.

I scooched further into my chair and began to relax. This wasn't turning into the weekly Gay Pride Hour I had envisioned after all.

We then spent the rest of the hour—50 minutes, actually—voicing our concerns and fears about our present and our future, and how we could both change to improve our relationship. I told Michael that I didn't want the gay stuff in my face all the time because I felt it meant he liked men better than me. He said he kept it out in the open, otherwise he felt he was back to keeping secrets. And we were able to say these things without yelling.

Wow. This was a good idea, after all.

Finally, Ron cleared his throat and pulled out his appointment book.

"So okay, do you think you'll benefit from a weekly session with me as referee?" he asked.

I smiled at Michael. "I think so."

"Me too," he said.

"Good. I can see the difference already. Now, let's talk about a good time to meet. Do you want to pick the same time every week, or do you just want to play it by ear?"

Michael and I looked at each other. "Let's play it by ear, okay, Em?" he said.

"Sure." I turned to Ron, wrote out the check, and tore it from the book. "We'll call you tomorrow about next week once we check our schedule."

"Fine," said Ron. We all stood up and headed for the door, me and Michael in front, Ron close behind. I was still clutching the check.

"You two did great," said Ron. "A lot of couples in mixed-orientation marriages make sexuality the main issue, and it's usually not. Instead, it's clear communication. Since you've made the decision to integrate Michael's sexuality into your relationship, you've already won half the battle. Learning and knowing what you can do for each other is the real issue for you, and that doesn't sound so difficult, does it?"

We both shook our heads. I can't believe I thought this guy was evil. Ron placed his hand on the doorknob and the other on Michael's shoulder.

"Now, Michael, of course you realize that it will be difficult at best to fully integrate yourself into the gay community," said Ron. The first red flag shot up and I heard the check crinkle in my hand. "In fact, many gay men will ostracize you because you're wearing a wedding ring. Maybe you'd like some private therapy sessions with me to learn how to cope with the inevitable rejection you'll certainly encounter because you choose to stay with Emily instead of declaring yourself as 100 percent gay."

The one red flag turned into ten and began to thrash violently in front of my eyes. I froze, unsure what to do, not really believing I was hearing these words.

Ron turned the doorknob, and I saw my chance. "Excuse me," I said and pushed past them into the waiting room. As I opened the outside door, I glanced back. Ron's hand was still on Michael's shoulder as they crossed the room. Their voices were lower, and I couldn't make out their words. I threw the check back into the air behind me and slammed the door.

I stomped out to the car and plopped down into the passenger seat, fuming. I leaned over to turn the ignition and sat back and stewed. The windows fogged up in less than a minute.

Michael opened his door and slid into the driver's seat. "Emily, what the hell is the matter with you?" he yelled, glaring at me. "We had a great session until you threw your tantrum. I can see real breakthroughs down the road! I thought you felt the same way, but now we're back to this!" He banged his fist on the steering wheel.

Fuck You, I'm Gay was back. Inevitably, after Michael spent any amount of time at a club or his Wednesday night meetings, he always came home with more of an inflection to his voice, sounding just a little bit more gay than when he left the house a few hours earlier.

I stared straight ahead, focusing my glare to melt the thin sheet of ice that had formed on the outside of the windshield. I turned to him and sighed.

"Michael, I'm going to tell you a story. Imagine that your marriage is like the foundation of a house. It feels like it's absolutely bulletproof and will last forever. You have a good idea of its history and you trust it to support you when you're upstairs. It gives you no reason to doubt it, and you live together peacefully."

I didn't expect him to react, so I continued.

"Okay, now imagine that after a few years, little cracks begin to appear in the foundation. Perfectly normal, but it's nothing that a little spackle won't fix. The relationship is still solid, and aside from the spackle drying out and cracking whenever it's windy or somebody stomps around too much upstairs or during the spring thaw, the foundation still does its job 99 percent of the time.

"Now imagine that there's something you don't know about the foundation, something that affects it to its very core. The house begins to shift, the walls start to crack, but you don't think it's the foundation because, after all, it still looks pretty sturdy.

"In time, however, the foundation starts to crumble in a few places, and you still don't have a clue why. In fact, you start to believe that it's your fault that the house is falling apart, so you give away the upright piano and stop stomping around. But you don't want to change anything about the house because you love it so. After all, most of the rest of the house is okay."

Michael stared at me, his mouth set in a tight grim line,

eyes stony. I continued.

"Now the house is in danger of caving in. That's when you discover the secret. To save money, the contractor had used too much water and not enough cement. Then you hear about something you can do to the foundation to make it almost as good as new. You're ecstatic! You don't have to leave! And you can save your house.

"So you hire a contractor who promises to do everything possible to help you fix the foundation. He tells both of you what to do with shims and this special glue and starts the work, and for awhile, everything's great.

"But then, the contractor throws a wrench into the formula. He pulls you aside and says he thinks that fixing the house is great, but the house will catch on fire one day anyway, so why bother fixing the foundation at all? He thinks he's helping you out, but he's really saying that you'll never be 100 percent happy with the house, so why not cut your losses and move out now?"

I stopped. Michael was still glaring at me, his lips tight. He put the car into reverse.

"Em." He sighed, then said, "If you really want to end the marriage, why don't you just say so?"

I banged my head against the window. "You just don't see it, do you?" I asked. Neither of us said a word during the whole drive home. Several times, he almost hit the play button on the cassette player, but he obviously thought better of it.

Chapter Nine

I'd like to be able to say that the episode at the therapist's was the beginning of the end and that Michael and I proceeded to act like mature adults and recognize there was no way in hell that our marriage was going to work, but of course it wasn't. Why would we act rationally when we both thought the other would change? I wished Michael would return to the perfect state he achieved during our honeymoon days, and Michael probably wanted me to return to my previous mouth-shut self so he could run off and be Mister Gay but still have the security blanket of heterosexuality whenever he needed to wrap himself in it. Instead, we both slipped effortlessly into a wall of indifference. We knew we didn't want to live this way, but until something came along to boot us out of our inertia, neither of us would make the first move.

In the meantime, we reached new levels of obnoxiousness whenever we did have to interact with each other. Like the night we went out to dinner and Michael happened to see a young man and woman sitting at a table holding hands. "Two men or two women couldn't do that," he huffed. Or when he was filling out the renewal form for his health insurance at the office, he stopped and looked up. "Spouse," he spat at me, his finger indignantly stabbing the application. "A gay couple couldn't get health insurance together," he announced before resuming his scrawl.

My obnoxiousness was more covert and more vengeful, but at least I had fun doing it. One day in early November, Michael and I met with Estelle Robbins, director of the Coventry animal shelter, to plan a special section for an upcoming benefit. Estelle was a lesbian, and Michael soon found a way to turn the conversation around to everything gay.

"You know, Estelle, I read last week in *The Advocate* about a new scientific study that says that not every cat and dog is attracted to a cat or dog of the opposite sex."

I looked at Michael, opened my mouth, thought better of it, and said nothing. I willed myself to get through the hour-long meeting without any sarcastic words coming out of my mouth. I wasn't overly optimistic.

Of course, Estelle had heard through the grapevine about Michael coming out. During most of the meeting she and Michael chatted away like old buddies, even making a few references to "the life." They all but ignored me, and talked very little about the benefit. I was tempted to walk out and head back to the office, but I stayed because of the animals.

At one point, we walked over to the cages of cats waiting to be adopted. The cards on each door gave the cat's name, sex, age, medical problems, and, the saddest of all, how the cat ended up in the cage. Estelle and Michael were in the middle of an animated conversation and happened to stop in front of the cage of a scrawny black female named Pookie. The card noted that she hadn't yet been spayed; Pookie was obviously in heat, yowling nonstop and rubbing up against the walls of her cage as well as against her food and water bowls. Michael stuck a finger through the cage to scratch her ears. The cat promptly turned around and stuck her butt in front of his face. He turned red and stepped toward the next cage.

"Don't bother," I murmured to the cat. "He's not interested."

When the meeting was over, Estelle and Michael hugged, while she offered me only a dry hand. "I'm really looking forward to the benefit," she said. I was already thinking up some newsworthy emergency I could come up with that would effectively kick her off the front page, relegating her to a few paragraphs on page 13 where no one would see them. I could possibly replace her article with a syndicated column from Pat Buchanan, but again, the thought of the animals got to me.

Back at the office, I had asked all of our regular free-lancers to come to the office that afternoon because Joel was there to set up email accounts that would automatically forward mail received at the paper to their home accounts. There was nary a Blue Hair in sight due to their propensity for quill pens and parchment paper. I don't think any of them even owned a touch-tone phone. Joel asked Gwen, one of the newer freelancers and a student at Richford College, what password she'd like to use.

"Sappho."

When I heard that, I glanced at them, Joel with his fingers poised over the keyboard, Gwen standing to his right watching the monitor. Poor Joel, he didn't have a clue.

"Uh, how do you spell that?" he asked.

Funny, she didn't look gay, I thought. But then again...oh forget it. That's when I hatched my plan.

I needed an interview with Estelle, but I didn't want to do it. I would send Gwen on the interview at a time when I knew Opal, Estelle's lover, would be at the shelter.

"I want an in-depth Q&A with her," I told Gwen, who was probably thinking that I was finally giving her a big break. "I know she's busy getting ready for the benefit, but she needs the press. Take your time and ask her anything you want."

Gwen looked startled. "What do you mean, *anything?*"

"Well, I've heard she's looking for a new girlfriend," I said. "She's been with the same woman for more than ten years and rumor has it that LBD set in after the first two years together."

Gwen nodded knowingly. LBD as in *Lesbian Bed Death*. I

wondered if anyone else at the Clueless meetings was able to use the stuff they learned there in direct subterfuge. "I know," said Gwen. "All they want to do is get the dirty stuff out of the way—just so they can say they've done it—and then get down to the business of every long-term lesbian relationship. All they really want is to live together like a couple of spinsters," she elaborated. "*That's* why I'm single.

"I would never let that happen to me," she continued. "I think that the older lesbians were never really able to fully express their sexuality because it's something that gay men had cornered the market on." She wrinkled her nose. "My women's culture professor told us that."

Here I go overdosing on gay stuff again. Where were all the straight people? Since it was Tuesday, I would get my dose of them in Burlington. As I drove north, I smiled as I thought of the sparks that would fly once Opal saw Gwen hitting on Estelle.

When it came to the Clueless meetings, I was starting to turn into a junkie. During those two hours every Tuesday night, I concentrated so hard on what everyone was saying that I was drenched with sweat by the time I stood up at the first break. It wasn't so much what was said; rather, here was a group of people who were intimately familiar with what I was experiencing in my marriage—with slight variations, of course—and I didn't have to explain why I did or said certain things—or why I was still married, for that matter.

Wednesdays and Thursdays, I was fine. Fridays, I was consumed with closing the paper. On Saturdays I started to think about the Tuesday night meetings, what I would say, or the update that Ted or Cheryl might give. Sundays, I began to think that the next two days would go too slowly for me to bear.

On Monday I started the countdown of the number of hours left until seven o'clock the next evening. By the time Tuesday evening finally rolled around, I was a wide-eyed junkie, wild for my fix. And from what I could tell, I was not alone.

At the meeting, it was Anita's turn to dump. She let out a loud sigh and her shoulders drooped down. "You know, I just don't know if I can take any more of the constant rollercoaster that Bill is putting me through. One night he's all cuddly and loving, like when we were first married, and the next night he's turned into a snarling, spitting tiger. Or he goes into a major depression." Heads around her nodded.

As she spoke, Anita would methodically shred one tissue at a time, tearing a half-inch-wide strip from one end before rotating the tissue a quarter turn and removing another strip. She wadded each torn remnant into her left hand while her right held the intact but rapidly shrinking tissue. Each strip would be progressively shorter than the last, until her right hand was clutching a tiny rectangle of tissue, which she'd add to the growing wad in her left hand. At this point, she would let the sodden clump drop to the floor, reach into her pocket, pull out a fresh tissue, and begin the process all over again. After only five minutes, a small pile of tissue clots was starting to build at her feet. She was totally oblivious to the growing mounds.

"It's almost as if our good times deliberately set him off, because although I know he's happy and loving with me and not just putting on an act, deep down, he knows that straight marriage is not for him." All eyes were on Anita's hands as they made their way through another Kleenex.

"The good old rollercoaster," said Cheryl. "When is it time to finally get off?"

"The problem is that when things are going well for us, I think they're going to last and Bill will see how good we are together. Then he'll have a change of heart and completely forget about men." A clump of tissue landed on the toe of her shoe. "This has been going on for so long I'm sick. He thinks he can bury being gay, and so I start to believe him. But that's just when all hell breaks loose and it's another ticket on the fucking rollercoaster." A clean square of tissue magically appeared in her hand.

Janet piped in. "I've been up and down on the rollercoaster with Tom so many times I've lost count," she said. "And as time went on, the ups and downs started to last much longer and look a lot different. Every time he went up or down, it feels like he rearranged the furniture. And I couldn't believe the number of floor plans this man has been able to come up with." She laughed. "You know the score: He's sick of the rest areas, so he comes back to me. Then he gets bored and horny and goes online to find his true love. He finds one, it lasts for two weeks, maybe three, and then he's back to me, swearing his undying love. A few weeks later, he's off to the club again to find a *real* male friend, nothing sexual, of course, while adding that I should start to make other plans."

She took a deep breath. "I think he was deliberately nasty to me because he felt that the gay male identity he was working like hell to develop would disappear into thin air if he happened to be nice to me. I've developed one hell of a tolerance to Dramamine." She smiled. "But Tom was so good at the art of furniture arranging—making me believe that this time everything would be different—that he could have gotten a job at Macy's, if nothing else."

"You know," said Anita, "there's an Indian tribe in northern Canada where every time a member of the tribe dies, the entire community goes to the house of the dead person and rearranges all the furniture."

"Why do they do that?" asked Ted.

"A couple of reasons. One, so that the people left behind can start living a new life. And second, so the soul of the deceased can't recognize the house and stick around to haunt it," she said.

"You think if we all go home and rearrange our furniture our gay spouses will become confused and choose some other place to haunt?" Beverly asked.

"Could be," said Anita. "Maybe I should just tell my kids to go at it." She smiled. "Most of the stuff in the living room is Bill's anyway."

"Rearranging the furniture," said Charlie. "I like that. So

whose house is first?"

"Mine," said Cheryl. "This week, I was thinking about why we put up with all of this shit, or at least why *I* do. You know what I came up with?"

"What?" Beverly asked.

"Well," Cheryl said, "this is going to sound stupid, but one of the things that I like best about Paul is that he doesn't snore. After he moved out the first time, I got up my nerve and had sex with another man. He was Paul's polar opposite: out of shape, not a great dresser, and loud, but I loved it because he wanted me, all of me. And it was great, until we fell asleep. He snored so loudly I couldn't sleep. I spent the night wrapped in a moldy quilt, wandering around this strange apartment with a German shepherd that growled at me constantly. Only the guy couldn't hear his dog because he was snoring so loudly. Since I couldn't sleep and was thoroughly miserable, all I could think of was Paul and how he didn't snore, and then, of course, I started remembering all the good things we had and that I had blocked out long ago.

"So I called him up when I got home, and the whole thing started up again." Cheryl started to cry.

Beverly patted her shoulder. "Oh honey," she said. "Don't you know that it doesn't matter if a guy snores as long as he wears you out enough beforehand so that you sleep right through it?" Cheryl half-laughed through her tears.

When I got home, the house was dark. The cats clamored at me when I opened the door. A scrap of paper with the words *went out* was stuck cockeyed to the phone. Well, *duh*. I read for an hour and then fell asleep. I slept until two, when the full moon illuminating the room woke me up. As soon as I opened my eyes, I knew something had shifted. I could see every detail in the bedroom from the brass handles on the dresser to the words on Michael's stack of gay books on the nightstand.

I wish I could have videotaped myself as I got out of bed, put on my robe, tucked the cordless phone into my pocket, and walked downstairs. It felt as if I had gone to sleep and woken up a different person. Everything looked so clear, yet so distant, that I felt I was on the outside watching this person—me—move far too slowly through the simple act of navigating a flight of stairs. If I knew I wasn't already awake, I would have thought I was sleepwalking.

The living room was so bright it looked like a spotlight was shining through the window. I felt myself drawn to the circle of moonlight on the living room rug. I needed the clarity, the certainty, of the moon. I curled up in the circle of moonlight and lay down in it. My body was partly on the carpet, partly on the floor. As the moonbeam slowly crawled across the floor, somehow my body followed. I was so comforted by the light that I slept on the floor all night.

I felt the cats scrunch up against me sometime during the night, moving with me. Whenever the furnace kicked on, I felt the vibration through the floor in my cheek. My senses were turned off except for the tiny bit of hearing I kept tuned to the frequency of the cordless phone, knowing it would ring sometime, but not caring enough to prevent me from sleeping. With my eyes closed, I still saw the moon.

The phone finally rang at 6:30, jarring me out of my strange non-sleep.

"Hi." Michael's voice was flat. He sounded exhausted, probably expecting me to react with hysteria.

I offered up an unintelligible grunt.

"I thought I should call."

"Oh." Silence.

"We can talk tonight," he offered.

"About what?" Stingily rationed words, parceled out lean and hard.

His exhalation was redolent with the aroma of *Fuck You I'm Gay.*

"I'll see you tonight."

I hung up. I was still lying on the floor. I needed more moon, but now it was a faint apparition, strong-armed by a weak sunrise. I reluctantly got up.

It was the first time that Michael had stayed out all night.

• • •

Some women say they know the minute their husbands become smitten with another woman. When Michael first came out, I thought of these women with straight husbands and remembered how a co-worker at the *Transcript* had reacted when she thought her husband was having an affair. At first she denied it, then reacted with full-blown jealousy. In the end, she shamelessly threw herself at her husband and they remained married. In a small way, I was jealous of her. Although women are conditioned to expect that men will stray, when it finally happens, it's still a shock. But they also intuitively know all that's required is to turn up the volume on their feminine wiles. The theory was that once the wheels were put in motion, he'd remember what he was missing, see the errors of his ways, and voilà, she'd win him back.

I remember my grandmother holding forth on the subject of dealing with wayward husbands: "Get a good big rolling pin," she'd roar, shaking her fist, "and don't hesitate to use it whenever necessary."

Women with husbands who had affairs with other women could follow a well-thumbed rulebook handed down through the years by previous generations of wronged wives. My situation was different: The wives with husbands who were attracted to other men usually didn't know where to turn first. Especially when the husbands declared their undying love for their wives and the life they shared, but categorized their need for a man as a very specific form of male bonding, what were we supposed to think? Were we denying their masculinity if we told them no, they couldn't go? So the first night that Michael stayed out all night, I didn't need a crystal ball to know what had happened.

On a chilly Thursday last week—the day before deadline—the paper was bustling as usual, with the Blue Hairs hobbling in with their columns and advertisers phoning with last-minute changes. I had scheduled an appointment with a new marketing guy from the college who wanted to arrange a coop ad for an upcoming Christmas gift issue. This was Michael's territory but, as he was out on a sales call, I agreed to see him.

When Brad Turner walked in the front door, Carrie motioned him to my desk. He sat down, opened a leather portfolio on top of my littered desk, and began his pitch. He was an attractive man, 30-ish, tall, sandy-haired, and the muscles under his suit were not hard to miss. After he sat down, Carrie smiled and winked at me as she walked away.

About ten minutes into his presentation, Michael walked in. He sat down at his desk, glanced over at me, and looked at Brad, who returned his gaze. Instantly, the air became charged, like the seconds before a thunderstorm when the fur on the cats gets staticky. I swear I smelled ozone. Brad stopped talking in mid-sentence and Michael stood up to extend his hand. I cleared my throat in order to introduce them, but they handled the formalities without me. They were totally oblivious to me and the chaotic buzz of the office. Their eyes were locked.

Finally Michael spoke. "I believe I'll take over from here, Emily," he said without looking at me. He grabbed Brad's portfolio. Still staring at each other, Brad switched chairs and rested his elbow on Michael's desk. I couldn't breathe. I gathered up my papers and headed to work at Carrie's desk.

• • •

That evening, if I closed my eyes, I almost thought it was a night long ago, ripped out of the Pre-Coming Out daybook. Michael and I had finished dinner, which he had cooked, and we were sitting in the living room, Chainsaw on my lap, reading and talking as if nothing had changed, including the incident with Brad at the office. I looked up from my book and glanced across the room at Michael. He smiled back.

The phone rang. The cordless was on the arm of my chair,

so I reached for it.

"Hello?"

There was a pause on the other end followed by the crackly voice of a man who sounded as if he had just left puberty behind last week, tinged with the high whine that seemed to be native to most gay men.

"Is Michael there?"

If I were a cat, my fur would be standing on end. I thought I had a respite from The Gay Shit tonight, but I guess it was too much to ask.

I put on my best smarmy smile and said, "Just a minute."

"It's for you." I repressed the urge to hurl the phone across the room and instead passed it to Michael. I pretended to continue reading.

Out of the corner of my eye, I saw Michael scrunch up his face.

"Who?" he asked. He listened for a minute. Suddenly his eyes opened wide and he flashed a quick glance in my direction. He stood up quickly and walked out of the living room and into the kitchen. I was able to catch a few words. Michael was doing his best to keep his voice down, but the word *sister* came through loud and clear. I couldn't believe he'd give out our home number. He stayed on the phone for a few more minutes. When he sat back down in the living room, he tucked the cordless phone in between his leg and the chair.

"Who was that?" I asked, smarmy smile still on my face.

"Oh, just some guy I met who wanted the date of the next meeting." He picked up his book and began to absently flip through the pages.

The churning in my stomach started to boil over. "Isn't it always on Wednesday nights?"

He shrugged off my question. "Yes," he said, his eyes still glued to his book, "but this guy is new and he wanted to make sure."

"Then why did you have to duck into the kitchen to give him a simple answer?"

Michael placed his book on the table. "Look, Emily, you told me you didn't want to know the details of my other life which—do I have to remind you—you've given me your blessing to go out and explore. I'm just sparing you details that wouldn't make a difference anyway. Besides, before you totally gave up on therapy, you asked me to keep it under wraps."

"Jesus, with every man who craves dick within a 50-mile radius currently after your ass, which now includes Brad Turner, how could I not notice? And now I have to see it right in front of me plain as day in the office!" Chainsaw jumped off my lap and ran upstairs. "You said you'd keep it out of the office and that you wouldn't give out our home number! And why the hell are you saying I'm your sister?"

"You've been spying on me!"

"I don't have to spy, you leave it all out in the open for me to see, as plain as day. Sometimes I wonder why you're so nasty to me, and I think I know why."

"Well then, Miss Psychoanalyst, why don't you tell the world everything you know about me so we can all have the benefit of your years of important insight."

I took a deep breath. "I think you know that you're gay, not bisexual, but you don't want to make a decision just yet, and you don't want to be the one to end the marriage. So you figure if you are passive enough and push enough of my buttons you'll piss me off so I'll say *enough* and tell you to leave and therefore turn into the bad guy. If this is the case, Michael, you're doing a great job. Christ, I always knew you would be a handful when you went through your midlife crisis, but what I didn't realize was that you'd experience your second adolescence at the same time."

He looked at me as if he had a thick pool of bile in his throat he couldn't swallow.

"You think you know everything that is going on with me," he said. "Let me tell you, Emily, you don't know shit. You don't have a clue about what it's like to go from a member of a respected group of society to one that is regularly spit on, beat up, and murdered."

I squelched the urge to start sawing on an invisible violin.

"You're right. I don't know what it's like, since I've never gone through it. But what I don't understand is why you have to be so nasty and hostile to me. Michael, it's not my fault. I didn't drag you kicking and screaming out of the closet. But you know, since you came out, I thought that if I did everything you'd want a man to do to you and for you, that short of having a dick, you'd be so fulfilled with me that you wouldn't need to be with a man.

"But what intrigues me the most is that this new persona you've adopted—that of a living, breathing, sexual being—simply doesn't jive with the image I've had of you for so many years. You've been like a pod person to me. And because I've viewed you as an asexual person for so long—aside from our brief honeymoon a couple of months ago—part of me feels like cheering you on, so you can finally discover what being sexual is all about. And also maybe you'll be able to tell me what I can do to turn you on. I thought I had already tried everything in the book, short of taping down my breasts and wearing a strap-on."

During my tirade, Michael continued to look at me, no emotion on his face, his lips clamped. He didn't attempt to interrupt, so I kept going.

I laughed, more of a bark, really. "And you know, for the longest time, I actually thought you were impotent, and I blamed your lack of interest on that, and the worst thing to do would be to nag you about it. So I left it alone—obviously."

I was treading in dangerous territory. I didn't care. I had a few more comments up my sleeve. Michael remained silent, stoic.

"For that matter, I can't believe you're still wearing your wedding ring, though knowing you're referring to me as your sister to all these young studs, you probably slip it into your pocket on the way into the club. I think that's smart, but I have a better idea."

I walked to the hallway for my wallet. I opened the change purse and took out a couple of rings and put them on the coffee table in front of Michael, who glared at them.

"Those are the wedding and engagement rings you gave me. I took them off a few weeks ago."

He pointed at my left hand. "Then what are those?"

"They're fake. I bought them at Kmart for five bucks apiece."

I slipped them off and gave them to him. He examined them closely. "I took off my real rings and bought fake ones. Fake rings for a fake marriage, you might say."

He cleared his throat.

"Are you done?" His voice was devoid of hostility. Now he just sounded tired.

I scooped up the rings and sat back down in my chair. I closed my hand into a fist and shook it like it was a maraca. I nodded.

"Okay, then." We sat there without a word, without looking at each other, for about an hour. Michael coughed, then got up and went upstairs. I heard the door to the guest room close. I fell asleep in the chair.

Chapter Ten

There was one question I wanted an answer to and I thought about it as I headed to Burlington for the Clueless meeting. It was based on something Cheryl had said in passing last week: "Why are they attracted to someone who has the same kind of body?"

Besides puzzling over everything else that was going on with Michael, I was absolutely stuck on this question. I've always believed that the best thing about the world was that it is filled with opposites: chocolate and vanilla, AC & DC, boy and girl. The contrast is part of the allure, with each side wanting to conquer the other for no other reason than it *is* the other. As long as I can remember, I've loved the idea of opposites. I figure that if I could gain a bit of insight into the *other*, maybe someday I could claim a tiny bit of it as my own.

I felt this sense of *other* more strongly with Michael than I had ever experienced with any other man. After he came out, of course, I knew why: he had not one, but *two* others, and I think this is why I was so eager to agree to anything Michael suggested: Part of me believed that if I kept agreeing, I'd get to the root of his *other*, or at least one of them. I was completely blinded by the *other* in him.

But even more, I loved his maleness, the way his bicep tensed when he did something as simple as brush his teeth or hoist himself out of bed. I'd stare at him to try to soak up the mystery of his maleness, the mystery that made it impossible to take my eyes off his body whether or not it was clothed. Is this how straight men feel when they look at women? Or, for that matter, is this how Michael feels when he looks at another man? I wondered if other women felt the same way about a man's body, *their* man's body. Did a quick glance at a taut male thigh evoke the same chills in their temples and nipples?

I'd stare at my husband with a passion and appetite that was palpable. It clung to me like a sweaty fog. These days, of course, Michael didn't like it when my gaze lingered. And he made sure to wear his robe whenever he was around me, so he wouldn't have to bear the edgy indignity of my desire.

Part of me, deep down, knew the truth. Our dilemma was that we were *too* much alike. The same things that made me think with my clit, my entire body, for that matter, were what affected him too. It wasn't the *other* at all; on the contrary, the problem was that we were both turned on by the same thing: We both loved men.

And now that we knew the truth, where could we possibly go with it?

Despite his recent behavior toward me, there was no denying that Michael loved me. We had built a home, a history, a business together. The love that was causing us to cling to each other in a vaguely unsatisfying life was quite real and strong. But how long could either of us live with this? After all, love's worst enemy is familiarity. And it was this familiarity that made us agree to pacts we would not have made with anyone else.

As I locked my car in the lot outside the Women's Health Center, I thought, here we go again. Hope somebody brought the Dramamine tonight. When we were all settled around the circle, I jumped right in.

"Hey Cheryl, you said something last week that got me thinking."

"Yeah, what was that?"

"Why would he want to have sex with a person who has a body exactly like his?"

"Boring!" Cheryl blurted out.

"Exactly!" I said. "But remember, that because it is so similar, there's no mystery, but also there are no surprises. They know what to do, what to expect, and how it's going to turn out!"

"*Boring!*" Cheryl repeated.

"Yes, but there's a certain degree of security to that as well, and a bit of obsession involved, like golf," said Ted.

Beverly burst out laughing. "Golf? Oh please!"

"No, I'm serious," he said. "Listen, the goal of every good little obsessed golfer is to get a little ball to go into a little hole."

More laughter. "Well, I guess the people we married were into other sports, which is why we're all here," Anita said.

The rest of the evening continued on a light note. But the talk about difference and similarities got me thinking. What *was* it about the sameness of another body that was so appealing to Michael? I had to find out.

The next morning, I called Janet to confide my plan. Her response was predictable.

"You're gonna what?"

"I said, I'm going to sleep with a woman to see what it is about having sex with a mirror image of yourself," I repeated. "I don't know why Michael would want to have sex with a man. Oh, sure, I know why *I* like to have sex with a man, especially with Michael, but that's because we're different. You know, Slot A goes into Slot B. But if Slot A has sex with another Slot A, well then, where's the attraction? Where's the mystery? Where does everything go?"

She paused. "You mean, you don't know how two men have sex? How old are you, Em?"

I laughed. "It's not that, it's just that I can't see what would be so fascinating about making love with a variation of yourself. It sounds like masturbating, and for that you could just stay home, right?"

She laughed. "So is this some kind of scientific experiment, then?"

"I guess. See, I already know about the differences. I *love* the differences. What I want to know is why Michael is attracted to sameness."

"You realize you're swimming in murky waters here," she said.

"What do you mean?"

"I mean, even if you do have sex with a woman, you'll never really find out why Michael is attracted to men. You do realize that, don't you?"

"Yes, but I don't care. I want to try to see what Michael sees in it." I felt like a broken record. "I just want to find out about the physical allure, if it would turn me on to have sex with someone who had a body exactly like mine."

She sighed. "Well, I know you'll do what you want to do anyway, but just be careful."

"Hey, do me a favor."

"What is it?"

"Don't let anyone at the group know I'm doing this, especially Charlie and Ted. I don't want them to think that the enemy won another one for their side." Janet swore herself to secrecy and wished me luck. We hung up and I sat down in front of my computer to do a little research.

In order to carry out my experiment, I needed to find a lesbian bar. I didn't want to complicate things by running into someone I knew, so I had to head south. I got online and typed GAY MASSACHUSETTS into the search engine. After scrolling through listings for S&M boutiques and queer feng shui interior decorators, I found a private club in Lowell that sounded as if it might fit the bill. The description for The Gas Lamp said that the mix of men and women was about 50–50 and proper attire was requested. I wanted to make sure, though, so I scrolled down and found a link for the AIDS hotline in Lowell. I figured somebody there could give me the scoop on the place.

I told the woman who answered that I was new in town and asked if she could recommend any places for women to hang out. She started rattling off a laundry list of what I could choose from. "You want lesbian-only, mixed, leather, strip shows, or what?" I didn't realize that such diversity existed just 90 miles from Coventry.

"Uh, I guess women who aren't too butchy, but I don't mind if men are there too."

"Oh, then you'd like The Gas Lamp, right off Worcester Avenue on Pine Street." I was right. "Pretty classy, lots of lipstick types, sometimes go-go dancers—"

She was going too fast for me. "Lipstick types?"

"Oh, sorry, hon, you must be new to all this," she said, dropping her voice and slowing her speech considerably.

"*Lipstick* as in lipstick *lesbians*. You know, they dress up a bit, wear makeup, and could never be confused with a farmer, like some of these dykes who come down from the boonies. You'd think that if they wanted to look like a man that much, they'd spring for the operation. Say," her voice assumed a purr, "you don't need someone to show you the town, do you? Tell me what you look like and when you'll be coming down and I'll look for you at The Gas Lamp."

I stifled a laugh—that was *all* I needed. Though it was appealing, I wanted to conduct my experiment on my own terms, to pick and choose—or to be selected myself.

"No, I don't think so," I answered. "Thanks for the offer, but I'm not sure when I'll be passing through."

"Well, if you change your mind, you can call me here the day before you come down. I'm Charlotte. Everyone at The Gas Lamp knows me."

"Okay, Charlotte. Thanks for your help."

What a trip, I thought as I hung up the phone. Lesbians seem to be as predatory as gay men. At least this one was. What do shy lesbians do?

My mind was getting ahead of me. A Grand Experiment, Em, that's all it's meant to be. I desperately want to know exactly what it is that Michael feels.

• • •

I had never before put so many miles on my car in such a short period of time since Michael came out. Only a month and it was time for another oil change for the 240. Having a gay husband was turning out to be tough on cars.

The Gas Lamp turned out to be a nondescript cinder-block building in Lowell's industrial district on a deserted but well-lit street. Deserted, that is, except for the cars that lined both sides of the street as far as the eye could see. A faint but fast thumping emanated from behind the cinder blocks. Every time the door opened, the reverberation washed over the people standing outside like a wave.

A couple of women milled around the gray steel door. No velvet rope here to keep out the riffraff, only one mean-looking bull-necked man dressed in camouflage from head to toe with a massive linked chain that dangled from a belt loop and snaked into a pocket. He looked as if he had just walked off the battlefield.

I double-parked in front of the club while I thought about what to do, since I didn't want to park too far away. One of the women walked over to my car, eyeing me suspiciously. "Can I help you?" she asked, curtness edging her voice.

"I want to find a place to park, but I'm not sure if I want to park on a side street. Is it safe to walk?"

She gave me the once-over and glanced at the maps lying on the passenger seat. I must have passed her test as her manner softened.

"Sure, but tell you what. I'll follow you down the block and if you can't find a spot on Pine, then make a right onto Elm, and I'll walk alongside you and then walk back with you. Deal?"

I shrugged. "Sure." She walked in the street alongside the car, resting her hand on the door handle as we moved. She looked kind of neutral, not too masculine or feminine, and she struck me as a regular at the place, a person who spent maybe three nights a week here partying with her friends. I had seen her type at the places I went to with Eddie.

She wore tight black cigarette jeans and a white tailored

women's blouse that I wouldn't have thought would go with the jeans, but the mix of opposites helped achieve her neutrality. It seemed studied, though, as if she didn't want any woman—butch or femme—to rule her out, so she staked out the middle ground to increase her chances. Of course, all of this was sheer speculation that flashed through my mind in the minute it took to drive down Elm Street. To be honest, I didn't have a clue as to how the lesbian mind operated when it came to the dance of seduction. All I knew is that it had to be different from the heterosexual mating dance, since it had been my experience that someone had to be the pursuer while the other was the pursuee. In my mind, two Slot As cancelled each other out.

My escort tapped the door handle. "Turn right here," she said. "See three spaces up in front of the Cherokee? You can squeeze in there." She hopped up on the sidewalk and watched me maneuver into the space.

I shut off the engine and got out. "Hey, thanks a lot," I said. "You didn't have to do that."

"No problem," she said, holding out her hand. "My name's Terry."

I had debated whether to use my real name, weighing the pros and cons, like telling someone a fake name and then forgetting to respond to it, but I hadn't yet made up my mind. "Emily," I decided, extending my hand.

We walked back to the club. A few more cars streamed by.

"Busy place, huh?"

"That it is," said Terry. "Where in New Hampshire are you from? I haven't seen you here before."

Of course she had seen my license plate. "Up near Richford." I didn't want to give too much away, but without giving my last name, it would be impossible to trace me. "I work at the college."

"Doing what?"

"I'm in the communications department," I replied, which wasn't entirely false, since when we needed more copy to fill the paper, I printed as many stilted press releases from the college as I could.

"What brings you down here?" Another question with an answer I had pondered but hadn't entirely decided on yet.

"I've heard about The Gas Lamp, and had nothing better to do tonight, so I decided to come down and check it out."

We rounded the corner. The thumping from behind the cinder blocks got louder. "You came down alone? No friends?" She paused. "No girlfriend?"

"Nope, nobody could make it tonight."

"Well, I think you'll enjoy yourself," said Terry. She waved at a Subaru packed with women as it sauntered down the street. It beeped back. "Just let me know if you want me to introduce you around or give you the grand tour."

"Sure. I think I'm going to find a bar stool where I can camp out and watch the parade for awhile," I said.

We reached the door of the club. The man in fatigues stepped aside. "Make yourself at home," Terry said, opening the door with a flourish. "Just yell if you need anything. Sheila," she said to a woman standing just inside the door, "take care of my friend Emily. This one's on me."

Oh, God, the last thing I wanted was to be obliged to any one woman there, but Sheila waved me in. "Sure, Terr," she replied as Terry went back out to the street. She must be the Unofficial Greeter, I decided, getting first dibs on any fresh meat that walked in the door.

Sheila pointed to the bar. I followed her hand as my eyes got used to the dark. "Yell if you need anything." Second time in less than a minute that I'd heard the same exact phrase. I wondered if it was some kind of code for new meat. I found a barstool unclaimed by jacket or human and ordered a beer. By the time it arrived, my eyes had adjusted to the dark.

Charlotte at the AIDS hotline was right. This was a classier place than the New Hampshire dumps. Black walls, swirling lights, and an elevated dance floor with a style that seemed a few notches above what I had expected of Lowell, an hour's drive from my old stomping grounds in Groveton. Leather upholstery devoid of cigarette burns, brass rails that gleamed with every pulse of the strobe light, and bartenders who bore no resemblance to the scruffy specimens I had seen in the clubs I visited with Eddie.

The mix was slightly more women than men. I watched the show—and felt myself being watched as I sipped my beer. Five minutes later, a woman tapped me on the shoulder and asked if the seat next to me was taken. She announced her name as Winnie and sat down before I had a chance to answer.

She was attractive in a suburban Massachusetts kind of way, far too feminine for Coventry and its environs. She was a bit shorter and older than me, brunette, and, I discovered when she leaned across me to reach for an ashtray, at least one cup size larger.

We talked about the weather and she bought me another beer. Four songs later, Winnie's hand was resting halfway up my thigh. I tried to fall into the seduction, not by imagining that she was a he, but by pretending I was inside Michael's brain and that I was becoming increasingly turned on by Winnie with each minute that passed.

Maybe another beer would help. Winnie signaled to the bartender, and before the drinks arrived, she grabbed me and we headed for the dance floor. As soon as we started to dance, the music changed to a slow number, and she pulled me close. Again, if I was Michael and I was currently dancing with a person who had the same plumbing as me, would I be turned on? I tried to remain neutral and open-minded.

Winnie ran her hand along the small of my back while gently pushing her groin into mine. Every time she exhaled, her breath caught the edge of my ear. Was I marked as someone who had come here just for sex? Or was it the norm to expect you'd get laid if you exchanged more than ten words with a stranger while sipping a Molson?

Whatever the case, I figured that as long as we were going to cut to the chase, I'd find the answers I had come looking for. And that's when my heart started to pound, not because I was getting turned on, but because I was becoming nervous. I was going to get my answer; did I really want to know?

Winnie must have felt my pulse start to race; she pulled back to look at me, surprise on her face. "Oh, Emily," she said, breathless. "Mind if we go?"

I tried to smile as if I was turned on—whether I succeeded was moot at that point. "Sure," I said, pulling her back and pushing my crotch against hers. "Let's go."

She told me she lived a few blocks away from The Gas Lamp. We grabbed our coats and left the club. Outside, Terry winked at the both of us as we hit the sidewalk.

Her apartment reminded me of the many nondescript dumps I had lived in across the Bay State: cinder block walls painted a pale gray, a small refrigerator where chipping the ice buildup in the freezer once a month was the aerobic equivalent of a four-mile run, and more locks on the door than I could count.

Once we were inside, she started kissing me. The Michael in my brain made me kiss her back, although it was nothing like kissing a man. There was no pronounced jawbone, no sandpaper face, no urgency. Her face felt a little mushy, and when I reached up to touch her on the neck, I was surprised that the sinewy cords I was accustomed to in a man's neck were nonexistent in Winnie's.

Her patterns of seduction followed the same schedule as a man's, or at least the men I had slept with before I met Michael: five minutes of kissing, then the shirt gets kind of scrunched off one shoulder, hands cup breasts, nipples get. tweaked. Then, impatience with the interference of clothes, off comes the shirt in a brief glimpse of urgency, followed by caresses all over the torso. Seven minutes later, the pants are yanked off, hipbones are briefly licked, and the ass is lightly squeezed in order to get to the main event. In this case, she wanted to bury her face in my crotch. And so, since it was an experiment, I let her.

It felt like I was a dispassionate observer watching a movie where I already knew how it would end. To be fair, I was well aware of the subtle intricacies and nuances that come when you're familiar with a particular body, and that the first time you become sexual with another person, the absolute novelty dictates that the passion be more physical than mental.

Oh, I had an orgasm—I've never been able to figure out how any woman *wouldn't* be able to come with a warm, wet tongue gently flicking across her clitoris, no matter who it belonged to—but the funny thing was that I wasn't even remotely turned on.

There was something missing, and it wasn't just Michael and it wasn't the lack of intercourse, or a penis, for that matter. Having sex with somebody with a body identical to mine wasn't charged with the sense of the *other* I so loved. And so there was no sense that here was an opportunity for me to try to decipher or overpower that *other* for even a minute. And while I'm sure it's not that predictable in every case of lesbian sex, I knew that if I couldn't understand Michael's pull toward a person of his own sex, I truly couldn't understand why he felt an attraction to me.

When I caught my breath, I pulled away from Winnie's mouth. I didn't know what I would do if she had demanded equal time, but fortunately, she just wiggled up and held me. Five minutes later, she was softly snoring, and so I gently rolled away from her and started to get dressed. "I have an early day tomorrow," I told her when she opened her eyes.

I let myself out of her apartment, and three hours and 27 minutes after I had first pulled up in front of the club, I was heading for home.

I hadn't decided when—or *if*—I would tell Michael about my adventure. But I definitely knew where I stood when it came to understanding Michael's attraction to somebody exactly like himself.

• • •

The next day, I went into the office a few hours late and stayed until just after five when Mrs. Fitzgerald came by to drop off her column. Since we started the cemetery series, I had been spending more time with her and viewed her as someone I could confide in. So whenever I needed to check a date on a story or the spelling of a name, I dropped by her house to sift through the collection. More often than not, we'd end up chatting about history, analyzing the town today, and gossiping about the other Blue Hairs. About a month ago, I had told her everything. She was the shoulder I needed: She didn't judge and she was very supportive. Michael knew none of this.

We had been chatting for a half hour when Michael walked in.

"Hello, Mrs. Fitzgerald," he said with a smile as he sat down at his desk. "On the trail of another hot story?"

"Always," she replied. "You know me." She stood up and walked around to his desk. She placed a hand on his shoulder.

"Listen, Michael, I just wanted to tell you that what you and Em are going through is tough," she said as Michael's smile slid off his face. "One of my cousins who was married for 32 years had to deal with the same thing a few years back. They're no longer together, but I know that the two of you can do whatever you set your mind to."

She patted his shoulder and started to leave. Michael said nothing, just glared at me. When the door had closed behind her, he banged his fist down on the desk.

"Emily, what the hell was that all about?" he said, his voice trembling on the last word.

"What are you talking about?"

"You outed me! I *never* said you could do that!" He pounded the desk again, then stood up and started pacing. "Now she's going to tell the whole town! What will that mean for me?"

"Oh, calm down, will you? Besides, with you going to every gay event in three states, you'd think you were the poster child for Coming Out Day."

"*That's* different!"

"How so?"

"I have to worry about my safety now, so I have to be careful who I come out to. If the whole town knows what's going on, who knows what could happen? Besides, it's my prerogative—all this has been much harder for me than for you."

I couldn't believe it. "How would *you* know what I'm going through? You never ask! You're so wrapped up in your new identity that you don't have a clue how I feel, and you don't care to ask."

"Well, I don't see that you've been emotionally crippled by the experience."

"I have a paper to run!" I yelled. "I don't have the luxury of running off to my daily therapy session and my twice-weekly coming-out group meetings at the drop of a hat. You come and go as you please, and it's all I can do to drag myself to Burlington one night a week where I don't have to explain what it's like to be married to a person who suddenly changes his mind and doesn't know if he likes women or men!"

"I don't see why you need to keep going there, anyway," he said quietly. "All it does is turn you against me."

"It does *not*," I said without moving my jaw. "Look, you have all the support you need. But you come gaily out with as many rainbow bumper stickers as you can slap on your car and sit there and tell me you don't like the fact that I need to talk about this with somebody, anybody. You've shoved me into a closet all my own because you decided to come screaming out of yours."

"Yes, but at least you don't have to learn how to live in an entirely new lifestyle. Honestly, Emily, I don't think you have a clue about what it's like for me, to be on the receiving end of open hostility from complete strangers, adjusting to a new culture, always being hit on—"

"Well, you probably just endure that for the sake of

furthering the cause of gays everywhere," I mumbled.

"Look, I'm not saying you're totally unscathed by this, but I sometimes think that if you were a little bit lesbian we wouldn't be having all these problems and you could better understand what my life is like."

Uh-oh.

"A little bit lesbian!" I barked out a laugh. "Where did you come up with *that* one?"

"Ron says that discrimination against homosexuals would disappear overnight if every straight person would just go out and have sex with someone of their own gender."

"Oh, really?" I asked. "You actually think that inside every heterosexual man and woman is a raging queen or bull dyke dying to come out? Jeez, if you believe that one..."

"Come on, Em, I just want you to get a better idea of what my life's been like, since you basically have shown no interest."

"I don't have to!" At this point I was shrieking . "Gay this and gay that are thrown in my face every time I turn around! According to everything you read and everyone you talk to, I'm just some castrating bitch who's bound and determined to keep you shackled to the straight world against your will. And of course you go along with it."

As I went through my tirade, Max stared at me dully from his perch on top of my monitor. Unlike the other cats, Max was totally blasé, probably because he had to put up with so many people traipsing through the office every day. "You say I show no interest," I continued. "That's a good one. Let's see, there are the PFLAG meetings you signed me up for without telling me, the horribly written *Loving Someone Gay* by some asshole gay Ph.D. who can't write his way out of a paper bag, the copies of *Out* and *The Advocate* lying all over the house—Michael, tell me something, because I don't understand. With all this information in my face every minute of every day, why on earth would I need to ask you about anything when it comes to being gay?"

"Well, you *could* be a little bit more tolerant, which I don't understand since you used to be such a fag hag."

"That was before I discovered that I was married to one!" I could tell he was losing patience with my tirade because he started shuffling through the papers on his desk.

He sighed. "I just think that if you could explore your attraction to women, you wouldn't be so hostile and our marriage would have a chance of making it."

Sure, so you'd have a misery twin to have your *Oh, poor me, I'm gay* parties with...

So I can do all the hard work for you that you need to do by yourself...

So you won't feel so guilty about what you've done to our marriage...

I couldn't take it anymore. I decided to use my trump card.

I sat back down, a coy smile on my lips. "So you basically think that the key to saving our marriage is that I should go out and sleep with a woman so I can understand what you're going through."

"Basically, yes." He paused. "All my friends think that everyone is a little bit gay, but they're just denying it. Look what happened in the movie *In and Out*. The poor guy denied it after he was outed, but it wasn't until Tom Selleck planted a big juicy kiss on his lips that Kevin Kline finally knew he was gay."

"So you're saying that if I go out and sleep with a woman, I might discover that I was a lesbian after all?"

"Yes," he said. "At least a little bit."

"I see," I nodded. "And what would that mean to our marriage?"

"Well, it would mean that we've both been in denial for all the time we've been together."

"And?"

"And we could finally be ourselves."

"You're not answering my question," I told him. "Would we stay married?"

"Well, why not? Given everything else we have together,

the business, the house, can't you picture it: you being who you truly need to be, and me doing the same. Why, we could even go out to Studebaker's together as a foursome, you with your lover and me with mine!"

I was getting nauseous. What was next in his mind, turning the *Courier* into a paean to gay life in Coventry? I shuddered.

"That's all well and good, Michael, but there's one problem with your fairy tale scenario."

Concern filled his face. "What?"

I looked down at my feet. I felt a tiny bit of cat litter lodged in between my sock and my heel. I scuffed my foot along the floor a few times to free it.

"Well, I wasn't going to tell you," I began, my voice drifting off.

"Tell me what?"

"Well, I did it."

"You did *what?*"

"I had sex with a woman."

I thought his jaw would fall off his face. "You *did? When?*"

At that moment, I decided to milk this puppy as far as I could. Coy, I thought. Try to look coy.

"Well, since you came out, all this gay stuff all over the place got me thinking exactly along the lines you've been talking about. What *is* it that makes someone decide that he or she is gay after living for years as an apparently happy heterosexual?"

Michael was grinning from ear to ear. "*Exactly* what I've been telling you."

Good. He bit. "Yes. Well, I know that you've been dealing with it longer than I have, but I started to wonder if the same thing could happen to me. So, instead of coasting along all well and good until something came along to trigger it, I decided instead to pull the trigger myself."

Michael leaned forward, wringing his hands. "Well?" he asked.

"Well…" I began. "I'll spare you the gory details, but suffice it to say that after it all was over, I could truly see that it was everything I had expected, and more."

At this, Michael was practically bouncing up and down in his seat.

"Really? Wow, that means Ron's theory is true. Boy, Em, I wouldn't have expected you to enjoy it so much."

"Wait a minute," I said. "Who said I enjoyed it? Michael, when I said it was everything I had expected and more, I meant it was even worse than I had thought it would be. I absolutely hated it. It was like having sex with my identical twin, and where's the excitement there? There's *no difference,* Michael, and it's the difference between us that I love about making love with you, besides the fact that I love you. Your body is so *different* than mine, Michael, and that's the attraction for me. I love how you go out where I go in, you're hard where I'm soft. Don't you understand? To me, having sex with someone who's just like me was the most boring thing in the world. In order to get turned on, I had to keep my eyes closed and imagine it was you instead of this, this woman! An inflatable doll would have been more exciting."

Michael looked as if I had punched him in the stomach.

"I did it because I wanted to understand what you were going through. And now that I know, I honestly don't know why you prefer to be with someone who's exactly like you."

He was staring at the floor. "You didn't have to tell me all this, you know."

"I told you I saved the gory details. Why would I tell you I liked it when I didn't? That I almost threw up in the car on the ride home? Not because of the act itself, but because I knew I would never be able to understand you, and when I realized that, I knew I had lost you."

He looked absolutely miserable. "But there is a way around this," I said.

"What?"

"Well, since it appears that we're going to take a stab at an open marriage, that means that if you're going to see men on the side, I can, too."

"You can too what?"

"See men."

His nostrils flared. "No, you can't!"

"Why not?"

"That would be cheating on me!"

"Well, do you think that your having sex with men isn't cheating? Sex is sex is sex, and one of our vows was that we would be monogamous with each other."

Michael exhaled heavily and frowned. "Emily, we've been all through this before, and you said you understood, but I guess you don't. How many times do I have to explain to you that having sex with you is making love because of the emotional attachment we have for each other, while for me, having sex with men is a purely physical need?"

"Well, it's a physical need for me, too, and what if I get an urge to have sex with a man while *you're* out having sex with a man? What am I supposed to do?"

He grinned. "Wait until I get home."

"You think I'm going to want to have sex with you after you've been fucking a man? Or, for that matter, what makes you think that you'll want to come home and make love to me after you've been—I'll use your words here—exercising your purely physical needs with a man? You'll want to come home and be tender with your wimpy wife?" I slapped my lap. "Why am I having trouble believing this?"

"You're overreacting, Em."

"*I'm* overreacting? Jesus, Michael, if you can go out and have sex with anyone you want, I should be able to as well."

"Em, as I've told you, it's not that cut and dried. Besides, you've already seen how good it can be between us when I can claim all parts of me instead of constantly having to push one part down."

"Yeah, well, it's a pretty dim memory to me now. Give me just one reason why I can't have sex outside our marriage if you can."

"Because it would seem like a competition," he said,

shrugging. "I would think about what the other guy can give you that I can't."

"Besides the fact that he's heterosexual and you're not?"

"That's not fair."

"Michael, what makes you think that *I* don't feel competitive with the guys you're with?"

"Because, as I've explained to you time and time again, with you there's love involved. With guys, it's just sex."

"Well, Michael, *you* may feel competitive if I have sex with other men, but you know how I feel competitive when it comes to the guys you claim you're only seeing for the sex?"

"How?" He was starting to squirm, a sign that the conversation was starting to hit a bit too close to home.

"I'd worry that even though it's working for us now, that someday you would like to live as a 100 percent gay man where's it's not just the sex, but rather that you want to embrace the whole gay lifestyle. But most of all, I think you want to know what it's like to have a real one-on-one relationship with a man. You want to fall in love with a man and you want to know what it's like to have a man love you back, unconditionally, and without question."

"But I won't let that happen!"

"How can you say that? You can't control your emotions or who you fall in love—"

He cut me off. "You forget, Emily, that I controlled my emotions for all those years. Of course I can control them. Besides, why would I want to give up what you and I have together? I would never let anything interfere with that."

True, Michael was a master at not letting his emotions show, but look what happened when they finally boiled over. We had reached an impasse. We couldn't change each other's minds.

It felt as if we had crossed our own private line in the sand. And I believe that Michael was truly shocked that I didn't want to go along with him anymore.

Chapter Eleven

Poor Lonnie. Though she only came to the Clueless meetings about once a month, she probably viewed it as her civic duty to show up just to give her version of the positive side of having a gay spouse, since no one else in the group shared her opinion. The rest of us knew that any newcomers would not come to a second meeting if Lonnie was in especially rare form.

The last time she was there, Lonnie launched into a convoluted story about the delicate manners she and her husband, Jay, had to employ when they had approached a bisexual man about the possibility of forming a threesome, either temporarily or as a 24-hour live-in orgy. "Initially, it would just be for sex," she said, waving her arms around. When she wasn't wearing a Hawaiian print muumuu, she'd wear some sleeveless housedress, even in the middle of winter. Her triceps were so flabby that Ted and I once joked after a meeting that she might just take off in flight. "Then, if it worked out, we'd live together in a monogamous trisexual relationship," she intoned, the clanging of her numerous disco-era bracelets almost drowning out her words. It was painfully clear that Lonnie needed the meetings more than the rest of us, if only to convince herself that even if she was truly unhappy with her marital situation, she would dig in her heels and stay to avoid turning into what the rest of us occasionally resembled at meetings: bitter, depressed shrews intent on thwarting their spouses' true happiness.

A couple of months ago, a woman named Tracy came to a Clueless meeting. She was shy—like most newcomers—but she wore her emotions pretty close to the surface. Her clothes hung on her already-thin frame, her short black hair clung to her scalp, and her eyes were large from the newness of her situation and the resulting lack of sleep. Her eyes darted between all of us, no doubt anxiously waiting for one of us to tell her what to do about her marriage.

Fifteen minutes into the meeting, Janet was discussing the finer points of deciding whether she should tell her mother about the change in Tom's sexual habits before the divorce was final. Tracy seemed to relax a bit and slid back in her chair. Then Lonnie cleared her throat and I thought, "So long, Tracy."

"Yes, but the more people who know about your situation, the more networking you can do to help find a suitable partner for you and your spouse," Lonnie said in her booming voice, her arms all over the place as usual.

I glanced at Tracy and saw the initial shock in her eyes change to note-taking mode. How could she know how radical Lonnie's position was? Across from me, Janet sighed, shifted in her seat to turn away from Lonnie, and stared at the floor, obviously counting the minutes until Lonnie shut up. She droned on and I tuned her out. I started to mentally review my to-do list at work for tomorrow.

"Once your spouse is able to realize his full range of sexuality, your marriage will improve beyond belief," Lonnie said with a note of finality, leaning back in her chair.

Suddenly, Anita burst out laughing. We all turned towards her.

"Sex, sex, *sex*," she exclaimed. "That's all I've heard since I started coming here. I *had* sex once, or used to every few months when my husband got drunk and figured it had been awhile and he owed it to me. But after he came out and I finally stopped blaming my ratty self-esteem on me and started pointing the finger where it really belonged—at

Bill—I went out and got what I craved—sex with a man who had a hard-on ten seconds after I walked in the door. After going without for so long, that's what I thought I wanted. And I was ecstatic that a man wanted me and my body.

"After the first month or so—we met two or three times a week—the sex began to get predictable—you know, round the bases and head for home in twenty minutes or less."

Cheryl cut her off. "But we *don't* know, that's the point."

Anita glared at her. "Let me finish, okay? What I'm saying is that sex is pretty much sex with a definite beginning and end. And—sorry, Charlie and Ted—for women, it does the trick for awhile, but soon, it's not enough. Finally, it dawned on me that it wasn't the sex *per se* that I was missing in my marriage, it was the little things: the hugs and kisses that come out of nowhere, in the car, in the kitchen, or in the supermarket. It's the look you toss to your spouse on the other side of the room when you're at a party and your song comes on. Damn it, it's the little things that take up a proportionately longer percentage of your daily life than the act of intercourse could ever consume.

"*That's* what pisses me off most, not the lack of sex, but reading the books, hearing the songs, seeing straight couples who show their love with the little things, and knowing that what they have is something I will never share with my husband."

For one long minute, no one said a word. Poor Tracy; now I knew we'd never see her again. Anita was right. We all tended to focus more on the physical act of sex—on how the non-monogamous spouses among us were getting a full deal while we were doing without—than on the little romances we believed constituted a happy marriage. Of course, there were a few who had had only one relationship in their lives, and that was with their gay spouse, so they didn't know what they were missing, aside from the messages they picked up through the radio, *Cosmo*, the movies, and idle gossip with their girlfriends. I was sorriest for them, because they felt they were stuck the most, since they had nothing to compare their relationship to. They didn't realize that the amount of compromising they were doing was not the norm in most relationships.

But Anita wasn't finished. I glanced around at the others and could tell they were caught off-guard by what began as an accusation but had quickly escalated into truth. We nervously looked at each other when Anita cleared her throat. Some of us needed to hear the bare truth, to be hit between the eyes with it, but I knew that some in the circle would plug their ears against whatever she would say from here on.

The sad truth is that I felt some of the people in the group used the meetings as an excuse to avoid making a decision about their own marriages. "I want to weigh all the options before I make up my mind," their crossed arms and closed body positions proclaimed. "I need to examine all the angles and *then* decide." Well, if they took the time to examine all their options, they'd be in limbo for the rest of their lives. I had heard the same complaint about the old-timers in A.A. meetings from Charlie who told me he had been going to A.A. for three years when he met Linda.

"They're only replacing a smoky bar and cheap booze for a smoky church basement and bad coffee," he told me when I had brought it up with him a few weeks earlier. In fact, even though I first started going to Clueless meetings as a way to cope after Michael came out, at times the meetings tended to lull me into an almost uncontrollable sense of inertia as I listened to stories that were better—and worse—than my own. Sometimes, I'd compare the minutest details of my life to what other people talked about that night. I wondered if Michael did the same thing at his meetings.

"I know what a decent straight marriage is like," Anita continued. "Yeah, it had its problems—they all do—but in retrospect, they were minor compared to being married to a gay man. Every marriage and relationship involves some degree of compromise, but when you're married to a gay spouse, there's a lot more compromise than in a heterosexual relationship, and most of it falls on the shoulders of the straight spouse, especially if the gay spouse is not willing to put aside The Gay Shit in order to work on improving the marriage as a whole.

"I filed for divorce last week, and what surprised me is that I'm even more pissed off than before. Why did I wait so long? Why did I initially, stupidly, think it could work? Why did I become an expert at repressing my instincts?"

She was on her soapbox now, and no one was about to interrupt her. "So let me ask all of you this: Imagine yourself ten years from now. You're still married to your gay spouse, probably more in name than in spirit, and you've put up with a decade's worth of crap. Your spouse, on the other hand, has been indulging since first coming out, and the two of you decided that the issue of having gay sex with someone outside of the marriage wasn't even on the same level as staying married. God, I remember thinking, 'If he was happy, then the marriage would be happy.' The sex part—or even the little romantic things part—didn't mean that much to you, or so you told yourself, right? After all, menopause was right around the corner, and all the stories you heard about living in *that* camp were about how you wouldn't want to have sex at all, and so you decided to hang on just a little bit longer, and then it wouldn't matter.

"Well, ladies and gentlemen, here's the other part of the scenario a decade into the future: Your husband spends three nights a week at your house, eating dinner with you and your almost-grown kids, watching TV, and helping out with the joint 1040 at tax time. But he sleeps in a different bedroom and spends at least 30 minutes on the phone every night with the man who's his main squeeze—whose house title has your husband's name on it as joint owner—on the four nights each week when he's not at your house. How do you fill up your days and nights when he's not there? Friends? Lovers? Drugs? Overtime?"

She paused and looked around the circle at each of us. Obviously, this was an issue that most of us weren't ready for, judging from the looks of discomfort on our faces. The truth is that I did want somebody to take me by the hand and make the hard decision for me. Here, finally, was somebody telling it like it is, but none of us were entirely sure how we felt about it. At the same time, I'm sure we felt that our own marriages were different from the others in the group, that we alone had what it takes to make the marriage work despite the odds.

"Of course, there's always the matter of children—did you always want more than you got? Did you ever consider applying to adopt a baby as a single parent? Of course, the agency would have thrown out your application in a heartbeat if you listed your spouse as gay. But how else would you have another child, immaculate conception? After all, if your husband doesn't want to have sex with you, how do you expect to get pregnant? It's a hell of a lot harder—I know! I will always be amazed at the fact that I did manage to have one child—and I can tell you the exact day that Mark was conceived, too!"

We all laughed and shifted in our seats a bit.

"In fact, my luck in getting pregnant despite the great yawning chasms of the sex life I had with my husband made me believe that I should never ever take a chance on Russian roulette!"

She waved her arms over her hips. "I mean, look at me. I'm not exactly centerfold material. And I don't have to tell you that being married to a man who has absolutely no physical desire for you doesn't do much for your self-esteem. I've never heard a woman complain that her husband pays her *too* much attention. I mean, I think it would be a terrific feeling to go out for a night on the town with your spouse when it's not your anniversary—which for me in recent years has meant that we get to have a pizza delivered instead of going to pick it up—both of you dressed to the hilt. You go out to a party and you look across the room to see your spouse staring at you as if you were a big juicy steak and he hadn't eaten for days. Being married to Bill, though, made me feel like the equivalent of a hamburger when he wanted nothing less than filet mignon. Either that or he had just gone totally vegetarian. You know, it's hard to be a Big Mac when you're waiting for a vegetarian to ravish you."

She cleared her throat again. This time nobody cringed. "There is one saving grace being married to Bill if we *were* planning to go to that hypothetical party, however."

She glanced around the circle, waiting for a response. I threw up my hands and asked with a smile, "What?"

"Well, he may not be willing or able to ravish me with his eyes when I put on that little—or, in my case, *big*—black dress, but at least he would be able to suggest a few drop-dead accessories to go with it."

Peals of laughter followed. Anita frowned. "The downside of this scenario—besides the obvious, of course—is that his attitude toward me provides me with absolutely no incentive to look good. And so I don't."

• • •

The rest of the week proceeded as usual: We put out a paper, Michael wasn't talking beyond what was necessary, and he wasn't around much at home. After our last blowout, I thought it was the definite last straw, but then Michael surprised me by asking if I wanted to spend Saturday with him to do some Christmas shopping. Two weeks left until the holiday, and we hadn't discussed what we were doing or which presents to buy. My hopes soared. Will this be the day he tells me he's giving up men and is ready to devote himself entirely to me? As usual, any sane counterthought that surfaced after that was drowned out.

"Sure," I told him. "What do you have in mind?"

"Oh, I figured we could hit some of the stores, drive around, you know, like the old days."

I fought to keep my excitement under control. Maybe he's planning to give me *himself* for Christmas this year, and he wants it to be a surprise, which is why he hasn't said anything yet. Even though I wanted to jump up and hug and kiss him, I stayed in my seat. "Sounds good," I managed.

"I want to get an early start, too."

"Great."

That Saturday morning, just after seven, I was working on my first cup of coffee, trying to hold onto my optimism. Michael wasn't home yet from his gay night out. Suddenly, all three cat heads jerked up, their ears yanked by an unseen thread attached to the ceiling, linked via some warped Rube Goldberg contraption that was activated whenever a car crunched its way up the driveway. Michael dragged himself through the door after taking what seemed to be twice the normal time to navigate from car to house. When he pushed the door open, he looked exhausted.

"Hi." His voice sounded as if it were caught on a branch and had gotten stuck. I felt a pinprick in my stomach.

"Are we still on for today?" I asked.

Michael shrugged. "Sure, let me just sleep for a few hours," he said, heading up the stairs. I noticed that neither our voices nor words jived with what was really going on. My brain twisted as I swerved away from reading something into his actions and catching the rollercoaster to hell as my hopes were dashed. I tamped my evil thoughts down to a place where I could almost ignore them.

A few hours doubled in on itself. Nine o'clock turned to eleven. I decided to do some work. I turned on Willard's radio show, which had just started. The first hour was devoted to warped Christmas songs, à la Dr. Demento. Perfect.

Willard and I had talked about publishing a retrospective of his Carnage photos over the last couple of years as a special supplement to entice more auto dealers to advertise. So I spent the morning leafing through back issues of the paper and reviewed some unpublished shots that were just too weird. Like the closeup of a fly on the cracked windshield of a totaled Buick at Hogg's Salvage Yard. Or the eerie overhead shot of a long row of crunched Taurus wagons in varying stages of disrepair, also at Hogg's. Actually, they weren't that much weirder than some of Willard's other shots—we planned to have a contest in the supplement asking readers to vote for the strangest Carnage photo—but at the time Michael didn't want to run the junkyard shots because he thought they might offend the car advertisers we did have. Fuck 'em, I thought, as I sifted through the shots.

Twelve noon. I had been staring at Willard's slides for hours and all the cars began to look alike. Willard started one of his skits, a conversation between a flatlander and a reclusive backwoods type. Kind of Mr. Yuppie meets Mr. Gorton's Gloucester Fisherman.

Willard turned up the volume on these scenes during foliage season and again at Christmastime. He figured that if any visitors had the lame-brained idea to move to Coventry and happened to tune into his show, they would quickly change their minds, thinking everyone in town was hostile to newcomers. It must have worked, since Coventry county had the lowest influx of urban-country transplants than any other county in New Hampshire, including Coos, way up north, easily the coldest, most barren land in the state. The people up there tended to think anyone from away who moved in must have just been released from either the state pen or a mental institution. Who else would want to live there?

I needed to hear only a few lines to know that Willard was using a recycled script. I figured he had spent too much time in the last week sifting through his stockpile of photos for the Carnage supplement to write a new skit.

"You can't change a cat into a dog," he drawled in an exaggerated North Country accent. "And even if the cat wants to change, it'll only work for so long. After all, a cat's a cat. Can't make him bark."

I was staring at a photo of a 1967 MG upside down that was being used as a chaise lounge when Willard cleared his throat.

"Now, one of my favorites, from that old smooth duo, Walter Becker and Donald Fagen, 'Barrytown.' I don't have to tell you which album it's from, or do I?"

The MG looked familiar, but I couldn't recall its owner. On Willard's question, I drew a blank.

"Well, just think back to those lazy late nights when a certain substance took hold of your brain, when you suddenly became so incredibly famished that if you didn't stuff something in your mouth right then—I'm talking foodstuffs here, kids—you thought you would absolutely die from hunger." He had a suave, Steve Martin brand of delivery, which always surprised people when they first met him because they expected a beatnik but got Frank Zappa instead.

"Yes, kids, I'm talking about a wonderful bag of salty, crunchy things, a bag that I carried around with me constantly, earning me a certain nickname which today is tossed around, sometimes with admiration, sometimes with consternation, but always with love."

Willard loved to toss these loopy pop quizzes into his show at least once an hour. It was one way to guarantee listener feedback. I was stumped.

"Yes, my sons, if you can remember that wonderful nickname, and that means if you're a flatlander you're automatically disqualified, because no way were you anywhere near Coventry in those days, or if you can name this Steely Dan album give me a call right now."

How could I forget? Willard was the Pretzel Man! The album: Pretzel Logic. I froze. *Pretzel Logic.* The term perfectly described what had been ruling my brain for months. I had twisted myself in so many directions to make Michael happy that I had turned into a pretzel.

I sat motionless, staring at the photos but seeing nothing. I listened to the mellifluous strains of the music, the smooth jazz phrasing, and the utter cynicism in Donald Fagen's voice.

I closed my eyes and envisioned a pretzel, the kind you buy from a street vendor. Soft, chewy, quickly yielding while most of the grains of kosher salt jumped ship with the first bite. And twisted beyond recognition.

I didn't like the person I had turned into. I did it to make Michael happy, but instead we were both miserable.

Willard's show continued for another couple of hours, during which he played selections from U2, the Kinks, and Stravinsky. I still hadn't budged from my seat. All I could play over and over in my mind was that I had turned myself into a fucking pretzel, and for what?

I hear the water run in the pipes upstairs. Michael must be awake.

A few minutes after Willard signed off at three o'clock, Michael finally straggled down the stairs. Eight hours of sleep had no effect on his grimness. If anything, grimness seemed to be permanently set in the stone of his jaw. He clicked on the coffeepot, nuked a mug of room-temperature coffee, and then sat down at the table across from me. I continued to stare at the photos. Michael tapped his fingers on the tabletop. I still didn't look at him.

The acrid smell of Michael's nuked coffee reached my nose. I heard him take a sip. "Well," he said, "are you ready?"

I don't think I've ever heard more lack of enthusiasm than I heard from Michael at that moment.

"No," I said without looking up. "I don't think I want to go."

He walked over to the back door and swung it so hard that it dented the wall. He stomped outside and leaned against the porch railing.

A fear I hadn't yet admitted to anyone was my fear of the unknown, of what my life would look like without Michael in the personal side of it, without him in this house. The professional life we shared at the office would be no hassle. I knew exactly what to expect, and once we got used to the dearth of secret signals and rolled eyeballs exchanged across the desks, I could easily accept him as just a business partner who was good at his job and helped make the paper profitable.

I realized now that it was a question of the personal stuff

I shared with him that had made me twist myself for so long. Even though the last nine months of our marriage had been stressful, it was still familiar. It was as if part of me feared the void more than the crap we hurled at each other. At that moment, the cats emerged from their hiding spots. Despite the yelling and banging, their little cat brains registered the fact that somewhere in the house, a door was open. I didn't know it at the time, but Michael had slammed the door so hard that it failed to latch and was a few inches ajar, enough for the enticements of the outside world to tempt three frightened cats from their hiding spots. And since they were indoor cats, they weren't going to let such a golden opportunity pass them by, even when it was only 15 degrees out.

I was still sitting at the kitchen table with a tight grip on my coffee mug. I didn't even sense a cat was nearby. Then Michael began to bellow. Bellow was the perfect word for it, since it brought back the memory of countless afternoons spent watching Fred Flintstone complain about some aspect of his life that wasn't running particularly smoothly as he stamped his feet and pumped his four-fingered fists into the air in prehistoric frustration.

"What is it, Fred?" Wilma would appear stage right, always the good wife standing at the ready to pat Fred on the shoulder and tell him, "There, there, now, everything's going to be all right."

Wilma played the mother to Fred's bratty whiny kid. And then it clicked. I wasn't Wilma or any other female TV character whose primary function, week after week, was to placate the males in her life, whether husband, father, or son. I would be spared any new insight for a few minutes because Michael started to bellow again.

"Emily!" Drawn-out, more insistent, in a voice I'd never heard from my husband. That's when I saw the open door. I poked my head out to see what Michael was yelling about.

Chainsaw had gotten out. He probably was nervous enough already, his little wet cat nose quivering a mile a minute at all the new smells, even in winter, but Michael's screams had sent him cowering, and now he was wedged between the garbage cans. As I rushed to rescue the cat, all I could think about was how different Michael must be now because he didn't care if the neighbors witnessed his outburst.

Ignoring Michael, I tiptoed toward the. cat, who was shaking violently. I knew he would claw me. Right then I cared more about how Chainsaw felt than about Michael, so I didn't feel like mustering up the energy to glare at him for not closing the door. I gingerly gathered the cat up in my arms and held him close as I walked across the porch and into the house. I carried him upstairs and into the bedroom and laid him down on the bed, caressing him and talking softly. After ten minutes, his shivering stopped and a weak purr came from his throat. A few minutes later, Chaos and Lionel ventured onto the bed. Five minutes after that, I heard Michael's car pull out of the driveway.

That night, Michael got home about an hour after I had gone to bed. Wordlessly, he climbed in beside me and under the covers and held me close. One by one, the cats joined us, anchoring us at the butt and shoulders. It was the first time in months I slept through the night.

The next day, I dragged myself across the hall and into my office around eleven thirty. I sat at my desk, thinking and not thinking, doodling on a scratch pad for a couple of hours. Michael came in around two and stood in the doorway, watching me. For about five minutes, neither one of us said anything. Then suddenly, I just wanted the whole thing to be over. I felt his eyes on me, but I didn't look up. Suddenly, Michael burst into tears, big silent tears. If I looked at him, so would I. He got up and left the room. I continued to scrawl gibberish onto the pad for another hour before I dragged myself across the hall and into bed.

The smell of burnt coffee startled me awake around 5 a.m. Michael hadn't turned off the coffeepot. He had turned the pot on when he first came downstairs and never turned it off. Suddenly, it felt as if I had a phantom limb, a physically overwhelming ache in a limb somewhere off to my right; a third arm, but an arm that was no longer there. I needed to get out of the house, and fast. I ran down the stairs, turned off the coffeepot, quickly fed the cats, and got into the car.

When Willard opened the door, he pulled me in over the threshold. I could count the number of times I've been to Willard's house since I moved back to Coventry on the fingers of one hand. I never knew when she'd be at his house, and I didn't want to create any friction between them. I didn't much care for Carolyn, a sentiment she shared about me. I thought the idea of her cat-fur afghans and sweaters was kind of macabre. Although I loved to snuggle up with them, I would never bring one home because my cats would think I was a traitor.

Willard was silent as he steered me into the living room. I noticed even more cat fur tumbleweeds than in my house, judging from the unclaimed clumps spread around the room. Willard was ordered not to touch them, but since he didn't own a vacuum cleaner it wasn't an issue—he and Carolyn must have had a fight recently.

He gently nudged me into the cats' chair, so-called because it was the sole piece of furniture in the house the cats were allowed to destroy, which he insured by regularly spraying the arms and back with catnip spray and tucking several ounces of the herb into the seat cushion. Willard tossed a cat-fur blanket onto my lap and headed for the kitchen to put water on to boil.

I pulled the blanket up to my chin. Almost immediately, three cats of indeterminate gender and gene-pool background began to sniff at my feet. Five minutes later, Willard set down a cup of hot water and a plateful of peppermint tea bags on the table beside me. I took two and plunked them in the cup, weighting them down with a teaspoon.

Willard sat down on the ottoman and warmed his hands on a cup of espresso. As he looked at me, he arched his right eyebrow, a trait I thought was a permanent affliction due to all the time he spent squinting behind a camera.

"So?" he asked.

I took a sip of tea. "So *what?*" I then proceeded to fill him in. His eyebrow scooted even higher.

I sipped my tea. "Help me out here, Willard, maybe you know. Why are Michael and I still stuck?"

"It's really not too difficult," he said. "You think he'll eventually come out as straight, while he probably thinks you just need to get used to the idea that he's gay. After all, you did accept him once already after he came out. Besides, you're still the rock in his life. Like it or not, you're really all that Michael has."

I snorted. "As though he treats me like that." I set my cup down. "At this point, he only comes to me when he wants something and he expects me to feel sorry for him."

"Well, Emily, look at it this way: When Michael came out to you, he was already used to the idea. He probably went back and forth for several years, trying to decide if giving up the certainty of the life he had with you was worth going out on his own into a life filled with the unknown. I mean, this town is pretty accepting as long as you don't wave it in their faces, but in the larger world, who knows what he would face? But for you, the news came out of nowhere, which must have been particularly devastating because you also work side by side with the guy."

He sipped his espresso. "So when Michael finally told you, he had had time to think about how it would affect your marriage. He probably was resigned to the fact that you'd boot him out immediately. He's probably wondering why you're still with him."

I nodded. "Me too."

We spent another hour talking before exhaustion overcame me. I slept in Willard's spare room. I got under the covers and within minutes the same three mongrel cats that had checked me out downstairs staked their claim by wedging me under the blankets. Just like home, I thought, and immediately fell asleep.

When I woke up the next morning, Willard was gone, but

he'd left a full pot of coffee on. I drank a few cups. When I got back to the house, the cats tripped me as I walked in the door, yowling their discontent. Michael's car wasn't in the driveway, but something didn't feel right. The house felt unsettled.

After I dished out a can of wet stink, I headed upstairs to the bedroom and saw that half his clothes were gone. Across the hall, I found a note from him on the desk in my office.

Em, I'm sorry for everything I put you through. I don't know what I want, but I do know I need some time on my own. I'll be staying at Ron's house for awhile. Don't worry, I'll still get my work done, but I won't be in the office. You don't need any more of this in your face. I'll fax you any new contracts and send in the artwork.

Love, Michael

He still doesn't know what he wants? At least I do, now.

I called Ken Carville, the attorney who had drawn up the papers when we bought the newspaper. He wasn't in, so I left a message for him to call me at home.

Chapter Twelve

Sometimes you file certain conversations away in a readily accessible recess of your mind, even though at the time it seems like an interesting factoid with no relevance to your life. For some reason, I remembered a particular conversation with Eddie as if it were yesterday. I replayed the film in my mind on Tuesday as I headed to Burlington for the Clueless Meeting.

"For a gay man, making love to a woman is nothing but work, plain and simple," Eddie informed me on one of our aimless drives through the White Mountains.

Michael and I had been married for almost two years at that point and I was spending less time with Eddie. When he called out of the blue to see what I was doing one weekend, I agreed to go for a drive with him just like the old days since Michael was going to be in Malden visiting his sister. Back then, I thought it was odd that Michael always made himself scarce whenever Eddie called or came to the house to pick me up. He studiously avoided eye contact not only with Eddie, but also with me whenever Eddie was around.

I reached over to poke him in the ribs. "And how would *you* know, Mister Gay From Birth?"

He looked at me out of the corner of his eye. "Well, I was married to a woman once, you know."

"No!"

"Yes," he answered. "But don't let it get out. It'll spoil my reputation."

"How long were you married?"

"Oh, only a couple of years, when you were away at J-school."

In my rush to explore the world after high school, I had left Coventry behind in a flash. I cut off all contact with anything that was remotely connected with the town—including Eddie.

I couldn't believe his revelation. I had known Eddie since the first grade, and though he did go out with girls when we were in high school, I also knew he was matching up accessories in his mother's closet when no one was home.

We were heading north on I-93, going through Franconia Notch, probably the only two-lane interstate highway in existence. Concrete barriers effectively ruled out a passing lane. "Why did you get married?" I asked.

In an effort to convey his displeasure to the car in front of us, which was adorned with a "Save the Cape" license plate from Massachusetts and going ten miles under the speed limit to get a good look at the Old Man in the Mountains, Eddie sped up until his front bumper was inches away from the rear bumper of the car in front, before braking abruptly. I saw the driver nervously glance in the car's rearview mirror.

I braced my arms against the dashboard. "Damn Mass-holes," Eddie muttered. "Em, you were asking why I got married?"

I nodded wordlessly, letting go of the dashboard long enough to peel off a stick of peppermint gum to stave off my impending nausea from his stop-and-go driving.

Eddie let out a big sigh. "Well, these days I'd be laughed at for sitting on the fence. But I truly loved Rita. I wanted to marry her, and I thought it would work. Besides, I had always wanted to see how the other half—the *straight* half—lived."

I found my voice as the level of bile in the back of my throat receded slightly with the minty gum. "I thought you always knew you were gay."

He hit the brake as the car in front turned on its emergency flashers and slowed to fifteen miles below the speed limit. "No, I didn't. What I *did* know was that even though I enjoyed spending time with women, there was always this unnamed *something* in the back of my mind. I had a different feeling toward men than toward women, and I knew it wasn't how most men felt toward other men. For years, I couldn't put my finger on it."

Eddie slowed down and began to keep a respectable one car-length behind the other car. "Gimme a stick of gum, will you?" I handed it to him and with one hand he unwrapped it and curled it into his mouth. "Part of me knew that I didn't really want to find out, that my life would change more than I could imagine. I was comfortable with my life. I didn't *want* it to change." He pushed in the cigarette lighter. "Not much, anyway, because I still thought about men. A lot. After we were married about six months, I finally had to tell her the truth."

Eddie fished out a cigarette from the pack of Merits stuck in the cupholder as the lighter popped out.

"So what did Rita think of all this when you told her?"

He made a sour face as he put the cigarette between his lips and tried to prevent the gum in his mouth from touching the paper filter. "What do you *think* she thought?" he shot back. "She was shocked, she screamed, she slapped me, she told me her life was over. Then we started to wheel and deal. We drew up a contract that attempted to dictate my behavior. In other words, what I could and couldn't do based on what *she* was comfortable with." He lit his cigarette and inhaled deeply to get the nicotine effect. He exhaled. "Of course, my behavior didn't change a bit. It was Rita who had to constantly talk herself into what was and wasn't acceptable to her. And as I got a taste of a little bit of the sex I had always fantasized about but always pushed away, I kept bending the rules. Occasionally, I would ask to renegotiate one of the clauses in the contract, but most of the time I would just ignore the contract and not tell her."

He took a drag on the cigarette and cracked open the window. "In a very short time, I began to view Rita as my warden, a somebody to rebel against. I became more and more resentful of her. We didn't talk about it, but we both wondered what we were still doing in the marriage. It was one big game of limbo. I kept lowering the bar while the music played and fully expected Rita to go for whatever I asked. Most of the time she did, only because she didn't know about most of it."

Once we left Franconia Notch, the interstate doubled from two to four lanes. The Massachusetts car scurried off to the shoulder, a scared rabbit in search of some breathing room. Uncharacteristically, Eddie stayed in the slow lane.

"I'm not proud of what I did, Emily. Looking back, I realize I wanted to see how far I could push her. I wanted the security of our marriage, but with the excitement of the forbidden fruit I was suddenly allowed to indulge in, it was all too much. I wanted it all, and Rita wanted our marriage more than anything else. *That's* why she put up with me for so long. Because it was so important to her, I felt like a heel for even thinking about leaving."

"So what happened?"

He held the cigarette to his mouth, twisting it between his lips. I watched his jaw twitch as he continued to chew the gum.

"What usually happens—she met somebody who didn't play games with her, who wanted only her and who didn't need to be with anyone else in addition to her." Eddie took a long drag, then flicked the cigarette out the window. "And I didn't blame her one bit. But the day the divorce was final was the saddest day of my life. I haven't seen her or talked to her since the court hearing."

I could see that he needed something to snap him out of his mood. Just then, a blue Infiniti Q10 with Connecticut plates passed on the left. The drive turned into a drag race, as Eddie suddenly swerved into the fast lane behind the Infiniti.

"So what was it like for you in bed with her? Was it always

like work?"

"I enjoyed it for the first year we were married, before I came out. Remember, I liked women and I *loved* Rita. She always wanted me to be more sexual with her, but I thought she was comparing me to previous boyfriends who *I* always thought just wanted her for the sex and nothing else. I had to constantly reassure her about this—that for me it was more of a question of quality than quantity. I frequently asked what would she rather have: a relationship based mostly on sex, or one based mostly on love."

"What did she say?"

"Love, of course, but she always wanted more sex than I did, since she viewed it as a testament of my love for her. Yes, it was that, but I always felt I showed my love to her in a lot of other ways. We had sex often enough for me."

I couldn't resist. "How often was 'often enough' for you?"

"Once every three or four weeks."

I opened my mouth, but Eddie cut me off.

"Yes, yes, I know. It wasn't enough for her, but it did the trick for a while. I think from the beginning she thought I would change." He smiled slyly. "You know, now I don't blame her one bit, because it definitely wouldn't be enough for me now."

"Yeah, well, what's enough now?"

"Three times a day!" He laughed. "But when I was with Rita, I was never *not* there. I mean, I wasn't pretending that she was a man that I was fucking. It's just different. With women, it's making love. It's work. With men, it's fucking. And there's a world of difference."

I'd spent lots of time with Eddie over the years, but the only conversation I recall in detail was that one. Do I remember the talk because I sensed that Michael was gay? I'm not sure, but I think that during that entire conversation, the topic of Michael didn't come up once. And because my best friend was a gay man, did part of me always know I would marry a man who would turn out to be gay? Back then my views toward sexuality were pretty much black and white.

If a man is in a gay bar, that means he's gay. The same for a woman, unless she happened to prefer the company of gay men, like me. I didn't have a clue then that the lines would become so fuzzy.

By the time I parked the car in front of the Women's Health Center, my mind was reeling. Deep down, did I know Michael was gay when we met? Should I have known? Hell, here I was, putting it back on me again, I berated myself. Pushing open the door to the meeting room, I was surprised to see a party in full swing. Of course. I had forgotten all about the Clueless Christmas Party. Anita greeted me at the door.

"I forgot," I told her, jangling my keys. "Maybe I should go out and get something."

"What, and miss the festivities? We have everything we need, Emily, except you," she said, leading me by the elbow. "Come on in."

The room looked quite different from our normal Tuesday nights. People were dressed up with paper hats on their heads and holding drinks. A scruffy Christmas tree leaned against one wall, beer and wine bottles had replaced the coffee pot, and our chairs were arranged around a long table heaped with construction paper, glitter, glue, felt, tinsel, and baseball caps.

"What's all this for?" I asked Anita.

"Oh, that was Beverly's idea. She thinks we should all make straight spouse Christmas presents this year and give them to each other and screw our spouses."

"But they don't—"

"Screw?" she laughed, finishing my sentence. "I know! That's why we need to have some fun!"

Over the next ten minutes, everyone took a seat around the table, a drink by their elbow.

"Okay, guys," Beverly announced. "Welcome to the First Annual Clueless Spouse Arts and Crafts Christmas Party!"

The room quieted down for a few minutes as we dug into the piles of what amounted to second-grade art supplies.

Cheryl began to giggle.

"What's funny?" asked Ted.

She held up a piece of green construction paper folded in half.

"I made a Christmas card!" she said.

"What's it say?" asked Janet.

Cheryl stood up and cleared her throat.

"Santa and his sleigh,
Seem very far away,
When your love's gift to you
Is, 'Hey, I think I'm gay!'"

Everyone in the room cracked up.

"Hey," said Ted, "maybe we should start a line of greeting cards—how to tell if your wife or husband is gay."

"How about a card with two women that reads, 'I've learned to use sex as a weapon. When my gay husband won't do what I want, I threaten to insist on having sex,'" said Beverly.

"How about a quiz?" offered Anita. "Does your husband prefer skimpy briefs and g-strings to boxers, but never wears them in front of you?"

"Or does he carry his tools around in a Victoria's Secret shopping bag?" asked Janet.

"Hey, who put up the tree?" asked Charlie.

"I did," said Beverly. "You wanna make something of it?"

"Yeah," he said. "It doesn't belong here."

"And why not?"

"It's not straight."

Beverly shook her head. "Yeah, well, neither is my husband."

"Forget about the cards," said Ted. "What about the books? I was wandering around in the Radical Womyn bookstore last week to look for a Christmas present for my wife, and it seems there's a conspiracy to help women leave their husbands. I found a book called *From Wedded Life to Lesbian Life*. No way was I going to buy this."

"I'm surprised they even let you in," said Charlie, "but

what did you expect? You think you're going to find a book on how to grill a steak at a vegetarian bookstore?"

Everybody laughed. I began to think that maybe we should have a party every Tuesday night; this was certainly an improvement over the intensity of our usual meetings.

Charlie held up a baseball cap. "What's this for?"

"What do you think it's for?" Anita asked. "That's for the Celibate Martyr's Hats we're all going to make."

"Except for Lonnie," said Cheryl. "But she's not here anyway."

"You know, I don't think that Lonnie and her husband have sex," said Beverly. "I think she just gets off on flaunting the fact that she has stuck by her man when the rest of us are too weak to swear off ever having sex again."

"That's only because she's gone through menopause."

Beverly snorted. "I heard that," she exclaimed indignantly, huffily putting a fist on her hip. "I've been through menopause, and I'm not celibate...except when it comes to my husband, that is," she added with a grin.

Charlie started digging through the pile in front of him. "So what exactly does a Celibate Martyr's Hat have on it, anyway? A couple of horns like a bull?"

"Nope," said Cheryl as she picked up a cap and placed it backwards on her head. "I think it needs one of those ah-oo-gah horns like on the old cars."

Charlie reached over to swivel the cap around on her head. "No offense, Cheryl, but ever since the day she came out, my wife has been wearing a baseball cap that way on her head. I think she even sleeps in the damn thing."

"Well, it has to have horns, so let's see who can make the horniest hat," I suggested.

Ten minutes of laughter, snipping, gluing, and sprinkling glitter passed. That's when Janet asked, "You know, one thing I think about is what if it happens again? After all, I couldn't tell that my husband was gay, and now I walk around thinking every man is gay, except for you guys, that is," she said, nodding to Ted and Charlie.

"Well, I have a gay friend who has insisted on meeting all of my prospective dates before we go out," said Cheryl. "His gaydar is pretty accurate."

"I have a better idea," said Anita. "When I was complaining to my husband about the fact that I wanted to make sure the next man I dated would be straight, he generously offered to hit on him as a test."

"Well, at this point, I'm at the stage where expecting a spouse to be straight is a bit like looking for a husband who puts the toilet seat back down," said Beverly. "Nice if you can find it, but a bit of a luxury."

"Why don't we just get t-shirts made up that say, 'My next spouse will be STR8'?" I said.

"Yeah, but on the backs of the shirts we should print a list of the best lines we heard from our gay spouses," said Ted. "Like, 'I love you, but I can't have sex with you.'"

"Or, 'I want to stay friends with you...but I don't have any time to spend away from my gay friends,'" said Anita.

Janet coughed. "How about, 'I promise you, there's no one else...well, there were these five different times.'"

"What about, 'Maybe we can have sex on your birthday, if you're good,' then, 'Sorry, can't do it...it's your birthday, not mine, so go take care of it yourself,'" said Charlie.

"What gets me is that when they still have one foot in both worlds, there's someone from the gay welcome wagon telling them that everything will be all right if they just hurry up and be gay, meaning, if you leave your spouse," said Anita.

"And there will be a big party too," added Cheryl. "All I know was that Paul left me quicker than shit when he found a shoulder to cry on, among other things. But when Gay Camp wasn't more fun than home, he wanted to come home even faster. Guess Mister Gay found out the grass wasn't greener, it just had a different kind of tree growing out of it."

"Well, you know, I just sometimes think that Bill tried for years to be Mister Fixit for all these years," said Anita

"What do you mean?" Ted asked.

"Having babies are just the final symptom in the Mister Fixit syndrome. Somewhere along the way, Bill thought he could will himself to be straight. First he slept with a woman, but that didn't fix it, so then he married a woman. Again, that didn't work, so then he figured if he could father a child, that would mean he was straight once and for all. But when that didn't work, he finally gave up."

"Well, when I was pregnant, things were touch and go for a while," said Cheryl. "I almost miscarried a few times. I remember thinking it was really strange that Paul wasn't upset that I might have lost the child, although he was just thrilled by the fact that I was pregnant. I think he was surprised that he could father a child when he knew deep down that he was gay."

We spent the rest of the evening talking, laughing, drinking, drawing obscene pictures, and throwing tinsel at each other. The party ended at ten thirty, well past our usual ending time, but with the tension we all faced in our everyday lives coupled with the usual angst of the holidays, I'd bet that our Clueless party was the season's highlight for everyone there. More importantly, the party showed me what life could be like again without always wondering what stage of the rollercoaster Michael was traveling on and trying but always failing to predict the stage so I could alter my behavior in advance.

Reality returned with a vengeance the following afternoon. It had been two weeks since Michael had moved out, since I had seen him, for that matter. I was starting to get used to the solitude, the peace, the predictability of daily life. That all flew out the window when Michael called me at the office around three the next day.

"How are you?" he asked.

"Oh, fine." I took a deep breath. "I went to see Ken, you know."

"Oh good," he said. "I was planning to come over to the house tomorrow so we could talk." He paused. "I mean, I'd like to know if I can come see you, that is, if you're not busy."

This could be easier than I thought. The week after Michael moved out, I met with Ken, our attorney, to draw up a standard set of divorce papers that would at least provide us with a starting point. Ken had sent them over a few days ago, but I didn't want to look at them. The papers were sitting on the kitchen table, waiting for Michael's signature. "Sure," I said. "You can come over after work."

The next afternoon, I had been sitting at the kitchen table for over an hour when Michael's car pulled up. When I heard his footsteps on the porch, I grabbed a notepad and started scribbling.

Michael looked as if he hadn't slept in a week. His eyes were sunken, his hair was uncombed, and his jeans had stains on them. I hid my shock when he walked into the kitchen and sat down at the kitchen table across from me.

"Hi," I finally managed.

"Hi," he replied in a voice gravelly with exhaustion. Before I could change my mind, I pushed the short stack of papers towards him.

"Everything's there," I said without looking at him. "I had Ken go over it all, and if everything's okay, all we have to do is go over to the bank tomorrow morning and have Millie notarize it. I have to go to Fletcher tomorrow anyway, so I can file them while I'm there and—"

"What's this?" he asked as he leafed through the papers, not fully comprehending what they were.

Oh no, what had he been thinking?

He laid the papers on the table and looked right at me. "What are you telling me?"

It was no use. There was no delicate way to put this.

"I'm tired of all this, Michael. I want a divorce."

He didn't react. I think he was too stunned.

"Why?"

My blood pressure immediately ratcheted up ten points, but I kept my voice calm. "We've tried everything, but none of it has worked. Can't you see? This isn't you, Michael, and it isn't me."

He looked at me as if I were speaking Latin, but he didn't get angry. "But that's not what I came back for," he said. "I came back because now I know that I'm truly bisexual, not gay, and that I don't have to act on my attraction to men. It's not worth it if it means I lose you, Emily.

"I'm not happy without you. I thought I wanted this life, this new life. I thought it would be the missing piece, the magic wand that cured everything. But it's not, it doesn't begin to compare with what you and I had, Em, and I miss it desperately."

I stared at him. As before, a small germ of hope started to develop, and I know if I did nothing, it would soon drown out my instinct, my reason. I wished he had just shown up, kept his mouth shut, signed the papers, packed the rest of his stuff up, and gotten the hell out of there.

But what if he was right? What if he had really gotten it out of his system this time and was ready to come back and we could live like we were before? My brain was soaking in this stew of questions. But as I looked at him and thought of the rollercoaster we had been riding all these months, I could feel hope shrink inside me.

"We've been all through this before, Michael. You try to deny it, and then I start to deny it. But it always returns. Can't you see we've been repeating the same crap over and over? If I took you back now, part of me would be obsessing about when the other shoe would drop."

I didn't know what else to say. I wished he would leave. But one thing was true. I still loved the man. Even after everything we'd been through, this one fact remained clear.

He reached across the kitchen table and clutched my hands.

"No more," I said, twisting my hands away.

I got up from the table, leaving the papers, and headed upstairs. About five minutes later, I heard his car start.

• • •

I've always looked askance at people who leave the television or talk radio station blasting all day. They never come right out and say they're lonely, only that the house is too quiet without the static background noise. The day Michael came back to the house to pack up the rest of his things, it was so quiet I had no choice but to turn on the radio. I tried to ignore Michael as he puttered around the house, but I kept noticing that the stack of boxes placed at the front door was growing smaller as the day wore on. As he worked, I sat in the living room trying to plow through a stack of *Editor &* *Publisher* magazines that had piled up at the office, but it was impossible to read about an industry where Michael and I owned a business together, soon to be the last connection we had.

After I spent half an hour reading the same paragraph, I finally gave up and picked up a collection of short stories by Shirley Jackson, author of "The Lottery," the infamous short story where a small town picks one of their residents to stone to death each year. I needed to pour my thoughts into anything that would distract me from seeing Michael out of the corner of my eye as he wrapped mugs and plates in last Sunday's *Globe*. But even the kitschy gothic stories couldn't help. I watched Michael's every move as he carried another box out to the U-Haul parked in the driveway.

A couple of times, Michael asked me to help him lug out a particularly awkward box or piece of furniture, and I obliged, though while we struggled over a threshold or down a flight of stairs, we studiously avoided looking at each other.

And then it was over. The last boxes were stacked in the truck and the house was quiet. Michael walked down the hallway, probably for the last time, I thought. The wooden floor seemed to creak more loudly than before.

I burrowed into my book and purposefully squinted at the pages. Michael walked over to where I was sitting and stood in front of me, his legs slightly spread. I glanced up at him and saw a look of exhausted defiance on his face. I tried to look nonchalant, but didn't have the energy to fake it. When he cocked his head to one side, I thought of a parakeet I had when I was nine.

"See you tomorrow?" he asked, his tone fully expecting me to refuse him.

"I guess," I said, and turned back to my book. He stood before me a few seconds longer and let out a breath he had obviously been holding a second too long. I refused to look up again, so I turned my attention to his feet. He was wearing the steel-toed Timberlands I had bought him for Christmas three years ago.

I noticed that the flannel lining of the boot looked a bit frayed. If I had my manicure scissors handy, I would have leaned over to trim the stray threads. However, his left foot pulled back slightly, hesitantly. His toe rested on the floor as if he were about to execute a pirouette. But his right foot was in an obvious rush, and suddenly I was staring at the bare floor where his shoes had stood. I heard Chaos scrabble up the stairs as Michael clomped toward the back door. My eyes stayed locked on the floor, but I felt the antennae of my hearing tune in on Michael.

I listened to the fabric of his clothes rustle as he walked through the kitchen on his way to the back door. His wedding ring—I was surprised he was still wearing it—clinked when he reached for the doorknob. I heard a wet snap as his mouth opened slightly and stayed ajar for a couple of seconds, before he thought better of what he was about to say. The back door opened, closed, and he was gone. The U-Haul's diesel engine protested slightly before it caught. I heard handfuls of gravel spitting, crunching, and popping.

The crunching was still going long after I could no longer hear the rumbling diesel, and I realized that it was Lionel eating his dry food, a hint that it was time for wet stink. He knew that Michael was out of the house and it was safe to come out of hiding. When the crunching stopped, I clumsily untangled my legs from under the blanket. My left foot had fallen asleep. I wiggled it and struck the book against my ankle to speed some sensation back into it.

I stood up, shakily at first, and headed for the kitchen. Chaos walked in front of me in her crazy, drunken style while Lionel slithered beside me. Chainsaw was asleep in front of the woodstove. Might as well feed them early. At one point, when Michael was rooting around in the kitchen, packing dishes and silverware, I was worried that he would take the can opener, and how would I open the cans? Then I remembered that the cats had only dim memories of the sound of a sharp wheel cutting into metal since most canned cat food came with poptop lids. One less thing for me to worry about.

Epilogue

Before I opened my eyes, I knew something had shifted. Two months had passed since Michael had moved out, and every morning had felt the same—gray and blah. No matter what I did, I couldn't shake it.

An uncontested divorce was in process and our relationship at the office had become relatively neutral after the first awkward week. Things had settled down, except when I was home by myself. As soon as I walked in the door and the cats flung themselves at me, a thick cloud of dread enveloped me, refusing to budge until I left for work the next day.

So when I woke up that morning and felt different, it was a start. It was Saturday and I had no plans for the day. I climbed over Chaos and Chainsaw twirled up underneath the blankets in the indentation that had been Michael's side of the bed and walked over to the window. Several times since Michael moved out, I had tried to sleep on Michael's side of the bed, but it didn't feel right. My body didn't fit on his side. Trying to sleep in the middle of the bed made me feel untethered. So the two cats took over Michael's half by eminent domain and began to sleep there every night. Their low growls would gradually become muffled as they burrowed their way under the covers where they'd sleep in their makeshift tent, purring all night long.

I stretched and glanced outside into the bare branches of

the trees, searching for a robin, a redwing blackbird, anything that would give me a sign that today was indeed going to be different. The temperature must have already been well above freezing for several hours; I saw a thin cloud of mist floating above the receding snowdrifts. The fog resembled the clouds on the cemetery soundstages in the 70s horror shows on TV.

A stream of water ran down the tire tracks in the driveway. The gray crust had fallen off a drift in the yard and I saw the layers of snow that had formed during the winter's storms, separated by layers of ice. The rapidly melting top coat was from last week's storm, the thin layer beneath was from a snow squall two weeks ago, and so on. About halfway down, a dotted black line divided the layers. That layer was left from just before Michael moved out, when the squirrel attacked the birdfeeder, scattering sunflower seeds across the hard crust of snow.

When that snow fell, Michael was still living here. When I was a kid, we did a similar thing when a huge maple tree toppled over in the schoolyard after a storm. "There," I remember Mrs. Fitzgerald pointing to a ring near the middle of the tree. "When that tree was growing, George Washington was alive," she told us. I thought of taking a cross-section of the snow, putting it into a terrarium and then into the freezer, right next to the top layer of our three-year-old wedding cake, covered with freezer burn and several bags of frozen broccoli.

I knew that I would get in the mood to throw out the cake someday—it certainly hadn't been on Michael's packing list—but right now it required too much energy. After all, it's not like I need the freezer space, I thought, staring at the snowbank.

I suddenly had a thought. I knew just what I would do today. I headed up to my office and opened the lower drawer of my file cabinet. I pulled out a stack of envelopes stuffed with photos from our wedding. I pulled the gluey flaps apart and unceremoniously turned each one over so that photos and negatives spilled onto the rug. Then I sat down with my legs crossed and began turning each one right side up, spreading them out to get a better look.

It was kind of a ritual. Michael and I used to look at the photos once a year. We bought an album with *Our Wedding* inscribed on the front in fake gold leaf, but never got around to putting our photos in the album. I used to carefully examine the photos a few days before our wedding anniversary as a way to take stock of the previous year and put it in some kind of perspective. I knew that today would be the last time I would go through the photos. Michael didn't ask for them when he was packing; I figured it would only serve as a reminder of the years he had spent living one big lie. I felt the same way. As I looked at them, I scoured Michael's face and the other people at the wedding, looking for clues. Did he know, even back then? And, for that matter, did I know what was going on?

I picked up a group shot and gazed at the faces of the commingled families and friends. Aunt Alice would be dead of liver cancer not one year later. I reached into my top desk drawer and felt around until I located the magnifying glass. I picked up a shot of me and Michael at the head table at the reception. We both looked happy, holding hands, eyes a bit bloodshot and wide from the stress and wonder of everything that had happened in the previous two months since moving to Coventry. I focused the magnifying glass directly above Michael's face. Each pore became huge. The carnation on his lapel seemed to explode. I looked for a squint, a grimace that would reveal that even back then Michael knew full well what he was hiding. If only I had looked this closely at his face in the photo before he came out, or even before the wedding. Could I have prevented all this?

Lionel sauntered into the room and began licking one of the photos in the pile. Several years ago, I had to take down one of the wedding photographs I stuck on the refrigerator because the salt and chemicals in the photo finish attracted Lionel like a bowl of tuna. I came home one night to find tiny cat tooth marks and dried cat spit where Aunt Alice's head used to be. But now I let the cat have his fun. He was licking a photo showing me with my mouth open and my eyes half-closed. Of course, Michael looked great, as usual. Lionel began to gnaw on a corner of the photo.

I set the magnifying glass down on the floor and reached over to pet him. I wasn't going to find the truth by looking at old photos. I started arranging the pictures in piles to put them back in the envelopes, then stopped. I scrambled to my feet and headed downstairs to make a cup of tea. While the water was heating, I kneeled in front of the woodstove and opened the door. Red hot coals. Perfect.

I closed the door and went back upstairs to my office and gathered up all the photos. I couldn't carry them all, so I grabbed the first thing within reach: Chaos and Chainsaw's cat bed. I pulled out the cushion—it was so thickly covered with clumps of gray cat fur that I had forgotten it was blue—and dumped the photos into the wicker basket. Lionel followed me downstairs. On the way, we passed Chaos and Chainsaw, dozing on a stack of laundry in the hall that was clean when I took it out of the dryer a few days ago. Intrigued by the activity, they raised their heads and quickly followed. I set the basket in front of the woodstove and went into the kitchen to pour my tea.

I was more energized than I had been in weeks. I opened one of the kitchen windows a few inches and bent down to breathe in the cold air. Still cold, but not cold like winter. I opened the freezer door and pushed aside the bags of frozen vegetables. Then I saw it in all of its freezer-burned glory: the now-inedible top of our wedding cake. With one hand I grabbed it while the other held back an avalanche of bags of frozen vegetables, Tupperware containers, bricks of ground beef, and Ben and Jerry's containers so ancient the flavor had been brought back as a flavor flashback—*twice*. I removed the cake from the freezer, carried it into the living room, and set it on the wedding photos in the cat basket.

I couldn't believe what I was about to do. I opened the

door of the woodstove. A piece of coal spat at me. I grabbed a couple of photos and tossed them in on top of the bed of coals. Instantly, they began to curl up, the faces glowing red for a split second before the paper shrank and turned in on itself. All three cats were watching the woodstove: Kitty TV. Lionel began licking another photo while Chaos and Chainsaw sat inches from the open door of the stove, whiskers twitching in the heat.

I threw in a few more photos, then a handful. I was amazed at how quickly an event that had reached epic importance in my mind could perish so completely in seconds. When I had gone through half the photos, I knew what was next. The cake was frozen too solid to hack into pieces, so I heaved the whole thing into the woodstove's hungry mouth. The bed of coals angrily reacted; it sounded like popping corn. Six cat ears looked like they had been yanked straight up with invisible string.

The sweet smell of spun sugar instantly transported me back to the reception, so I grabbed the fire poker and prodded the cake, willing it to burn faster. It resisted; the poker got stuck in the cake and wouldn't budge. Forget it, it seemed to say. You can't undo five years of frozen memories that quickly.

I left the poker in the cake, sticking out of the woodstove, and watched as the frosting oozed and bubbled and melted, and then began to burn. The cake thawed, smelling freshly baked, but eventually charred beyond recognition. I watched until the air turned from sweet to burnt, and the coals turned to warm ash.

If you'd like more information
on resources for straight spouses,
please visit our web page:

www.straightspouse.com